EXCALIBUR

EXCALIBUR

Sanders Anne Laubenthal

FANTASY

First printing: Ballantine Books, August 1973
First Science Fiction Book Club printing: December 2000

Published by arrangement with the author.

ISBN 0-7394-1442-9

Visit our website at: http//www.sfbc.com

PRINTED IN THE UNITED STATES OF AMERICA

1. Rhodri

"We were not born," said Linette out loud, "to sit and look at the rain."

Her words echoed strangely in the empty house. As she sat at the open window, the candles burned behind her in the silver candelabra, for the storm had blacked out a part of the city. The lightning flickered behind the old roofs opposite, showing for a second the wet street; there was no other light anywhere except the remote gaslights of De Tonti Square. A man was walking along the street, his face bent against the rain. The darkness fell again, and in a moment she heard the heavy growl of the thunder. The storm must be moving out across the bay.

They'll be getting it at Silverthorne, she thought. But it's always candlelight there.

She rather wished she could have gone to Silverthorne with the others, but they had left her at home in case the wretched archaeologist called. Just as well, she thought with a flurry of scorn; Anthony might be there. He was there often now, doing research in Aunt Julian's library.

I'd rather be an old maid like Aunt Julian, Linette thought. I even look like her—black hair, grey eyes, the Silverthorne nose. I'd make a good old maid.

She stared out at the darkness and the remote pinpoints of gaslights which lit nothing around her. The wet July night poured in its smell of recently sun-baked earth now quenched with rain.

Through the sound of the rain she could hear the man's footsteps as he came along the sidewalk, and could even make him out as a vague dark movement. Suddenly, for no reason, she felt that sense of impending glory which sometimes descended on her out of nowhere, the sense of fabulous adventure and the piled-up splendor of life; it was the rain and the wet earth-smell and the dark movements outside that released it, and suddenly she could have laid her head on the windowsill and shed tears of happiness.

Then she realized that the man had stopped walking; he was standing on the pavement looking at the house. She thought of moving away from the window. But in her unreasonable happiness she did not move after all, but sat and watched him trying to see the number.

He opened and shut the wrought-iron gate, came up the short path and onto the gallery. Then came a short, heavy tap of the brass knocker.

Shall I open it or not? she thought, strangely excited. But already she had picked up a candle and was going. She opened the door as far as the chain would permit and looked out.

A man in a glistening-wet dark raincoat stood there; she thought he might be in his late twenties. His dark hair, slightly long, was plastered down by the rain.

"Good evening," he said with an accent she could not quite place. "I wonder if Malcolm Silverthorne lives here?"

"That's my father," said Linette.

"I'm Rhodri Meyrick, of the Caernarvon Archaeological Society. I thought I'd call; I hope it's not inconvenient?"

"No, it's all right. But my father's not in." She looked at him through the crack, wondering what had brought him out in such weather.

"Well, really," he said, "what I wanted was the key. Do you have it here?"

"To the old MacLeod place? Yes, of course."

"Could you, do you think—?"

"I don't know why not. Excuse me a minute."

She shut the door for a second, undid the chain, and opened it to let him in. He took off the dripping raincoat and looked around for a place to put it. Linette took it and carried it into the laundry, then returned to find him still standing by the door.

"Come and sit down," said Linette, leading him into the drawing room.

He looked appreciatively at the fine plaster moldings of the ceiling, at the silver candelabra over the fireplace, at the long windows and the eighteenth-century portrait of an ancestor. "A handsome old house."

"It was built in the eighteen-fifties. This is one of the older parts of Mobile; you probably noticed the other houses as you were coming."

They had sat down now. In the full light of the candles, she could see him clearly for the first time. She had already noticed he was about the same height as herself, lean and rather lightly built; she saw now that he was also rather good-looking, with a ruddy British coloring and dark blue eyes. What was most striking was the excitement in his face, a controlled keenness like a hunter's. She was suddenly quite sure that he was a very good archaeologist.

"Yes," he was saying, "I could see them quite clearly when it lightened, at least—the high roof-lines against the sky, the shutters, the wrought-iron balconies. It gave me the strangest sense—well, of walking back into the last century, away from the whole modern world."

"You'll find it's really like that," said Linette. "I know, because I've read a great deal, that life in some places is very different now. Superficially, I mean, we have the ordinary conveniences; but there's a certain undercurrent, a different way of looking at life."

"The MacLeod house is about the same age, isn't it?"

"Yes—oh, I forgot to get the key." She started to rise, but checked herself. "You can't go out there tonight, anyway—not in this rain, on an unpaved road. Besides, somebody'll have to talk to Aunt Julian first. My father hasn't told her anything about it." The thought came to her that perhaps that was what her father was doing tonight.

"Is that Miss Julian Silverthorne?"

"Yes. She's joint owner, and of course it can't be sold without her permission; my father was a bit hesitant about raising the question. I think he was waiting for you to appear on the scene, to back him up. Have you heard of Aunt Julian, though?"

"It was her article that brought me here."

"The one about the wall in the basement, which she thinks is twelfth-century?"

"Exactly."

"You know the story, of course—about Prince Madoc's colony that's supposed to have come from Wales in 1170. Then, they say, Madoc went back to Wales for more people, but couldn't find the colony again; people think a hurricane changed the coastline, the way one did in the eighteenth century. Later the Indians drove the colonists north into the mountains; you can still see the forts there. But there's nothing down here that we know about, except Aunt Julian's wall. We don't even know the name of the colony. Catherine Windeatt, the poet, called it Belmary; but that's out of Chaucer."

"The name in the Welsh records is Caer Mair Brydferth—the Castle of Mary the Beautiful. Like so much in the Middle Ages, it was named after the mother of God."

"Our big basilica still is. You must let me show you the city; you'll find it unusual."

A brief silence fell. "Listen," said Linette suddenly, "let me show you the way, tomorrow. The turnoff is narrow, and you might miss it. And I'd like to have another look at that wall myself; I haven't seen it since I was a child."

His expression kindled. "Are you interested in archaeology, Miss Silverthorne?"

"Well, I've read a good deal about it—the finding of Troy and so on. A friend of mine actually went to the Yucatan, on one of the expeditions; but I've never done anything like that. I'd like to, though."

"Why don't you help me with this, if you'd like to? That is, if your aunt lets us."

"Yes, I'd like to very much." She felt again that upsurge of happiness and excitement; here at last was something of that ever-imminent adventure.

"Please don't expect Troy, though. It might not even be a twelfth-century wall at all."

But she saw that his eyes had grown very bright; he certainly was expecting Troy, or hoping for it. Every archaeologist, she thought, wants to be Schliemann.

"About the key," she said. "I'll get it."

"If you would, Miss Silverthorne."

"Please call me Linette, since we're going to be—what? Co-archaeologists?"

"Colleagues, at any rate. Please call me Rhodri, then."

She went for the key and brought it back into the drawing room—a big iron key with an unfamiliar coat of arms engraved on the head.

"I'd better be going," said Rhodri. "Is eight o'clock tomorrow too early for you?"

"No, not at all." She brought his raincoat, and they paused at the door. A certain warmth had risen between them at the prospect of a shared adventure, and the idea of rainy streets and an empty house seemed a little desolate.

"I'd better go," he said. "Good night, Miss Silverthorne—Linette."

"Good night, Rhodri. I'll see you at eight."

She stood a moment in the half-closed doorway, watching him go down the street in the illumination of the lessening lightning. Then she went back into the drawing room and sat thinking about fabulous archaeological discoveries, the frescoes of Knossos, the gold of Mycenae, till her thoughts drifted into sleep and tangled in fantastic dreams. She was walking under an early morning sky along a white seashore that was, and was not, the bay; west of her, out of the sand, rose wonderful Romanesque ruins of rose-red brick, full of arches like the arches of

Fort Morgan where the Prince Madoc monument was. She went among the ruins and passed in and out of the arches; everything was bright and empty and full of a fresh daylight magic.

Then she was wakened abruptly by the noise of the family coming home. The lights had come back on again; she blew out the remains of the candles and went up to bed.

2. Vines and White Stone

"Tell me exactly," said Linette, "what do you hope to find, besides a twelfth-century wall?"

She put her hand to her hair, trying to keep too many strands from blowing out of its smooth, flat folds. They were going rather fast down the shore road, and the bright morning air poured past her with a steady force. The storm had cleared and cooled the air; everything seemed brilliant, and Linette felt an unusual gaiety that made her want to talk.

"Well, if it is a twelfth-century wall," said Rhodri, "it ought to be associated with other structures. In short, I hope to find Caer Mair." He did not look at Linette as he answered; he concentrated on the road, his face serious, his black hair blowing back.

"What will it look like, if you do?"

"That depends on the state of preservation. Also it depends on what the structures are."

"Romanesque arches?"

"Possibly. Are we near the turn yet?"

"You'd better slow down," she said, "or you'll pass it." She felt a little put off by his refusal to talk, and also more curious than before. If he had no idea what to hope for, why this intense excitement? Was it natural to archaeologists?

They were on a peninsula now between a river and the bay. The city had thinned out behind them; now outlying houses showed infrequently between tracts of trees Ahead, the arch of the bridge across the river mouth rose white in the sunlight.

"Be ready to turn right," said Linette. "There! Turn!"

They swung off the shore road onto an unpaved track covered with ground-down oyster shells. Wild land edged it on each side, grassy wastes of pine overgrown with magenta fireweed. Rhodri had to drive slowly now; the road was rough, and once they crossed a dry stream bed over a rattling bridge of boards.

"The old MacLeod house," said Rhodri. "Who owned it?"

"My Uncle Neal—great-uncle really. We used to come out here in the summer, thirty or forty people sometimes; he'd make ice cream, and we'd have a picnic under the trees. He was a bachelor, though; and when he died, he left the place to my father and Aunt Julian."

"But he didn't build it?"

"No, it belonged to another family before. They called it Camelot."

"Why?" asked Rhodri, hitting a bump rather abruptly.

"Oh, probably no reason. Old houses often have grand names here, like Rosedown or Carlyle Hall. Look—there it is."

The trees opened onto an area of tall grass, overgrown with fireweed and yellow hibiscus-like flowers. Out of it rose the house, a fading white, with four square white columns rising two stories across the front. The columns and most of the porch were half-screened by rampant vines that wound upward, their broad, coarse yellow-green leaves translucent to the sun. Behind the house the ground vanished sharply, dropping towards the river.

"Those vines," said Linette; "if they're not stopped, they take over the place. Drive round back; there's some shade there."

They got out in the shade of the house and stood for a moment looking down the slope at the smooth, lead-colored water of the river. Then Linette led the way around the house.

"It never was as elegant as the house in town," she said; "but I liked it. Aunt Julian keeps it in repair, and has the vines cut back now and then; but it seems so desolate with no one living here."

They climbed onto the porch, over thick vine stems that sprawled over the steps. The house and the vines gave out a soft, sun-baked, dusty smell; last year's leaves lay drifted in the corners of the porch. Linette touched a column, and some of the whiteness came off like a dust on her hand.

What will they do with the house, she thought, the Caernarvon Archaeological Society? Tear it down, likely as not, for the excavations. And suddenly she felt sorry about the house; she thought of Uncle Neal and the summer afternoons—all that gone then, soon not even a memory. And the people who had called the house Camelot—gone, with their romanticism and their secrets.

Rhodri stood at the large sun-faded door, turning the key in the lock. The lock gave, reluctantly; and the door swung open. They stepped into the hallway, amid dark panelling and old wallpaper where all the colors had been faded into dusty, soft shades. The sunlight pouring in around them was filled with little motes of dust.

"Someone'll live here, I suppose," said Rhodri, "if the excavation turns up anything. To act as curator."

"Assuming that Aunt Julian co-operates," said Linette. She was not sure she liked the idea of strangers intruding on those well-remembered rooms, but it was better than having the place torn down.

They went through the house, opening windows and shutters to let in the fresh air. There was no furniture; all the rooms were alike now, bare, full of the soft peace of long summer noons. Silence lay like water over the soft, faded-out wallpapers and dusty floors, disturbed for a little by their feet and voices, but flowing back inviolate as before.

"If the foundations are what I hope," said Rhodri, "I can get a little furniture and stay here during the excavations."

Linette's nostalgia about the old long afternoons died instantly in an uprush of excitement. "Let's look at the foundations now," she said. "But there's no electricity, you know. Have you got a flashlight?"

He made an impatient gesture. "Left it at the hotel."

"Never mind, I think one of the old lanterns is in the kitchen. Aunt Julian uses it sometimes."

They found it in a cupboard, and with it the kerosene can. Rhodri helped her light it, and they went down the cellar stairs into the dim, unfrequented depths of the house. The air was cooler, with a damp, long-closed smell; there were no windows, only small overgrown grates through which flecks of daylight came greyly. The yellow light of the lantern showed a large cistern in the middle of the floor; there was nothing else, only the old walls of mellow clay brick, mixing toward the north end with courses of white limestone. The north wall was white stone entirely, finely-cut massive blocks; it was marred only by a great irregular patch of white plaster, where a large broken place had apparently been mended.

Rhodri took the lantern and went on his knees by the wall, holding the light close against the stones. He bent over them as over some work of art, intensely, for a long time, touching them, examining the joints; Linette watched in silence. The cold of the cellar pressed around her, and the light seemed small in the vast shadows. She became slowly aware of the age of the house—older than her father, older than grandfather or great-grandfather, a house that had known old troubles and many deaths. But beyond that, deeper, these massive stone foundations—what were they, then? For an instant they seemed like walls in some dark ageless castle, Inverness or the House of Atreus, where fearful things had happened in forgotten years, things that had left a taint on the very stones. Rhodri, kneeling in the flickering lantern-light, seemed a shadow out of that enigmatic past; she was half-afraid that when he turned, he would turn toward her the face of a stranger. She shook her head to clear it: What is the matter with me?

Rhodri rose, and the movement broke the spell of her thoughts; she felt as if a dark, overshadowing presence withdrew from her. His face was eager and excited, and she felt herself lifted on the wave of his mood.

"It's medieval work, all right." His voice, filled with controlled excitement, echoed from the shadowed walls. "What else can it be but part of Caer Mair? Look at it—the north wall almost perfect, and traces of side walls on the east and west; other stones set in with the bricks, some of them cracked and chipped as if from falling. It looks as if this was a cellar or crypt of some kind, evidently smaller than the present cellar—you notice there are no stones visible at the south end? Evidently all the walls but the north were partly destroyed when the upper building fell—when it was burnt, I would say, because some of the cracked stones show traces of fire."

Linette listened to him in his earnestness; his keen face was flushed, his hair falling forward across his forehead. He did not appear to see her; she guessed that his mind was fast at work reconstructing the history of those stones. Why do I like him? she thought suddenly. Because I do like him. Is it because he seems so purposeful, so intense?

"We'll know more, of course, when the excavations get under way."

"What do you think it was?"

"A cellar or a crypt—I would say perhaps a crypt, the crypt of a church. Perhaps the one—" He stopped suddenly, with a slightly shut-up expression.

"Perhaps which one?" persisted Linette.

"They say there was a church outside Cair Mair itself, specially connected with the princely house, dedicated to Saint Michael the Archangel. The angel with the fiery sword—that accounted for its popular name, Annedd Cledd, the House of the Sword." He glanced quickly toward the stairway. "Come, let's go see your aunt."

"Not yet," said Linette, following him up the stairs. "Aunt Julian does her scholarly work in the mornings; she might be annoyed if we interrupted her. She's translating the *Poetic Edda* right now."

"What can we do, then, while she finishes her work?" He swung the lantern with an impatient gesture; Linette guessed that he was disappointed by even that slight delay.

"Well, it's almost noon," she said; "and I did bring that picnic lunch."

As they sat under a sweet-bay on the riverbank, eating under the rustle of silvery leaves, Rhodri said, "Tell me about your aunt. She sounds like an interesting person."

"Oh, very interesting," said Linette. "She lives in a castle."

"Didn't know you had them here."

"She built it with most of her inheritance, although she still has an estate up the country. Actually the central tower is older; Catherine Windeatt, the poet, lived there a long time ago. But Aunt Julian added the top story, the outer wall, and so on. She lives there alone, except for one servant and occasional company."

"That is interesting."

"There's more to come. She dresses to match the house—long, flowing medieval dresses, a silver circlet, and her hair down. She looks magnificent, but it surprises people when they first see her—so I thought I'd better warn you. Another thing: when they got electricity out here, she wouldn't have it except in the kitchen. She prefers candlelight."

They had finished eating by now; they gathered up the picnic things and went back to the car.

"Silverthorne is almost across the road from here," said Linette as they drove once more over the track of shells. "Oh, I forgot to tell you about her library. She inherited the Caldwell-Myers Collection, besides what she already had; it's a rather famous one full of rare books. So now she has probably the finest private library on the Gulf Coast, and people are always coming to consult it. There's a lady staying there now, writing some kind of treatise on the occult—a Miss Cornwall; she's British. I haven't met her."

They had reached the road. "Careful, now," said Linette. "It's the next turn to the left."

Rhodri turned; once more they were on an oyster-shell road leading through trees. But this road was smooth and well-kept, and led between a handsome pair of wrought-iron gates that stood open. Down a vista of overhanging oakboughs they could see a gleam of white stone, and a certain openness suggestive of the sea.

Silverthorne appeared suddenly as they came out of the trees, dazzling white in the sunlight amid the green lawns and the pale-blue summer sky. Walls of white limestone rose foursquare out of the grass, with a square tower at each corner; over the top they could glimpse the red tile roof of the tower in the central court. The east side of the house faced the bay; on the other sides, woods of oak and pine hemmed in the lawn.

Linette and Rhodri left the car at the end of the drive and approached the round-arched gateway. The massive oak door stood open, showing a round-vaulted passage closed by an inner gate of delicate wrought iron. Through the gate could be seen a grassy court, where a pair of peacocks in splendid turquoise walked with their peahens before the white keep.

A small bell hung by the gateway; Linette pulled the chain, and it gave out a sharp, clear sound. Out of the keep, across the bright sunlight of the courtyard, a woman came towards them, the light catching on her red dress and the gold of her earrings. Her hair was whitening, and in her delicacy and the creamy-brown of her coloring she was like an image of very old ivory.

"That's Aramelissa," whispered Linette as they stood at the inner gateway; "she's been with Aunt Julian as long as she's been here."

Aramelissa shaded her eyes and looked into the shadowed passage; her brown eyes were bright and ageless amid the lines of her face. She took them in with a gaze that was both humorous and enigmatic.

"Aramelissa, is Aunt Julian home?"

Aramelissa raised her hands in tremendous mock-alarm. "Oh, Miss Julian, she's up in the keep, pacing up and down like a queen lioness. Oh, isn't she in a powerful frame of mind?"

She began unlatching the gate, regarding Rhodri through the iron tracery. "Well, Miss Linette, I always thought it was Mr. Anthony."

Linette's color rose. "Oh, Aramelissa!—This is Mr. Meyrick, an archaeologist; what will he think of me?" Her head lifted haughtily. "As for Anthony, he was predestined from birth to be a Professor of Middle English; and I haven't seen him in three months."

Aramelissa, instead of replying, opened the gate; but the humorous glint was still in her eyes. She glanced at Rhodri. "Just take care what you say to Miss Julian, if you want to dig for any Celtic treasures." And she started away across the courtyard, toward one of the arched walks that connected the keep to the outer walls.

"You forgot to say Aramelissa was interesting too," murmured Rhodri, as Linette led the way towards the keep.

"Oh, she knows everything."

"Evidently—including what I've come for. Is that a bad sign?"

"There's no telling. But probably yes."

Linette still felt ruffled by her exchange of words with Aramelissa; she was irritated by the reference to Anthony, and then the presumption that Rhodri had replaced him—! She paused near the base of the keep, where a fountain flowed out of a stone lion's head into a rectangular basin, dipped her hands in the water, and smoothed her hot cheeks before going to face her aunt. Then they entered the keep.

They passed through an almost-round dining room with arched windows that looked out onto the court. A curved stairway wound steeply up the wall; Linette led the way up.

They emerged into a sliver of hallway, through which the stair vanished upward. A door opened on a large, airy room that took up the whole floor. Rhodri had a confused impression of arched windows, tall shelves of books, a long table, green wall-hangings; then he saw, and saw nothing else but, Julian Silverthorne.

She was pacing up and down by the windows, indeed like a queen lioness. She was tall, and her violet dress embroidered with silver swept magnificently about as she moved. Her hair, black slightly streaked with silver, streamed from beneath the silver circlet to below her waist. At the sound of their entrance she turned; he saw a face not unlike Linette's, though older, a long, proud-featured face with a clear pallor and calm, deep, grey eyes. He felt for a moment as if he stood before some perilous mythological queen, Maeve or Deirdre, more reverend than Guenevere, stranger than Iseult.

Her gaze singled out Rhodri, and the anger evinced by her pacing changed instantly into graciousness. "You must be Mr. Meyrick. My brother told me about you. Come in, both of you, and sit down. Have you eaten?"

"Yes, Aunt Julian," said Linette. "We thought you'd be busy translating."

"I would've been, but I had something else on my mind."

All three sat down in large carved chairs near one end of the table. Rhodri had time now to study the room, which was full of daylight from the arched windows. Between the windows, tall shelves of books alternated with green wall-hangings embroidered in white patterns of foliage. At the windows were cushioned green windowseats, on one of which lay a carved Irish harp. The massive table was almost hidden under books and papers; there were many sheets covered in a large neat script which must be Julian's, and he guessed that these were the translation of the *Edda*.

"Do you like my library?" asked Julian, amused by his intent, fascinated gaze.

"Yes, very much."

"I'll show you the whole house, if you like. But first, let me offer you some—?"

"Tea, thanks," said Rhodri. "With milk."

When Julian had left the room, he glanced again at the harp. "Can she really play it?"

"Of course."

"If I were a generation older, I think I'd be in love with your aunt."

Julian came back into the room, bearing a tray with the tea. All three of them now sat in the carved chairs, sipping the tea and looking out at the green courtyard across which the shadow of the west wall was beginning to fall, and where the peacocks still walked to and fro. Linette was beginning to feel sleepy with the long richness of Silverthorne afternoons; she thought of her dream, then of the strange-named ancient cities of Dunsany's tales, Bethmoora, Merimna, Perdóndaris. Then she came suddenly wide awake, for Julian had at last come to their real business.

"Malcolm has put me in a rather awkward position," she was saying to Rhodri, "by never mentioning this to me till last night. I don't know whether he's talked to you today or not; but the fact is, I don't intend selling that property. It's to go to Linette when she marries."

"This is news to me," said Linette, meeting Rhodri's startled glance.

"But, Miss Silverthorne," said Rhodri, "I came all the way here just for this excavation. And it was your article that brought me!"

"Just a minute," said Julian. "I said you couldn't buy; I didn't say you couldn't excavate."

"Then we can excavate?" Rhodri's face, in that second, was filled with an overwhelming excitement.

"Wait, wait. I'm not sure yet. I'm not sure those ruins ought to be excavated. You don't know the story of the discovery of those walls; but I do." She paused. "I don't suppose you ever heard of Mary Caldwell Myers."

"She owned the Caldwell-Myers Collection," guessed Rhodri.

"Yes. She came out with her husband's friend, who owned the place, to see the foundations of the house being dug; and it was then that the wall was discovered. They sent away the workmen—perhaps they hoped they would find treasure—and were alone there at the wall during a sudden storm. It seems Mary saw something then, something very strange. And at that time she was a sensible, practical young woman. I've always thought the ruins were responsible for her meddling in the occult; and latterly it was occultness of no good kind."

"What did she see?" demanded Rhodri almost sharply, nearly rising from his chair in excitement.

Julian looked at him steadily. "I don't know clearly. A shining thing of some kind, a golden light. Nobody ever knew what it was."

"And you want us to let it alone," said Rhodri. "Just because this woman saw something and didn't know what it was."

Julian continued to look at him. "I haven't finished thinking about it," she said. "Stay for supper. I'll tell you then whether you can dig or not."

3. Supper at Silverthorne

After tea, Julian kept her promise to show Rhodri Silverthorne. She began by taking them up to the round chapel at the top of the keep—a jewel-like vaulted place of white stone faintly tinged with gold by the amber windows. There was a single statue, a delicately carved and painted image of the Virgin as a young girl. The white altar stood detached from the wall, on a low platform of marble; the tabernacle behind it had doors of sculptured bronze. Before the altar, in a brass stand, burnt a lamp of red glass; its fiery color glowed amid the gold and white of the room.

Julian did not speak while they stood there; her gaze rested on the sculptured doors, and she seemed to draw herself to her full height. Only afterward, as they were going downstairs, did she explain, "Years ago, there was no church out here. People used to come—oh, in the summer sometimes, when a lot of people stayed at their summer houses on the bay, it would be quite crowded. The sculptor who gave me the statue was one of my guests, though."

She led them through the dining room into the kitchen, where Aramelissa was calmly reading *Paradise Lost*. Rhodri concealed his surprise and commented, "I see you've got a wireless."

"It's short-wave," said Julian, glancing at the bulky object in a corner, "sending and receiving. Malcolm insisted I have it; and really it's quite good, we often pick up New York and Mexico. But he thought we should have something in case of emergencies, since there's no phone."

She led them out through the arched walk to the door of the north wall, then upstairs. Both corridors, upstairs and down, had arched windows opening on the courtyard.

"My painting room is on this side," she said, "and a few of the guest rooms." She opened a few doors on white-walled rooms full of afternoon light, one with half-finished panel paintings in medieval colors, others furnished with handsome carved furniture and wall-hangings of blue or green, rose or violet or pale gold.

"I'll just give you a glimpse of the towers," she said. "This is the Atlantis Tower, where Miss Cornwall is staying."

The tower was on the northeast corner and overlooked the sea; it had its name from a tapestry that hung there, picturing Atlantis glittering in the path of the tidal wave. On the northwest corner was the Garden Tower, with Julian's room, which overlooked the rose garden. The southwest tower was the Eagle Tower, so called from a wall-painting of St. John with a tremendous shining eagle; and the southeast tower, again overlooking the sea, was called the Treasure Tower, from the strong-room for valuables on its first floor.

Julian led them back northward from the Treasure Tower. For half the east wing, the corridor became a gallery looking down into the great hall of Silverthorne, which had large windows opening to the courtyard and the sea. Square wooden pillars with painted dragon-carvings on the capitals rose to the gallery and the dark roof-beams. A long, heavy table, with massive candlesticks on it at intervals, ran the length of the room.

She brought them downstairs and out into the courtyard. The sun had disappeared now behind the walls of Silverthorne; only a long path of yellow light streamed through the gate, marked with the intricate whorls of the ironwork, and touched the white stone and softly-falling water of the lion fountain. The peacocks passed in stately procession across the rich light; their colors were kindled by it into an almost unearthly brilliance before sinking again into shadow.

"My guest should be back from town soon," said Julian. "She's British; her name's Morgan Cornwall."

"That's an unusual name," said Rhodri. "Morgan is usually a man's name. The only woman I ever heard of that had it was Morgan le Fay."

"Now there's an entertaining idea," said Julian. "You know Morgan le Fay in the Charlemagne legends is immortal."

"So of course she comes to Silverthorne," said Rhodri, "and does research in your library. What is she doing exactly, anyway?"

"She's editing a manuscript of the *Oracles of Patricius*," said Julian. "It's a magical text in the Caldwell-Myers Collection."

"Of course; I should have known," said Rhodri. "It's all in Malory: 'she learned so much that she was a great clerk of necromancy.' "

" 'And set the land on fire with ladies that were enchantresses,' " said Julian.

"And all the time," said Linette, "she's about forty, with short yellow hair and chilly eyes and a thousand angles, and lives with two striped cats in lodgings in Bloomsbury."

"Torquay, and the cats are white," said Julian. "You haven't met her yet."

"White cats," said Rhodri, "instead of black ones. She must be one of those white witches one hears about sometimes."

"Seriously," said Julian, "she may be, for all I know. I've seen her wear flowing white robes that ought to belong to some ritual. Anyway, here she comes."

There was the sound of a car stopping at the end of the drive, the slam of a door, and the sound of quick, light steps on the oyster shells. Linette felt suddenly a strange hastening of the heart, like fear; it is the quality of the light, she told herself, it is Aunt Julian and Rhodri's fantasizing. The steps sounded fast and sharp in the passage. Julian stepped to the gate and unlatched it, and moved back.

Someone came rapidly to the gate and pushed it open, then stood still in the gateway, framed by the yellow light. Linette had an impression of supernatural tallness, of red hair blazing like flame. A sense of nightmare came on her; her very heart and breath seemed to stand still.

The figure moved quickly out of the doorway; and Julian was saying, "Well, Morgan, did you find what you wanted?"

Linette felt the instant's spell break. It was only the light, she thought.

In the rational twilight of the courtyard she saw that Morgan was not, in fact, strikingly tall. She was a delicately-made woman of about thirty, wearing a white summer dress. She did indeed have splendid red hair, thick and Titian-brilliant, which spilled down her back in slight waves. Her face had the fine transparent pallor proper to that hair; her features were delicate and had a slightly abstracted look, as if she lived deep in her own thoughts. Only her eyes were truly strange; they were violet-colored, intensely secret and deep, under dark lashes.

"No, in fact," she said. "The libraries here don't have that sort of thing. But I can manage without it."

After introductions they went into the keep, where Julian lit the candles in the round dining room. Then they parted to get ready for dinner. Linette washed her hands and face, adjusted her hair, and returned to find Rhodri and Julian already sitting in the dining room in the candlelight. By now it was quite dark outside.

"What have you decided?" asked Linette.

"I haven't said yet," said Julian, "though I was about to. Here comes Morgan."

Morgan came in from the courtyard. She had dressed for dinner, in a long white flowing dress without sleeves; it was unbelted and utterly unadorned. Her only ornament was a necklace of twisted gold, made in one piece, about the length of a string of pearls.

They all took their places at the table, and Aramelissa brought in dinner. The warmth of the July night came in through the open windows; the land breeze brought at moments the scent of elder-blossoms from the woods, and the sound of the bay came faint in the pauses of conversation.

"Your name rang a bell for me when I first heard it," said Julian to Rhodri; "and now I remember what it was. Meyrick—it seems to me I read that some Meyricks were descended from Prince Madoc. That wouldn't be your family?"

"It would," said Rhodri. "The descent comes through his daughter Gwenllian, who married the Lord of Menai."

"That makes your quest more interesting, doesn't it? Well, we have our traditions too, like the second-sighted Malcolm."

"What quest is this?" put in Morgan, with some interest.

"Mr. Meyrick wants to excavate for the lost city of Caer Mair. And I've decided that I'm going to let him." Julian turned to Rhodri. "How long do you think it'll take?"

"That depends on what we find. For the preliminary work, say, a few days to a few weeks."

"In that case, why don't you stay at Silverthorne? I have all this room, and it'd save you the trip back and forth. You could stay in the Treasure Tower, and I could put Linette in the other room of the Garden Tower."

"I'd be delighted. I'd been rather longing to, but I didn't dare ask."

"What is this place Caer Mair?" asked Morgan.

"It was Prince Madoc's settlement in the twelfth century," said Rhodri.

"Madoc—he was descended from Arthur, wasn't he?"

"That's what they say about the royal line of Gwynedd, yes."

"Do you think you might find any—well, Arthurian relics?"

"No. What for? What kind?"

"How do I know? You're the archaeologist."

The conversation had become, inexplicably, a little irritated. Julian, to pour oil on the troubled waters, said to Morgan, "We were talking about your name earlier. It's an interesting one."

"Yes, I've always thought so."

"It's Arthurian itself, isn't it? Even the last name fits, since Morgan le Fay was one of the princesses of Cornwall."

"I'd forgotten about that," said Linette. "How does that come in?"

"She was one of the three daughters of Avalloc and Ygerna," said Morgan. "The other two were Morgause and Elaine. Afterwards Ygerna married Uther, Arthur's father."

"I've often wondered about Morgan le Fay," said Julian. "Why exactly did she hate Arthur?"

"She didn't hate him," said Morgan. "Though she could have, very reasonably."

"Why do you say that?" asked Rhodri. "After all, she tried to kill him."

"It's difficult to explain," said Morgan. "But after all, sharing a name with her, I've thought a lot about her myself. The evidence is there in Malory and the other sources, if you know how to interpret it. I reconstruct the story something like this."

She paused for a moment, looking thoughtfully down at the table. "There were three of them; she was the youngest. And after the tragedy in Cornwall, her sisters were married off by Uther to two of his subject kings; but she was too young. The Cornwall dynasty worshipped the old gods; and Ygerna—Igraine in Malory—placed Morgan in a college of priestesses on an island. They were nine maiden priestesses, the servants of Arianrhod; and they had the power of prophecy and other gifts that were not common. She was made chief priestess after awhile, the representative of the goddess. And she was happy there, glad to be there in the service of the Lady and to belong to her, body and soul. This place was Avalon, the apple-tree island, what they called Glastonbury later; that is to say, it was the Avalon of this world.

"You know the *Mabinogion* story, of course—how Arianrhod gave weapons to her son Llew, the young sun god? The story was differently told in Morgan's day; Arianrhod gave them freely, with no enchanter to trick her. She was the first person, so to speak, of the supreme triune goddess who was once worshipped in Britain.

"But this did not last. Uther died, and Arthur became king. This was the time of the Saxon invasions, and the British were having little success against them. Then a man named Gildas, a monk, said this was a punishment because the king tolerated the old religion in the land; and he made such an outcry, and got such a following, that the king was forced to act against the island shrine. The holy grove was cut down; the priestesses were scattered; and the king's half-sister, the servant of the maiden goddess, was taken away and married to a stranger."

There was a brief silence at the table.

"I think you've missed your calling, Miss Cornwall," said Rhodri. "You should have been a novelist."

Morgan smiled. "Is it such an implausible theory?"

"No, though unproveable, of course. I meant that you tell it rather well."

"Another aspect of the story that puzzles me," said Julian, "is why she tried to take Excalibur."

There was a complete silence, through which came faintly the endless sounding of the sea. It grew long; Rhodri pursued the last of his dessert with his fork, and Morgan looked intently at the spider lilies in a bowl on the table.

"Perhaps she did it out of vengeance," said Linette finally. But still nobody else spoke; and Julian watched her guests with a quiet, thoughtful gaze.

Aramelissa came in, cleared away the plates, and brought coffee. This seemed to break the spell; everyone moved as if awakened, and Julian went to the window and looked out at the night.

"It should be a good day tomorrow for your excavations," she said to Rhodri. "Speaking of the Arthurian legend, I was reading something not long ago—did you ever hear of the Pendragons?"

"Arthur and Uther—," said Rhodri in a curiously surprised voice.

"No, I mean the idea of the Pendragon—how does the book put it?—'the successors of Arthur and Uther and Cassibelaun,' that work in every age, with whatever few followers they have, to try to keep England closer to its ideal self and farther from its anti-ideal. Logres and Britain, I think they were called respectively."

"Well, I," said Rhodri with his color mounting, "I'm not familiar with the books in your library; but yes, I've heard of the idea."

"What do you make of it?"

"Well—" Rhodri stared thoughtfully at the table, as if concentrating on his words. "*Logres* does well enough for one name; in Modern Welsh, *Lloegr* is only England, but in the romances it refers to all of Arthur's kingdom. Though I don't see why *Britain* should be the other—it only means the Island of the Mighty. But I suppose it had to be called something."

"I meant the Pendragonship itself," said Julian.

He frowned still more intently at the polished wood. "Well, it's an interesting idea, isn't it? Although I would think it was rather a hard job. In books, people like that have big houses and ancient treasures; but in reality it might not be like that, he might not have such resources. He might have to depend mostly on himself, while his neighbors might think he was just anything, a writer, a scientist—" He gestured vaguely, as if he did not know what else to add. "That, anyway, is how I imagine it."

"And it sounds quite probable," said Julian lightly. "Who knows? Such a person could really exist."

Linette, who was watching them, saw the expression in Julian's eyes as she spoke; she fixed on Rhodri a gaze thoughtful, quiet, and unreadable, though the candlelight gave her face a luminous look.

Rhodri meanwhile was glancing at his watch. "Since you asked me to stay, Miss Silverthorne, I think I'll go get my things tonight. That way I can get an early start in the morning."

"I'll ride back with you," said Linette; "I have to get mine too."

"I'll show you to the gate," said Julian, rising. "You can take the other candle, Morgan, if you want to."

Linette, following Julian across the courtyard to the gate, looked back to see if Rhodri was keeping up. She saw, over his shoulder, Morgan passing among the arches of the north walk; she had a candle in her hand, and it made a ring of radiance around her. In her white robes, amid that unreal light, she had a spirit-like look; once again Linette felt her hair prickle as if with cold.

Nonsense, she thought, quickening her steps in the wake of Julian's. But nevertheless the impression remained, a vague and formless oppression of the heart, like a distant echo of foreboding.

4. Doors

"Linette!"

Julian's voice came through the door and through Linette's rapidly vanishing sleep; she sat up abruptly, half-dazzled by the muted sunlight. "Yes?"

"It's seven o'clock, and Mr. Meyrick's waiting for breakfast."

"I'll be there."

Before Julian's footsteps had faded, she sprang up and drew the drapes. Under the tower, the rose garden was in full bloom; eastward the bay was full of light. She dressed quickly in a dark-blue dress and put up her hair. She did not care for too much brightness or softness in her clothes; a certain severity suited her more, made it clear that she was serious and intellectual. Extravagances of purple and silver were all very well for a splendid eccentric like her aunt, but not for Linette Silverthorne. Still, she looked with satisfaction at her image in the mirror; this plain style became her.

Julian had decided to eat in the rose garden, and she and Rhodri were sitting at a wrought-iron table when Linette came out. Aramelissa followed with the serving cart.

Rhodri rose as Linette approached, looking at her directly and frankly, as he had looked at the stone. She sensed that now, with the roses heightening the fair and dark of her color, he was seeing her clearly for the first time; and her cheeks brightened under that appraising gaze. But there's nothing for him to find fault with, she thought, with a lift of her head, and approached the table.

"Well, Rhodri," she said, "let's go and look at your stones of Caer Mair." She felt, for some reason, a need of bravado; but she did not clearly know what disturbed her.

"I was just telling Julian that there's been a little contretemps," said Rhodri, recollecting his impatience. "I was unpacking my boxes last night, and I found my light's missing. Left it in Caernarvon, evidently; and I don't know where I'll get another."

"Do you really need it?" asked Linette, sitting down. "The lantern gives a pretty decent light, and I'm sure Schliemann didn't have anything better."

"You have a point there," said Rhodri, "though it is rather a nuisance." Nevertheless his face cleared; there would not be any delay after all.

"Where's Morgan Cornwall?" asked Linette.

"She never eats breakfast with me," said Julian. "In fact, she sleeps late; I rarely see her before noon."

"I told you she was a white witch," said Rhodri, half-laughing. "Up half the night casting spells. Divining the future by the power of Arianrhod."

"It's a good thing she isn't at this table to hear you," said Julian, laughing.

In the cellar, by the light of the kerosene lantern, Rhodri laid out his tools and surveyed the wall. "The first thing, obviously," he said, "is to get this plaster down and see what the break is like. That's going to take a while."

"What do I do?" asked Linette.

"Nothing yet. Maybe hold the lantern as I need it."

"How soon will you know whether it's your crypt?"

"I don't know. Tell me—who was the second-sighted Malcolm, anyway? The man your aunt mentioned last night."

"Oh, just an ancestor; I think he was my father and Aunt Julian's great-great-grandfather. His name was Malcolm MacLeod, and he foresaw his own death in war. In fact he wrote a poem foretelling it; it's printed in the genealogy."

"Extraordinary story."

"Oh, there are more. Second sight is supposed to be hereditary in that branch of the family. Why did you ask about him?"

Rhodri looked intently at the chisel he had just picked up. "Well, the second sight—I've known someone that had it." He placed the chisel against the plaster and gave it a sharp blow with the mallet; for a while there was too much noise for conversation.

Linette held the lantern up so he could see. She watched his intent face and the flying flakes of plaster, and heard the hammer-blows echoing in the dark. She felt vaguely depressed, as if the cool, earth-smelling darkness were weighing down on her; some restless and elusive disturbance stirred in her.

After a while, Rhodri stopped for a rest, and they sat down against the side wall, away from the mess of fallen plaster.

"Who did you know that had it?" said Linette.

"Had what?"

"The second sight."

"A woman. She lived in Caernarvon."

"Tell me about her. Was she old or young?"

"Young."

"What was her name?"

"Cristant Aberglas."

"Pretty name."

"Yes."

"What did she see?"

"Various things. She was very good at it." He rose and picked up the mallet and chisel. "I'll just get back to work on this wall."

Once again the conversation stopped. There was the circle of lantern-light, the steady thud of the hammer, the rattle of falling plaster.

Linette again felt the vague insecurity of the darkness. Standing with the light in her hand, she seemed to herself to be getting drowsy; the noise seemed far away as if it came across a stretch of dark water, from a shore from which a ship was slowly receding. Malcolm, she thought vaguely. Cristant Aberglas. What did they see?

Far away. Old stones marked by fire. She was not receding from a shore; she was sinking deeper and deeper into an inner darkness, into another world that lay in her mind like a lighted crystal sphere. Old stones—Cristant, not Aberglas, a slight girl with black braids and a thin circlet of gold; she was Princess of Caer Mair, and she stood in torch-light with a handful of others before a heavy wooden door.

"Linette!"

Rhodri's voice came sharp, dragging her out of her inner depths. I should be a writer, she thought as her mind flashed upward; I imagined that so clearly.

He had stopped hammering. "Hold the light over here," he said in a breathless voice. "Yes. Clay brick."

Linette stared at the brick showing through the flaked plaster. Why not? she thought uncomprehendingly. Why not clay brick?

"Look how it joins on," he said in the same voice. "A straight joint—clay and then stone. Does it go on like that?" He began to hammer again with redoubled fury; the plaster fell like snow. Linette watched the violent downward pace of the hammer. A straight line began to show amid the cracked whiteness, dropping vertically from the point of discovery, a clean jointure of brick against stone.

Rhodri laid it bare to the floor. Then he rose and turned to Linette; his face was strangely pale, and his eyes like half-hidden blue flames in the lantern-light. "What does it look like to you?"

His voice was level, but Linette could feel the strained-in intensity. Something in herself answered to it, so that she could hardly breathe. "It looks as if the stone ended straight, not like a broken place. Like a doorway."

Without a reply he turned back to the wall and began to hammer more fiercely than ever. The plaster showered down like a miniature avalanche. But even now, Linette saw, he did not strike recklessly; the thick and fast blows fell as cleanly as they had ever done. Yet at unbelievable speed he traced out a rectangle, following the jointure of brick and stone, and then with heavier strokes laid the brick bare.

Finally he stood back, breathing hard, with the sweat streaking the plaster-dust on his face even in the cool of the cellar. He was unable to speak, but his eyes were a blaze of exultation.

Linette took the hammer out of his hand. "Come outside. Catch your breath and wash your face and tell me what this is. And eat something. It's past one."

She herself was almost as overcome with excitement as he was. She could not have said which was uppermost, excitement or curiosity or a concern that she suddenly felt for him.

They came out of the cellar. Rhodri washed in the kitchen, and they sat on the back porch and ate the lunch Aramelissa had prepared.

"What do you think it is?" said Linette when he had caught his breath.

"I don't know," said Rhodri. "Obviously it was some kind of doorway. It could be the stairwell that led to the upper level; or it could lead to a completely collapsed part of the lower level, closed off for safety."

"But you don't think that," said Linette. "I see what you're doing; you're thinking of the most pessimistic things you can, to stop yourself from hoping too much. And I don't blame you. I feel a hope in me, though I don't know what I'm hoping for; and I want so much for it to come true, that the thought of its failing seems to choke me. I want something wonderful, something glorious to happen—something worth remembering, just once in my whole life!"

Rhodri looked at her, startled. "But I would have thought you were happy—"

"Many people would think so. I have a good family, a fine house, an education—by all the proper rules, I should now marry some promising young man and settle down to live happily ever after. In fact, by the rules I should have married long ago; I'm twenty-five, and that's rather late here. The girls I went to school with have been married for years; I see them sometimes, and I'm filled with horror. They're old; all the life has gone out of them—just ordinary, ordinary, ordinary. I couldn't bear that. I'd rather be an old maid like Aunt Julian. If I were really like Aunt Julian, that might be all right; but her way is closed to me. I know what I'll do; I'll go on in my education, get a doctorate, and teach in some university. That at least is not ordinary. But still it's not enough. I want more, much more, than years of lonely work, keeping up a position and watching myself grow older.

"I don't know why I'm telling you all this—I suppose because you represent something different from anything I've ever known. I wish I were an archaeologist; or I wish I'd lived in Caer Mair, or in Arthur's Britain that Morgan was talking about. It might have been different for me. Oh, if I'd been Guenevere, Lancelot might never have existed for all I'd have cared; I would have stayed with Arthur and helped him, with all my ability, to hold off the barbarians and keep what was left of civilization alive. But there's no chance of anything for me now. The world now is flattened-out and huge and dead; in it I have nothing and I am nothing. Aunt Julian's right to turn away from it; there's nothing worth staying for."

Rhodri watched her; her head was bent, her mouth tightened into a hard unaccepting line. He wanted to speak to her; words trembled in his mind. But around the two of them shone the fierce July sun over this harsh and strange land, over the heavy waters of the river. It was impossible here.

He rose abruptly. "Come down to the cellar."

Linette followed him, her bitter mood unbroken; everything around her seemed nebulous as a dream. The cool darkness relieved her; it did not mock her as the daylight did.

Rhodri sat down on the floor where they had sat before and stared at the lantern. She sat down beside him; the flame seemed to draw her gaze too, so that neither of them looked at the other. The cool silence closed for a moment around them, stilling his reticence and her distress.

"Let me tell you about that door," said Rhodri slowly, without looking away from the flame. "I was hoping it would be there."

Linette glanced at him, with a glimmer of light breaking her dark mood. "What are you really looking for?"

"I told you about the church of Saint Michael the Archangel. It was outside Caer Mair, at the place where Madoc made his first encampment before choosing the site of the city; actually it was only partly finished when he sailed away. And it was the special church of the princely house, or so the records seem to hint.

"The truth is, I am looking for treasures. Madoc is said to have taken certain precious things with him, and I have reason to think they were hidden in a secret treasury opening out of this crypt."

"Like the gold of Troy?"

"Yes, that sort of thing—the wealth of the princely house. But according to the tradition, there were certain other things—a talisman, for instance, supposed to have been given to the royal house by the famous Brigid of Kildare. It was only a glass vessel with water from a sacred well in Ireland; but it was called the Water of Vision, and the story says it had miraculous properties. Supposedly, if someone with proper faith let a drop of it fall in still water, he would see whatever he needed to know on the face of the water. Anyway, if this vessel really existed at all, and hasn't been destroyed, it might be with other royal treasures in that secret treasury."

Linette said nothing, but he felt that she was looking at him. He glanced at her quickly; her face held pools of shadow from the lantern-light, but her eyes looked out with a half-awakened brilliance. Ice with the reflection of flames, he thought suddenly; but not ice altogether.

He rose abruptly. "I'm going to take out the bricks."

Once again the strong, careful pounding began, and the mortar broke and crumbled. Linette held the lantern in silence and watched Rhodri. She saw how he did not remove any bricks at once, but loosened several; she thought, He wants to be able to see something when he moves them. His face was half-hidden by the shadow and by the dark hair falling forward. Why did I tell him that? she wondered. Now he knows my secrets—do I like that or not? Will I dislike him now for knowing?

She thought of what he had told her. It was a secret too, of sorts—but not personal, not intimate like hers. It was only a practical secret, to keep people from grabbing.

Surely he'll tell Aunt Julian, though, she thought. He's honest. Ah, Aunt Julian.

She sighed. Rhodri had put down the mallet and chisel now and was carefully working out a brick; he heard her. "What is it? Are you tired?"

"No—I was just thinking about Aunt Julian. How does she have a right to be so beautiful and happy? She lives in a world outside the world—is that right? I don't mean that she isn't concerned about people—everyone knows how kind and charitable she is. But she seems to set her peace somewhere else, where people don't go nowadays. It isn't the writing and scholarly work I mean; it isn't the medievalism; it isn't the love of nature, though I've seen her go out in a howling storm just to watch the sea. And she keeps a big black horse which she rides for hours sometimes through the countryside. But it isn't any of that. It's that she never seems to be disturbed about things that disturb other people—not about being an utter contradiction of the modern world, not about dying there alone perhaps some night—I don't think she'd be afraid of the Day of Judgment. It's as if she found a meaning somewhere that isn't accessible to other people—but is there any such meaning?"

"There is meaning," said Rhodri. "Why do you say 'not accessible to other people'?"

"I don't know. I suppose I mean 'not accessible to me.' "

"Give me the light!"

His voice startled her. She saw that he had pulled out all the loosened bricks now; a large hole opened black in the bricked place. Rhodri took the lantern out of her hand before she could move; she saw his face completely transfigured with something that was not excitement but steady and relentless; in it she and her doubts were swallowed up like a stone in the sea. She felt a flicker of desolation at being left like that, but it was lost immediately as she bent to look beside him into the gap.

He held the lantern at arm's length into the hole. The yellow circle of light fell on white stone walls, a passage leading spear-straight away from the cellar, and on a great heap of earth mixed with stones and tree roots that choked the passage within six feet of the doorway.

"Look here," said Rhodri in an almost breathless voice. "At the edge. Rust-marks from hinges. There was a door." He straightened and looked at Linette with an intensity that frightened her. "This is what I came from Wales to see."

The light fell strongly on his features, making sharp shadows. Linette felt an excited terror rise in her to meet what was about to be spoken, knowing a raging determination in him as powerful as Julian's peace.

He stared at her as if he were dragging her with him into some enterprise, without pity for either. "I am going to tell you the full truth at last. I am the Pendragon of Logres. We are looking for Excalibur."

Late that night Morgan Cornwall stood in the Atlantis Tower alone. Before her, on a round table of dark, polished wood, lay the playing cards of the Tarot pack divided into the four suits—coins, staffs, cups, and swords. She laid the numeral cards overlapping in a great circle like a wheel, with the aces at the four points of the compass; the court cards, page, knight, queen, king, ran from each ace to the hub, which was the Fool.

Nine times clockwise she circled the table, chanting softly in an ancient language that Rhodri might have half-understood. Then she stood still at the western point of the circle, facing the moonlight that came across the table from the open windows.

"Mother of all the living, Arianrhod, Blodeuwedd, Cerridwen; noble lady, you who were called Druan Gwen in this land—by that name I call on you now. Let my questioning of the cards be fruitful for the fulfillment of your will.

"Cards, cards, cards—coins, element of earth; staffs, element of air; cups, element of water; swords, element of fire. You I invoke, you I question, in the name of the ever-living Goddess.

"Cards, cards, cards. Who is it that has come over the waters?"

She closed her eyes and laid her hand on a card, then looked to see what it was.

"The King of Swords. Yes, it is he. It is the Pendragon.

"Cards, cards, cards. What does the King of Swords seek?"

"The Ace of Swords. He seeks the Sword.

"Cards, cards, cards. Who shall help me against the King of Swords?

"The Queen of Staffs, the Queen of the Air, my sister."

5. The Queens of Earth and Air

Morgan, as usual, did not appear at breakfast, which this time took place decorously in the sunlit dining room. Julian did appear, looking startlingly different in a grey silk street dress, with her hair up.

"I'm going into town, to Oakleigh among other places," she told Rhodri. "That's the headquarters of the local historical society. Shall I tell them about your excavations?"

"Well, actually, I'd rather you didn't. I'll explain why this evening."

"Not this evening," said Julian, smiling. "I'm having dinner at the Ironwoods'."

"Oh, then," said Linette, "I know what I'd like to do. I offered to show Rhodri the city, but I haven't yet. Rhodri, let's have dinner in town; I'll show you Oakleigh, and the basilica, and everything."

Julian wondered if this sudden display of historical interest had anything to do with her visiting the Ironwoods. But since she did not know the precise state of things between Anthony and Linette, she could not interpret it more definitely.

"Who are the Ironwoods?" asked Rhodri, as they started their work. There was not so much noise now; they had gotten the rest of the bricks out yesterday afternoon, and now they were actually in the passage. The yellow lantern-light made a mellow radiance around them; Rhodri was carefully loosening earth from the mass that choked the passage, and Linette was putting it through a screen. So far nothing had turned up but bits of broken stone; but those, as Rhodri said, did prove that the passage had been blocked after the collapse of the upper structure.

"Hm?" said Linette. Her gaiety at breakfast had been a very transient mood; all her moods today seemed to chase one another like shadows. She was plunged now into a kind of darkness, neither gay nor sad but vaguely depressing, whose cause she could not find.

"The Ironwoods."

"Oh, they're a family that we know. I used to see their son fairly often."

"He's married now?"

"No, he's been studying; he's getting his doctorate in August. His name's Anthony, and his dissertation is called 'An Interpretation of the Grail Quest in Malory.' "

"Is he the one Aramelissa mentioned?"

"Yes, but I haven't seen him in months. I never really encouraged him, and I suppose he gave up finally—though I would have liked him as a friend at least. Rhodri—"

"Yes?"

"Are you really going to tell Aunt Julian about Excalibur?"

"I'll have to. We can't keep the passage secret and secure without her. And I think she already knows something is up."

"I expect so. I was watching her the other night when you were talking about the Pendragons. I think she brought the subject up casually, but then—she has uncanny insight sometimes."

A silence fell, broken only by Rhodri's scraping and Linette's putting the loose earth through the sieve. Linette's hands worked mechanically at the task; but it seemed remote, and the darkness seemed to crowd and press in around her. What's the matter with my mind? she thought. I'm not usually like this. There's no sense in this—foreboding.

"Rhodri," she said in a low voice, "tell me about that girl."

"What girl?"

"The one with the second sight. Cristant Aberglas."

"Cristant." Rhodri lowered the shovel and stood looking thoughtfully at the lantern. "It's difficult to tell you about Cristant, difficult to convey what it was like.

"I was in Caernarvon, a year ago, a summer evening. You don't know Caernarvon; it's a seacoast town with a big Norman castle and ruined medieval walls more or less engulfed by the modern city. This particular evening I was walking around in the old narrow streets, without direction, not seeing them really because of the thoughts that were in my mind. I walk half the night when my thoughts drive me. I hadn't been Pendragon long.

"What put my mind in that turmoil was partly something I'd been reading—one of the splendid old romances, Malory in fact, in which Britain was indeed 'this sceptred isle,' Logres, the glory of the western world. But what had struck home to me, at the last, was what the people did during the war between Arthur and Mordred. After all the glory of Arthur's reign, as soon as trouble came, the people turned against him, because Mordred offered them ease instead of endeavor. The words seemed to burn across the darkness before me: 'and the most part of England held with Sir Mordred, the people were so new fangle.' And it seemed to me that this was true, even in our day, as Malory said it was true in his—how readily people will do that, preferring what is base because it is easier. Where are we going even now? I thought—downward, to mediocrity, mass-produced trash, the nadir of greatness. I can't describe how my mind was—bitter, burning.

"And as I walked, I suddenly found myself in a dead-end street. It was the old wall that was blocking my way; but I came out of my thoughts with a shock, and it took me a second to recognize it standing ruinous and pale-colored in the moonlight. I just stood and stared at it, and then I realized that somebody was watching me.

"I looked around. In the house next to the wall there was a second-story window open, and a girl was standing at it with a hairbrush in her hand. There was light in the room behind her, and it came on her hair— long hair, the loveliest I had ever seen, a kind of silvery gold loose around her. And her face was lovely, very delicate, very fair. Even without coming close, as I felt her eyes on me, I felt my hair rise as if with cold. For there was something about her—a wildness, something supernatural almost—as if she were not like other girls, as if she might do anything, say anything.

"And then she said, 'Pendragon.'

"I had never seen her before. There was no way she could have known. A kind of cold shock went through me; I couldn't speak.

" 'Don't be alarmed,' she said. 'My name is Cristant Aberglas.'

"I got my voice then and came under the window. 'What do you want with me?' I said.

" 'I want to tell you something,' she said. I stood there watching her in that mixture of lamplight and moonlight that seemed to shimmer around her. She said, 'You know the secret tradition of the Pendragons, that the sword of Arthur is not lost.'

" 'Madoc took it to America,' I said, dazed, as if I were reciting a geography lesson.

" 'And you must find it there,' she said. 'I know that this is important.'

"And I found myself repeating the verse from the secret tradition; I said it in Welsh, but in English it would be something like this:

Three Pendragons of Arthur's line:
One to lay the sword in shrine,
One to find it in its tomb,
One to draw it and bid him come.

The first was Madoc—we knew he had laid it in the treasuries of the not-yet-finished Annedd Cledd; he left that word with his successor when he came back to Wales for more people. And the tradition of the Pendragons says Arthur must be summoned by drawing it, in the great need at the end of time. But I'd never thought much about it, though I knew the Meyricks were of Arthur's line through Madoc's daughter.

"Cristant listened while I spoke, very gravely, and then repeated, 'You must find it.'

" 'Where?' I said.

" 'That's what you have to find out,' she said. 'But it's there; I saw it.'

" 'Saw it?' I couldn't help saying, even though by then I'd passed beyond all surprise.

" 'In my mind,' she said. 'Oh, I know this is strange to you. But you must go, go now, and not lose any time. This is urgent, and I can feel that there's danger in every minute lost.'

"And the force of her words was so strong that I turned around and started walking toward my flat as fast as I could go, without even saying good-bye. When I realized I hadn't, I felt a kind of sorrow go through me; she was so beautiful, I can see her as if she were standing before me. A woman like crystal and silver.

"I haven't seen her since. I've written to her—oh, it was easy enough, I found her name in the telephone directory. She did have the second sight; she'd seen the Sword in her mind, as a fiery golden thing, and been made to understand the necessity of finding it. But we don't know what the urgency is all about."

"And I suppose," said Linette, "that the first thing you'll do, when you get back to Wales, is go back and find her."

"Yes—I'll have the leisure to, then, instead of all the research and arrangements. And, though nothing's actually been said, there's a kind of—I don't know—an understanding, a bond, something delicate and fine that I don't know what to call—"

"Love?" said Linette very quietly, with lowered head.

He did not answer. "Talking of every minute's delay being dangerous, do you know what time it is? Eleven and past." He began once more to attack the hardened mass.

Linette once again set to work screening the loosened earth. She was aware of Rhodri's shadow as a towering shape cast on the white wall beyond him, like a giant hewing at some obdurate mountainside. Once more the darkness seemed to crowd around them, pressing close and silent.

"And where do I belong in all this?" she said. "I told you yesterday that I have nothing. And you told me your secret, then—but where does that leave me? I'm not one of these people like Cristant, that can actually help you as Pendragon. All I'm good for is to put dirt through a screen. I tried to tell you how desperate I am. This'll end; you'll go. And I'll be left empty-handed as before. I can't stand playing my life away with things that don't matter, while other people have all the risk and achievement. If I have to spend my life standing behind a desk writing names and dates on a blackboard, and rising to be a full professor, and sitting in an office correcting spelling mistakes and making out syllabi, and going home at night to cultivate my lawn and prepare new lectures—Rhodri, I can't stand it, I'll go quietly mad."

Rhodri stopped and looked at her; he saw the lantern-light gleam on the tears that had crept into her eyes. A troubled, smothered feeling came over him; he could not move. Then, rather awkwardly, he bent over her and touched her hair. And she began to cry in earnest.

"Don't, now," he said; "ah, don't. It's not true; it won't be as bad as that. And you aren't playing your life away. What you're doing does matter; it's not just putting dirt through a screen, though that's important in its way. You have to help me; you're every bit as necessary as Cristant. I told you what she said, how urgent it was; there may be more risk than either of us thinks. And if we do find Excalibur, that'll be an achievement indeed, something to dream of, maybe enough to cast glory over every blackboard and syllabus that could be."

"Oh, I'm so sorry," said Linette, swallowing her sobs. "It's so stupid of me to behave like this; I don't know what's the matter with me today." She cleared her tears away roughly with her hand. "It is good of you to say all that. I don't believe it really, but at least I can pretend to be necessary."

"You are necessary," repeated Rhodri firmly.

"If it's as urgent as you say," said Linette, "you'd better get on with it and give me some more dirt to screen."

They set to work again and went on for a long time without speaking. Linette became conscious once more of the oppressive darkness of underground, the great stillness of lightless earth and the ponderousness of the years. Forgotten seas, fern-like forests, dinosaur bones; Adam and Eve and their children and their children's children sleeping in the earth, under the plowed fields and the cities; broken dishes and lost dolls and scattered necklaces, fragments of the vanished happiness of the dead; arrowheads, spears, cannonballs, rusted swords, the last many had known before the dark shut down on them: all were hidden in the ponderous masses of the earth, far under the grass stems. What could she say to all those silent generations waiting for her to give an account of her life? The ache of having done nothing brought tears to her eyes, as her soul shook with an intense longing for heroism and greatness to justify her life. Well, she might get it now; she remembered and tossed her head, defiant of the darkness. The adventure was here; her hands, working the dirt through the screen, were closed tight on it; she would not let go, whatever dangers rose out of the shadows. Her mouth straightened in exultant pride.

And yet, slowly in the back of her mind, the sense of darkness intensified, took form in a nameless awareness that something was wrong. She remembered how she had been oppressed by this place ever since Monday, though she had never been afraid of the cellar in her childhood. No, it was not fear of the place; it was a foreboding, vague as yet, but spreading through her mind like dark water, foreboding of something that was waiting for them, in the darkness and like darkness, wakeful and evil. Images, high-colored like those of dreams, floated through the dark of her mind: dragon-guarded apples of the Hesperides, demon-haunted paths to the Grail, the flaming sword at the gates of Eden. Was there any good in the world that was not dear-bought and overshadowed with doom? And yet, had she not wanted this? What, she thought with a sense of sinking cold, what have I wanted?

She looked up at Rhodri working earnestly at the clogging dirt; his face in the lantern-light showed only complete, restrained absorption in his task. Yet there was warmth in his presence, something to fight back against the foreboding and the darkness. He alone understood her and cared about her longings. Her heart seemed suddenly to clench tight inside her, with a kind of pain.

"Rhodri," she said, "look at me."

He turned, his face showing only surprise, then a kind of alarm at the expression in Linette's eyes.

"Rhodri. Do you love Cristant?"

He did not answer, only stood perfectly still, looking at her.

"You say you haven't seen her in a year. Are you sure this understanding isn't only on your side and not on hers?"

His eyebrows contracted violently, and he struck his shovel into the dirt again; earth fell down with a showering sound. Linette half-rose from the screen, watching him with a latent, relentless light in her eyes. Under his fast and fierce strokes the dirt showered to the passage floor.

"I've seen it in other women. They'll forget a man they don't see, and they won't tell him. You can be sure she's forgotten you by now."

For answer he went on shovelling; she could see his face, the black eyebrows almost meeting in his frown, the sweat standing out on his forehead from his violent exertion. She thought his eyes were closed, whether in anguish or so as not to see her she did not know.

She seized the handle of the shovel; and again he stood still, half-turning toward her.

"Rhodri, look at me. Aren't I as beautiful as Cristant?"

He looked at her wonderingly, as if once again seeing her for the first time. He let go the shovel, letting it slide back against the wall; and slowly, like a man in a trance, he touched her hair with great gentleness. Her gaze wavered a little beneath his, but did not turn away; the color rose slowly to her cheeks and brow.

"She has forgotten you," she said in an almost broken voice. "She is nothing to you now."

And as Rhodri looked at her, the remembered beauty of Cristant seemed faraway and unreal. Linette's nearness and power seemed to blaze around him like firelight. She did not move; his hands, trembling, touched her face, her lips. Then suddenly, with an inarticulate sound like a cry, he dropped on his knees beside her, drew her face to his, and kissed her.

There was no more working that day. In an irresponsible happiness they went up into the July sunlight and drove down the bay, sometimes through tall pines and sometimes along the open shore where seagulls cried out overhead or dipped down to fish. The seacoast opened out into broad marshland, very green, with fishing boats in small canals alongside the road. The Dauphin Island bridge came in sight, a long white arc across the sun-dazzling water, with bay on one side and the green Gulf of Mexico on the other; they drove across toward the island, which rose white and green itself, girded with high dunes and crowned with pine.

They ate their picnic lunch on the public beach, which was practically deserted because it was Wednesday. The rest of the afternoon they spent walking barefoot on the white shore, through the broken wave-edges of the gulf that stretched green into the southern distance. Linette had taken her hair down, so that it blew loose in the wind like an island girl's. They watched the sun set in great spaces of crimson over the darkening sea; the clouds seemed like unreachable islands washed by a sea endlessly deep and clear, a sea of light that grew more and more blue as the darkness came and the first stars glowed white there.

On the way back, they had supper at a seafood restaurant. Rhodri ordered all sorts of extravagant and expensive dishes; Linette, watching him through the bright candlelight, was obscurely impressed, as if he had poured out great heaps of diamonds on the table. The wineglasses gleamed in the soft light; and behind all their movements and all their words seemed to move an unheard music, too delicate to be perceived by the ear.

Afterwards, they drove among the old streets while Linette showed Rhodri the architecture of the city—the great double-towered Basilica of the Immaculate Conception, with its golden angels holding lights under the solemn darkness of the portico; old houses with delicate ironwork or Greek pillars, set in small gardens or under vast overhanging darknesses of oak trees; a college with its long avenue of oaks and flowerlike arched quadrangle. And she seemed somehow to be showing them to herself for the first time; never before had they been like this, so gracious and filled with light, as if in them too that unheard music moved and upheld them with its exquisite harmony as of crystal or stars.

They drove into the park, past shadowy lawns and high stands of trees, across a causeway between two lakes that spread like dulled silver under the moon. All the rolling expanse of shadow and brightness was still and in solitude; there was no movement except the distant passing of lights on the main boulevard. They drove around the little mazes of roads beyond the lakes, in an enthralled stillness of summer night; finally Rhodri let the car stop and the sound of its motor die away.

By an unspoken consent they got out and wandered across the grass in lyric exaltation. The grass was long and fragrant; the summer stars hung large and low, washed over with strong moonlight as with a shallow sea. Even the silver street lamps seemed alive, as if metal itself had grown like a straight, slender tree and flowered into light. Live trees, pines and hardwoods, tangled the varied radiance into mazes of shadow.

Rhodri, looking up, saw the stars shining through the pine-needles and felt that the stars too were young, laughing with the first splendor of creation. He stopped; and Linette, feeling it in the pressure of his hand, stopped too and looked up with him.

"We are Adam and Eve," he said solemnly, meeting her eyes. "We 'have dominion over the fish of the sea, the birds of the air, the cattle, and every living thing that crawls on the earth,' and over the green plants and the stars. This is our kingdom."

Linette felt his words like a revelation of truth and exultation. No one had ever been in love before them. A rabbit ran through a space of light, and it was theirs. She called out softly to it; it paused and looked at her with bright, unwavering eyes before disappearing into the shadows. She felt she could have stroked the grass itself as if it were the hair of some living thing that waited for her touch. They passed under a tree with low, trailing branches; she caught a branch-end and held the small leaves cupped lightly in her hand like a young bird.

"Look," said Rhodri, "even the lamps are ours." For they had come to another of the roads, and the lights flowered overhead. He laid his hand on the silvered surface of the lamppost and felt the cold, hard metal; but there was nothing hostile or alien in its coldness. He shut his eyes for an instant, feeling its hardness under his hand. Man, the master of metals—Excalibur? For a second the thought of it flashed like a flare across even the ecstasy of love. But he opened his eyes; there was Linette watching him, and he smiled back at her.

They left the road, moving across a wide, grassy expanse which sloped gently downward. The moonlight shone around them; a sudden light breeze from the sea stirred the scattered trees and made the black branch-shadows tremble across the silver.

"Are we still in the park?" asked Rhodri, not as if he greatly cared if they were on another planet.

"Yes," said Linette. "Only—I don't see the houses that ought to be up that way."

"They've gone to bed and turned off the lights."

"I expect so. We can't be anywhere but the park."

"Somebody's awake, though," said Rhodri, "and has a nice taste in music."

They stood still and listened to the music, though it seemed to come from somewhere in the park rather than from the unseen houses. Yet it came as from an immense distance, delicate and clear, a sound like harp music moving in an undefined melody. The sound wove itself through Linette's mind; she seemed to see slender shapes, green-clothed, with leaves in their hair, moving through tree-shadows and moonlight in the patterns of a dance. Other shapes, in opalescent blue and white that flowed and eddied in the moonlight like water, came up from the lake shore and moved toward the dancers.

She stood without speaking, unconscious of time. Then it seemed as if a mist shifted in her mind, as if a gap in a clouded night sky had drifted shut; and she returned to an awareness of the park and of Rhodri. The music was gone; there was no sound except the faint stir of wind-touched branches.

"What was it?" she breathed.

"I know what I would say if this were Wales," said Rhodri, "if I heard it at night like this on some deserted mountain—a place where the boundaries of the worlds were thin. But here. . . ." He shook his head.

Almost without speaking, they drove back to Silverthorne through the transfigured moonlight. But instead of going straight in, they walked hand in hand to the water's edge and gazed at the moon's white path across the bay.

As they turned to go in, Linette whispered, "Look," and motioned upward.

On the level top of the Atlantis Tower stood Morgan Cornwall, robed from throat to foot in flowing white. Her red hair spilled loose and dark; the twisted necklace glinted coldly as if it were silver. She stood rigid as marble, her arms uplifted towards the sky, her face turned up white and exultant as if in intense worship towards the full moon.

After midnight in the Atlantis Tower Morgan stood again before the polished table. Once again she separated the cards into coins, staffs, cups, and swords—earth, air, water, and fire. Laying aside the court cards, she took the numeral cards of earth, air, and fire and laid them in an inverted triangle, earth along the top, fire and air at the two sides. At the corners of the triangle she laid the Aces of Coins, Staffs, and Swords. In the center she placed the card of the Fool upside down, and upon it the Queen of Staffs, the Queen of the Air.

Taking the card of the Queen of Swords in her hands, she raised it high as if in adoration; and carrying it uplifted before her, she went nine times clockwise around the table, singing in the ancient language to Arianrhod, Keeper of the Sword. Then she halted at the southern point of the triangle, before the Ace of Swords; and still holding the Queen of Swords high before her, she prayed aloud.

"Mother of all the living, Arianrhod, Blodeuwedd Cerridwen; Druan Gwen, noble Goddess—I call on you, I, Morgan, your servant. I call on you by your power as Arianrhod: assist me in my endeavor to recover your holy possession the sacred Sword. I call on you by your power as Blodeuwedd, the Queen of all beauty, faithful beyond the knowledge of man: keep me faithful also to your service, though I am about to pass into danger; let me not be shadowed by the Shadow with which I must deal. I call on you by your power as Cerridwen, Empress of wisdom and Ruler of silence: let your command go out through the realms of the dead and bring to me my sister, Morgause of Orkney, though she is called the Queen of the Air and is dedicated to your Shadow."

A gust of wind swept out from the center of the cards and blew out the candles, a hot wind, as if it blew out of fiery wastelands. Then out of the dark another flame sprang up, a thin green flame that flickered over the surface of the central cards but scorched nothing.

Out of the flame a voice spoke, a woman's voice, not loud, but low, beautiful, and heartless. "It is eight hundred years, sister. Why do you call on me now?"

"By the will of the Secret Powers, who told me you would help me."

"The Secret Powers. And so at last you have had to turn to the Shadow. Can you answer me now—why does Blodeuwedd betray Llew to Gronw and Gronw to Llew?"

"She does not betray them. The inhabiting Greatness whom we call the Sun Lord passes from Llew to Gronw and from Gronw to Llew; to that Greatness she is faithful beyond the knowledge of man. The sacrifice of their earthly representatives, which took place in the ancient times, was the price of being the god's dwelling and the mode of their passing into final union with the Sun Lord. Just as the Goddess passes from Mother to Bride to Ancient One according to the courses of the moon, so the Sun Lord passes from Llew to Gronw to Llew with the growing and fading and renewing of the strength of the sun as year follows year."

"That is what they said in the Inner Circles in the sacred groves."

"It is the truth. I have not forgotten your belief, though, that Boadb, the dark Shadow of Blodeuwedd, truly betrays the Sun Lord to the Lord of Darkness. But you must not suppose that about the Goddess."

"Do you remember when we last spoke, sister?"

"It was in the twelfth century; I don't remember the year. Owain Gwynedd was alive, and his queen's brother was the Pendragon and had the sacred Sword."

"I remember the Sword. You wanted it back; and you tried to re-establish the worship of your Goddess in its ancient form, working through the changed cult that still lived half-hidden. The priestess Ancret was to be your tool; she instructed the bard Kynon in the ancient mysteries, and he in turn was to influence the Pendragon to become king of the secret groves. But Owain died, and in the wars the Sword disappeared and you left the groves to search for the Sword. When you came back, years had passed and the groves were empty."

"And I had not found the Sword."

"No—and now you know why. You might have asked me, sister; for I knew."

"You knew?"

"Kynon knew that Madoc was the new Pendragon, for he was Madoc's close friend; no one was closer except Madoc's sister, for his wife was dead and his daughter was a child. It was Kynon who persuaded

Madoc to let Ancret sail with them to the west. Sister, you had abandoned Ancret; I did not."

"What do you mean?"

"What do you know?"

"I know by the secret arts that Druan Gwen was worshipped in this land, at the ring of stones called Cerrig Mawr. I know that the Sword was brought here, that a place was built for it called Annedd Cledd, the House of the Sword. These things I learned not long ago, not easily; it is difficult to reach with the mind across such vastnesses of miles and years."

"You did not know then that Druan Gwen was not worshipped as you would wish. At Cerrig Mawr, Ancret took a new lover and he killed Kynon; it was not sacrifice but murder, and thus they invoked the Shadow who did not leave them. And Annedd Cledd remained beyond their reach; for Kynon's pupil, Bran, made it the shrine of other mysteries, for love of Madoc's sister Goeral who had passed from the world. It was not death that took her; she still lies there in the long sleep, waiting for the end. Because she was of the new faith, Bran made the images of the ancient mysteries into ceremony and symbol for the service of their mysteries. Thus the Druan of Cerrig Mawr was the Shadow, and the Druan of Annedd Cledd was a poet's symbol for the world or the soul. There was no room for the one whom you worship."

"There is more reason, then, for my serving her rightly now. You will have guessed that I want the Sword."

The flame seemed to laugh; the laughter in its voice made it tremble as if in a draft. "You should never have given it to Constantine, son of Cador, when it was returned to you from the Other Kingdom after the passing of Arthur."

"How did I know he would be faithless to the groves? And they were all faithless after that, forsaking her worship; I could never get it."

Again the flame laughed. "I have been watching this archaeologist, whom you found—how?"

"I have connections in the secret circles of London. I was told he was the new Pendragon; and when I learned he was coming here, I sent forth my mind by the hidden paths and found out why."

"And so you followed him. I myself was waiting here for other reasons; I have stood at the gate of the shrine and watched him, with this girl who works with him. Her mind has certain depths she does not know about; it is perceptive towards me, and my presence troubles her. Yes, I will help you, sister—for a price."

Morgan stiffened a little. "What is your price?"

"First—I am hungry, sister. You do not know that hunger, that desire for possession and power over a soul. I devoured Mordred like that, whom I conceived in hate and reared in hate as a curse to Arthur the son of Uther—Uther who killed our father and wronged our mother, and whom I killed at last for vengeance by a lingering sickness. And after my own death I entered into Mordred; but I was strong enough then to devour him utterly; I clung like a haunting at the root of his mind. Now and then certain souls have come my way; it is not all that I would consent to devour. But twice I have failed in this place: once with Christant, the last Princess of Caer Mair; once with Mary Myers, who nearly sold her soul to the Darkness, and who would have become one with the Shadow. The memory of her wakens my hunger even now. And what I propose is useful anyway for the work. If you give me that girl to possess, the Sword will come within reach of our hands."

"She is not mine to give you," said Morgan, frowning.

"But I will need your help. And I tell you there is no other way to work." The green flame trembled and was silent for a moment. "Second—sister, the Cup is coming here."

"The Cup?"

"The Cup which is one of the four holy things. You know them—Sword, Spear, Dish, and Cup."

"You are mistaken, sister. The fourth holy thing is a cauldron, the Cauldron of Cerridwen."

The flame stood still and seemed to pause. "You are right. And I can speak the more freely because the Cup does not belong to your mysteries. I have sensed it coming: all things are preparing for it; even the boundaries of the three worlds become indistinct, and they draw closer to one another. I will help you if you will help me. I want to destroy the Cup."

"Why? What is it?"

"A thing hateful to me and alien to you—the great Cup of those mysteries which destroyed your island."

"I give it over to your desire, then. But what do you want from me?"

"I want to use the power of the Sword to destroy it. And I warn you, sister—if there is anything you want to save here, send it far away before then. For when that power destroys the Cup, it would be better for this place if the earth had swallowed it."

"I would like to save the lady of this house; she has been gracious to me."

"See to it, then. But I want those two things, the girl and the Cup: one to possess and use, and one to destroy."

6. The Seeing and the Cup

Julian did not need to be told the turn things had taken. When Linette and Rhodri came in to breakfast, it was evident to her from the way they looked and moved. They had been in the rose garden as early as this, and a red rose with the dew still on it clung in Linette's dark hair. Julian guessed that Rhodri had fastened it there, half-shy at his own temerity, emboldened by the subtle change in Linette's beauty. For she seemed changed since yesterday; there was a new softness or perhaps wildness about her, like that ecstatic sweetness of the air when suddenly, in the end of January, the hard, furled peach buds open tentatively to the sun.

"Well," she said as they sat down, "you just missed Morgan. She came down to say she wanted her breakfast later than usual. Actually she said she was going back to bed—didn't sleep well last night."

Linette and Rhodri exchanged glances, remembering the white-robed figure with its face turned toward the moon.

Rhodri turned his gaze to Julian, wondering how to begin his explanation about the Pendragonship and Excalibur. Julian this morning reminded him vaguely of something; she was wearing a plain sea-blue dress of some light material, and around her neck was a reddish-gold amber pendant finely set in gold wires. With the silver circlet—of course; the recollection came to him: it was a book-cover portrait of Eleanor of Aquitaine.

Before he could say anything, Linette asked, "How was the Ironwoods' dinner?"

"Well, you can guess," said Julian, smiling. "They were all there, but Cecilia did all the talking."

"Like a Lewis Carroll duchess," said Linette, "very opinionated; but she's so full of vitality that people don't mind. And the rest of you could hardly say two words; but afterwards Mr. Ironwood showed you his new books."

"Three of them, on medieval philosophy."

"And Anthony talked about his dissertation."

"No, as a matter of fact he said very little about anything. But he did ask if he could come and talk with me this evening; so I invited him to dinner."

The conversation seemed to Rhodri to have strayed rather far from his explanation, and he sat wondering how to steer it toward an opening. Julian unintentionally gave him the opening by holding up the pendant and looking at it in the sunlight.

"That's a pretty thing," he said. "It looks like something Eleanor of Aquitaine might have worn."

Julian smiled. "Perhaps it really is twelfth-century, then. An ancestor of mine is supposed to have picked it up among the ruins the French saw in 1699, which are thought to have been Caer Mair. Well, who knows? If this sort of thing was lying around, you might even strike treasure."

"I hope to," said Rhodri, catching his breath at the excellence of the opportunity. In a few words he told Julian the blunt facts of his quest, putting them before her without decoration or apology, for he despaired of both. She listened with interest but without comment; he could see she believed in his sincerity but not particularly in his chances.

"Still, I don't blame her," he said to Linette an hour later in the lantern-light of the passage. "If somebody told me he wanted to look for Excalibur on my property, I wouldn't be very sanguine about it either."

Linette said nothing. Julian's attitude had disturbed her vaguely, and she wished now that they would stop early again and perhaps go back to the island. This seemed to have been going on forever, the days of lantern-light, the hard barrier of earth under the scrape of iron. She looked at the barrier; and the vaguely troubled waters of her mind rose darkly in their caverns, pouring darkness through her thoughts. Of course they were not coming to the other side of the barrier, because there was no other side. The passage was a dead end blocked with earth; and there was only earth, the endless dark weight of it, lying hard against the scrape of the iron. An image sprang out of the nightmare of her mind, of them tunnelling round and round the world, under the seas, in a blind crooked track like worms, digging for centuries and never coming to an other side.

But she was silent; better that Rhodri should hope on as long as he could, unpoisoned by her sense of futility. Her mind found relief by straying back to last night; she seemed to hear again faintly in her mind the music that had brought her the vision of the dancers. The melody hovered more elusive and out of reach than before, but the delicate harp-notes trembled in her memory over the shadow-image of the dance. The darkness pressed round that fragile imagery but could not flow through it. Rhodri had said he would have known what to call it if he had heard it on some lonely mountainside—

"It's through!" cried Rhodri, his words ringing against the walls. "Linette, it's through!"

Linette, scrambling up out of her shattered reverie, had already heard the new note in the sound, as if his voice echoed off some new dimension of darkness. She peered beside him through the hole that had suddenly gaped in the barrier, unconscious of the loose earth that filtered onto her hair and face; crowded together they nearly jammed out the lantern-light and could see nothing but the shadowy whiteness of stone.

"Stand away!" said Rhodri in a hoarse, excited voice. He seized the pickax from among the digging tools and with a few sharp blows brought down the remaining curtain of earth, so that there was only a low mound on the passage floor. He took the lantern from Linette and held it high, close to the low vaulted roof. Before them the white lines of the walls plunged straight into impenetrable darkness.

"There was no falling-in at all, then," he said in a low voice. "This is as perfect as the day it was made. That heap was piled up before somebody sealed the door."

"Why?" whispered Linette in awe. Her question seemed to echo in the dark beyond the lantern-light; the hollow sound lapsing into silence seemed to throw it back at her, compelling an answer. "They must have been terribly afraid of something."

And immediately she herself was afraid. Stories she had known came crowding back to her, deep sorcery and dark communion with unhuman powers under the earth, demonic visitors, horrors out of the hidden places far from the light. She remembered Julian's allusion to Mary Myers; a fiery golden brightness and a delving into dreadful and forbidden knowledge. Why should Excalibur be connected with that? Yet in the old books, dark powers lay in wait along the paths to the Grail.

Dreadful and forbidden knowledge. The phrase stirred something in her mind, an attraction, a fascination. She had always wondered about the occult, about strange forces and secrets that could be spoken only in darkness. Why had men built these night-bound corridors, driving a tunnel through the dark to what end? She had a second's vision of them as Columbuses of the darkness, driving on and on, hauling away earth and raising the vault, with no end in view except to plunge deeper and deeper beyond knowledge—

"Rhodri," she whispered, taking the lantern. "Let's go on." She did not want to raise her voice, though she did not know why; it was as if she might wake the darkness itself to some unthinkable cognizance of them.

Rhodri glanced at her; she saw his face in the light, almost blank with absorption except for the intense brightness of his eyes. It was as if he had forgotten about her. His gaze took her in. "Yes. Did you notice the air is good down here? There must be ventilation, though I can't think why it hasn't been stopped up." He frowned, thinking about it; then, still carrying the pickax, he climbed with Linette over the fallen earth into the unknown passage.

Slowly she led the way into the close-crowding darkness. The old stones, white and cold to the hand, shone pale as the light flowed across them, in their careful rows set by forgotten builders. The dry, cool darkness hung around the circle of light like waters around a boat, waiting to rush back into their old domain in the wake of its passing.

"Rhodri," whispered Linette, "limestone didn't form here. This was brought from miles away. Why?"

And again her voice seemed to reverberate in the walls, calling for an answer; but there was no answer.

They went on; and she thought of the age of the darkness, undisturbed for how many centuries, night unbroken, without lamp or moon or star, stirred last perhaps by the flaring torches of desperate Cymri on the edge of Caer Mair's ruin. Dreamlike the image of them formed in her mind, torchlight on the stones, cloaked shapes in procession two by two, something indistinct being carried—

The image broke with a change in the light. It was the sudden whiteness of a wall looming out of the dark just ahead. "Look," she said, stopping short. "The passage ends there."

"No, it turns a corner. West—towards the river, would that be?"

She nodded, without speaking. Yes, it turned, clean-angled as a house wall, and plunged away into new darkness. She glimpsed a kind of exultant terror in Rhodri's eyes and guessed his thought—the passage could not go far, then; any moment now, either Excalibur or the utter failure of the quest. But her own mind could not grasp it; her thoughts seemed awash with darkness, sinking slowly through deep waters without any bottom.

They went onward, very slowly, for Rhodri was scanning the walls minutely as if he were afraid of missing some faintest mark, or as if he were trying to delay the discovery of—perhaps—failure. But there was no change, only the endless rows of white stone caught for a moment in a shimmer of light and then drowned in darkness. Linette moved beside him as if in a dream, an oppressive dream more real to her than the flow of light over the stone. Once more the cloaked shapes walked two by two in the torchlight; it half seemed to her that she was one of them, since her feet too moved between the rows of white stones and her heart too was filled with some dark trouble, grief or fear; she must be one of the walkers, because she was certainly not the black-haired girl who lay on the bier, whose face, hardly out of childhood, was white and still as the stones, and around whose brows gleamed a circlet of thin gold—

"Look!" said Rhodri in a low, sharp voice. "The left wall."

Linette's mind struggled up out of the dream, and she looked dazedly at the stones. The rows were broken by two long slabs set into the wall, rectangular and white as the rest; over them trailed markings of some kind, curved, small things that, as her mind slowly focused there, resolved themselves into letters. But she could not read them and stood staring dully, drugged with the darkness of the dream.

"Hold the lantern closer," said Rhodri with a tense, restrained excitement. "Yes—they're tombs. But how unalike they are."

Linette perceived that slowly now, as she stared at the slabs. The letters of the eastward one were clear-cut, finely-curved Celtic uncials; a decorative border went round the slab, elaborate and interlaced. The other was bare of ornament except for a cross of two straight lines, and the letters straggled rough and brief across the stone. The language was not Latin; Linette guessed it was Welsh, and somehow it lapped around her mind like the levels of the torchlit dream.

Rhodri peered at the decorated slab, translating slowly. " 'Bran, Chief Poet to the House of Cadwallen, friend of princes. He died the fourteenth day of November, in the year of our Lord 1250, by the hand of Gronw the traitor. He was born in Wales.' He must have been very old."

Linette listened to him. A scene opened out shadowily in her imagination, a stone-built hall full of people, the gold-circleted girl half-rising from a carved chair, an old man in blue robes speaking threateningly to a man with a spear. The spearman struck suddenly and ran; the old man fell as people rushed toward him.

But Rhodri's voice was speaking again, translating from the rough-cut stone. " 'Christant, the last Princess. She was killed at the end. God give her peace.' "

" 'Christant, the last Princess,' " repeated Linette. The name tolled through the dream; the cloaked figures moved into the darkness, carrying the black-haired girl on the bier.

Rhodri was not paying attention to her; he was looking at the stone, talking out of some imaginative depth. "Think of it—the sorrow and haste of her burial. It's obvious from the stone; Caer Mair had fallen. Can't you see it—the torches, the smell of smoke and burning, the upper church not burnt yet but soon to be, the smoke and smell of the torches like a presage of that; the red light, the frightened faces of the people; they are listening with half their minds for the enemy even as they say their prayers for the dead Princess; they are carrying the bier on their shoulders down toward this place—"

"A young girl," said Linette. "Maybe eighteen, nineteen; black braids, a golden circlet. Her face like alabaster, so cold, so stern. And her brother, the new Prince, a little younger. He has red hair and is carrying a spear."

Rhodri had turned and went staring at her. Her gaze seemed drawn in; her eyes saw nothing but were like wells of darkness in her face. Her voice was without expression, low, like a voice in sleep. She did not move, and her eyes did not follow his hand when he moved it in front of her face.

He did not wait for her to see any more. He put down the pickax and turned her around, taking the lantern; it was like turning a sleep-walker. He kicked something as he moved; it had been leaning at the base of the tombs and fell with a thud. By reflex he stooped to look; it registered on his mind as a book, but by then he had stuck it under his arm and was hurrying Linette along the passage. He felt the return of awareness in her movements; she tried to speak, but she was breathless and he did not spare breath on words. He did not stop till both of them were in the upper house, in the bare kitchen with the sun casting a subdued light on the boards of the floor.

Both of them sat down, leaning against the plaster wall. "What was that?" said Rhodri.

"I don't know," said Linette shakenly. "I was seeing it in my mind; but it wasn't like imagination, it was as if my mind opened onto some other place, another real world. It was as if a hole opened in the wall of a cave and I saw a real world beyond it."

"I thought something like that. Did you say the second sight was hereditary in your family?"

"Is it that?"

"I think so. But there's something else—I don't know—a dark coloring in it—How do you feel?"

"Tired. Drained. My head hurts."

"Much?"

"No—a sort of dull heaviness mostly. But what's that?"

"What?"

"Under your arm, practically in your lap. It looks like a book."

Rhodri took it in his hands. They could both see it in the kitchen sunlight; it was small and not very thick, bound in dark leather, with clasps and ornaments of enamel and a yellow metal that might be gold.

Rhodri drew a long, sharp breath. "And I was carrying it like that— a wonder it didn't fall to pieces. I would guess, a missal or a gospel book. Now, this is treasure."

He pulled out his handkerchief and carefully laid the book on it, as if it were the most fragile glass. Then, bent over it, he began trying to undo the clasps; but he seemed so moved that he could hardly do it. Linette, watching him, forgot her headache; jewel-colored images moved in her mind, indistinct memories of beautiful gold-lettered illuminations pictured in Julian's books. The clasps gave. With hands almost trembling Rhodri opened the cover.

At the first glance Linette felt a blast of disappointment. There were no beautiful colors; there was no gold. The lettering, though strong and graceful, was small, close, and in plain black; here and there she could see ornaments in fine penwork, but they were also in ink and not very striking. The only colors besides black seemed to be a goldish yellow and different purples, with here and there a touch of green.

But she looked at Rhodri's face and caught her breath. He did not seem to be believing his eyes.

"What?" she breathed.

"*Llyfr Caer Mair*. It can't be. Can't. But is."

"What, what?"

"*The Book of Caer Mair*. Not a missal, not a gospel book. Not brought from Wales. And in a style of ornamentation completely different from anything known in the twelfth century. Linette, do you realize what this is?" He had recovered his power of speech; and, as he looked at her, his face was full of an exultation that transformed it almost beyond recognition. Every ordinary expression was gone from it, lost in the single look of complete, awe-struck joy. Linette, seeing it, felt a sudden upswell of love for him; that complete purity of devotion to his science, that losing of himself in it, moved something in her almost to pain.

"What is it?" she asked.

"A history. Ah, Linette, look at it; it was made in Caer Mair; look at the colors; they were made from berries and plants, though I can't guess what kinds. Think of it; think what if, in Troy, Schliemann had found a book telling the true story out of which the myths were made." He paused, as if once again he could hardly speak. "It might even tell us where to find Excalibur."

Both were silent, trying to grasp the significance of the find. "But why?" said Linette. "Why did they leave it?"

"Forgot it, maybe; it was there at the base of the tombs. Or decided they couldn't carry it, in their flight; or hoped someone would come from Wales and find it. We can't know."

Once more, they stared at it in silence. Rhodri roused himself to collect the lunch basket from the cellar, but during the belated lunch they did not talk. Linette could see that Rhodri was too absorbed in his thoughts, and she herself felt a little bad from the headache. By the time they got in the car and drove back to Silverthorne, she felt better; but it was late afternoon and the sun was edging towards the pines.

Julian was in the courtyard, feeding the peacocks. They showed her the book, without telling her about Linette's interior vision; then Rhodri withdrew to the Treasure Tower, asking to have his dinner sent up so that he could pore over the book. Linette went upstairs to straighten her hair before dinner.

As she came back out into the courtyard, Morgan emerged suddenly from outside the arched walk. "Linette."

Linette was startled to find the fire-haired woman at her elbow. It was twilight, and Morgan was robed from throat to ground in white; the gold necklace gleamed at her neck. Linette remembered suddenly the white face upturned to the moon. But she concealed her shock and said, "Yes, Morgan?"

"Have you ever been to a seance?"

"No, I haven't." In spite of herself, in spite of her daylight conviction that all those things were trickeries, she felt a cold wind of fear touch her, to be speaking about such things with this woman in the twilight.

"I'm having one tonight. I thought you might be interested."

Linette thought to herself that the experience in the passage was quite enough for one day. But there was the fear that seemed to sicken her; she would not give in to it, she would quell it if it killed her. And she did not want Morgan to think she was afraid. "Yes. What time?"

As she spoke, something else seemed to uncoil in her, something gleaming and dark; a passionate eagerness awoke in her, fierce and undeniable, to reach out and touch those mysteries of darkness.

"Come to the Atlantis Tower at ten. Don't tell your aunt; it's possible she'd rather not know."

Morgan slipped past her into the north corridor, and Linette walked rapidly to the keep. She stepped straight into the dining room before realizing that there were people there—Julian and a light-haired young man who rose abruptly as she came in. She paused. "Oh—hello, Anthony."

Julian spoke up, reminding her that Anthony had come to dinner. Linette sat down by Julian, opposite Anthony. "How's your dissertation?"

"They've accepted it; in fact, I've turned in the final copy. I'll be getting the degree in August." His eyes fixed themselves on her with an expression she was not accustomed to see; it seemed to estimate her, weigh her against something, not dispassionately but with something tragic in it. The look made her uncomfortable, and she defended herself by looking at him more critically than ever. He was certainly quite different from Rhodri. Definitely he was taller—a bit too lean for his height, perhaps. His hair, as light as the candleflames, seemed less pleasing than Rhodri's dark hair; his face was too serious, and she thought it lacked color. What you get for living in a library, she thought savagely. She disliked the look of his mouth; there was something too resolute about it, and she was not sure what the object of that resolution was. The eyes were worst of all, brown and luminous, full of that thoughtful expression; she wished he would stop looking at her.

"It's something to do with Middle English, isn't it?" she said, knowing perfectly well what it was.

" 'An Interpretation of the Grail Quest in Malory.' "

"It must be quite interesting."

Morgan came in; dinner was served, and the conversation turned into an animated discussion between the two ladies, about certain English and Scottish ballads. Anthony and Linette hardly spoke; Anthony kept his eyes on Linette, and she kept hers on the literary conversation.

After dinner they went up to the library, and Julian took her harp and sat down on the windowseat. "You know that poem by Catherine Windeatt I was telling you about," she said to Anthony; "I got the musical setting the other day."

" 'Like a Silly Fool'?"

"Yes; it's one of the Teleri poems." Julian explained to Morgan, "Catherine Windeatt lived here in the eighteen-forties—a sort of out-of-the-mainstream Romantic. She had a whole semi-Celtic mythology;

Teleri was a princess." Touching the harp, she began to sing a delicate ballad-like melody.

"My father was lord of Aear,
Gold-towered by the sea;
My mother's gems of fire
Lit evening starrily;
I might have had Prince Ingleu,
Bright as the break of day;
But leaning at my window
I heard a harper play
And fell in love like a fool,
Like a silly fool.

"The nobles of the mountain
Were led before me all,
The knights of shore and fountain
Whose armor lit the hall;
My harper sang a lay
And looked into my eyes;
I cloaked my silk array,
Slipped out before sunrise,
And followed him like a fool,
Like a silly fool.

"We fled through stony hills
Till my shoes were worn through;
The frost in the black ghylls
Sword-pierced us two;
Rain fell on his harp-strands
And his raven head;
He warmed my cold hands
And never a word said,
And I wept then like a fool,
Like a silly fool.

"At dusk on a wet road
Prince Ingleu rode down fast,
Cried come back, I owed
No penalty for the past.
When I paused, called by regal
Weddings and warm light,

My love turned a white eagle
And flew into the night.
I ran after him like a fool,
Like a silly fool.

"My silks are worn to thread,
My jewels sold for meat;
Rain falls on my bare head,
And stones cut my feet;
But by soul-eating regret
And longing oppressed,
I climb at sunset
In the red crags of the west,
Still seeking him like a fool,
Like a silly fool."

"I think you like that poem," said Linette as Julian finished. "I know you had the setting composed for it."

"But the eagle?" said Morgan, looking thoughtful.

"The explanation is in another poem," said Julian. "Teleri says,

"To know it was Terleu, harper of the gods,
Whose love I had and was false to, long ago."

She looked at Anthony. "You haven't said much tonight. Come, I want you to sing 'The Shores of Italy.' "

Anthony obediently rose and took his stand by the windowseat, next to Julian. Linette saw that he was, at least, not looking at her now; but he was not looking at anything else either. He seemed to be looking across the room and out the window at the darkened sky, but not as if he were seeing anything. Quite suddenly she felt a poignant, intense sorrow for the long years they had known each other and the end of their friendship.

Julian played the opening chords, and Anthony began to sing.

"Did you ever see my own true love,
As you came through Salisbury?
Her face is like the lily-flower
On the shores of Italy.

"Her hair is like the black, black cliffs
That fall down to the shore.

If England has lost my own true love,
I'll never come back any more."

He finished and sat down, still without looking at Linette. "Morgan, will you?" asked Julian.

Morgan rose. "No, I'm rather tired. I think I'll go now."

Linette glanced at her watch and saw that it was nine-thirty. "I'm going too, Aunt Julian. It's been an exciting day. Anthony, shall I walk with you to the gate?"

"I'm staying awhile, but I'll walk with you across the lawn."

Morgan had gone ahead. Linette and Anthony came out onto the moonlit grass; the shadow of the wall lay black along the east side of the courtyard. "Anthony," said Linette in a low voice.

"What is it?"

"Your feelings have changed toward me, haven't they?"

He looked at her; his gaze was no longer estimating, only troubled. "Yes—and no. I suppose I'll love you as long as I exist—but there's something else."

"I ought to tell you—Rhodri Meyrick is here, the Welsh archaeologist."

"Ah, yes—I see."

"No, it's not simply that. It's something utterly different from anything I've ever known—a different kind of life, more real than any I've ever had. We're looking for something truly important; it's a kind of quest."

He looked at her with a kind of surprise, though his eyes were still full of distress. "Then you'll understand better what I mean. I too have a quest."

"Not for Excalibur, surely," said Linette, startled beyond secrecy.

"Is yours? No; mine is for the Grail."

They drew apart in a second's silence. Linette looked at him with a sense that her impressions of him were altering like a shifting of mountains. "I never thought you would do anything like that." She caught her breath a moment. "But can you? Excalibur, after all, is a real object, something that can be looked for; but is the Grail?"

"That's partly what I want to discuss with Julian." He looked at her resolutely. "I won't ask you to wait, or to consider things longer; I don't know what I'm doing myself, so I have no right to stand in your way. Nor do I know what else to say to you."

"Neither of our quests is finished," said Linette. "There will be time, afterwards, to become used to whatever has to be."

They had reached the door of the north wing. Linette stood in the doorway, watching him go back across the lawn, realizing that that was not what she had brought him out to say. Nevertheless this must be the end; and she felt again a poignant sense of loss.

Anthony came back into the library; the place seemed strangely larger with the others gone, its edges washed over with darkness. Julian had put the harp down and sat in a chair by another window, far from the candles; she was looking out at the sky over the water, and her face was in shadow.

Anthony brought another chair and sat down beside her. She seemed strangely subdued, remote, even sad; her face was still, and her eyes seemed dark with distance. He asked in a low voice, "Why did you ask me to sing 'The Shores of Italy'?"

"Because it once meant something to you and Linette. After all this time, it seems a pity that she should turn from you to a stranger."

"Perhaps it's better. You remember I wanted to talk to you; you'll see what I mean."

"Go on, then."

"I wanted to ask you, Julian—what is the Grail?"

"You've written a dissertation on it; you should know."

"I know what the scholars say—ten thousand theories, from the cauldron of Cerridwen to the cup of the Last Supper. But that doesn't tell me what I want to know."

"And why do you think I would know?"

"You do know."

"In some way, partially, darkly." Her voice sounded weary and heavy; as she turned her face toward him, the distant light caught a brightness of tears along her eyelashes. He felt a poignant shock; he had not known Julian ever wept.

"Where is it, then?" he asked in a lowered voice. "I don't know what it is or why I am drawn to it in this way; but I am drawn to it, obscurely and strongly, from the very depths of my being."

She did not seem startled. She merely asked in the same voice, "Where do the books say?"

"Some scholars say in the Metropolitan Museum—that the silver cup set in the Antioch Chalice is it. Malory says it was taken up into heaven."

She was silent. He went on, "Say that it's the cup of the Last Supper. That existed, and the cauldron of Cerridwen was never anything but an idea. Say it still exists somewhere. I don't believe it's in the Metropolitan. That still doesn't say what it really is. It's not simply a relic."

"No," said Julian. She paused, then spoke slowly, looking once more out the window. "Do you know the stained glass in the Providence Hospital chapel? The glass in the apse, I mean, in strong colors, with words and symbols."

"I remember mainly the Justice window. It had a flaming sword in it, very bright gold—I suppose the fiery sword of Eden, the sword of the archangel Michael."

"Take that for an example, then—think of power, the power of Justice, being embodied in a definite object; not embodied, exactly; think of it as a point of convergence, a kind of concentration of power. Yet not only a point of convergence, but also able, for that reason, to give forth power, like something charged with electricity."

"Then the Grail is an object of power?"

"In part. The greatest of all, and the most complex."

"But what is the quest of the Grail, then? If I understand you, it's not something that you could organize an archaeological expedition and dig up."

"You could dig up the object, if it were buried somewhere—though I think Malory is right in saying that it isn't. But that in itself would mean little."

"I thought not. But what would, then?"

"What is the quest like in Malory?"

"After the knights saw it veiled in Arthur's hall, and after it departed suddenly, they all vowed to seek it in the hope of seeing it more clearly. And the next morning they rode out, each one in the direction he thought best; but few of them ever saw it again. Lancelot glimpsed it, but only for a moment. Only three fully achieved the quest—and of those, two of them, for its sake, had renounced all earthly love."

He lowered his gaze, and his voice changed as if he found it difficult to speak. "That was why, until tonight, I hadn't seen Linette since April. I had to know whether, if that price were exacted of me, I would have strength enough to pay it. Because I must do this thing, whatever it costs—I can no more refrain than iron can refrain from being drawn to the magnet. To deny it would be to deny the most central thing in my being. And I learned. I know now that I will love Linette as long as I have a will to love with, because of her noble excellence and because of the way the splendor of the universe is manifested in her. But I know too that, if I had to, I could love her from a world away, without ever looking on her again. Julian—must I do that?"

Julian paused a moment before speaking. "I do not think that price is always exacted. Sir Bors, the third knight, is said to have been married to the Lady Elaine. There is always a price, but not always that."

She looked down a moment, thinking, then again met his gaze. "I think you will find your answer in the quest itself. Whatever you have to do will become clear to you."

"How do I begin, then?"

"You know from Malory that it can't be searched for geographically. You can only put yourself at its disposal, and it will let itself be found or not."

He was silent, looking hard at the white stone of the sill. "Julian— am I out of my mind, wanting to do a thing like this? Is it presumptuous? Is it even possible?"

"It has to be possible," said Julian, looking out into the star-filled darkness. "That doesn't say whether you'll achieve it or not. But it's something like the eternal desire of the world."

7. Night in the Atlantis Tower

Linette sat in her room in the Garden Tower. She had picked up a book of Julian's, an edition of Shakespeare that happened to be lying there, and was flicking through its pages in the light of the single candle. But she kept glancing at her watch and not seeing the pages, seeing instead scenes in her mind, imagined flashes of what would happen in the Atlantis Tower. The image of Morgan seated at a table, like a fortune-teller or a medium, came again and again to her mind; but she had glanced at the witch scene in *Macbeth*, and that mixed itself with her thoughts so that there also came the image of Morgan in red firelight, moving in slow circles around a cauldron—*What is't you do? A deed without a name. Seek to know no more. . . .*

A dark play, full of a close blackness more than night. —*hair is like the black, black cliffs that fall down to the shore*—

She frowned, as the thread of music crossed the dark universe of the play. What had Anthony to do with all this? But, surely, her true love's hair was as black as those fallen cliffs. She had a sudden vivid image of Rhodri standing with a broken bronze sword in his hand, his face in strong light against a background of night forest, his eyes fixed in horror on something she could not see. His hair seemed blacker than all shadow, as if night itself had fallen on it. The image passed like a landscape lit by lightning; her mind recoiled from it and was hurled back into the silent room. She looked at her watch again; it was ten. In a single movement she rose, blew out the candle, and went into the corridor.

Pools of moonlight from the courtyard windows lay on the floor. She walked rapidly the length of the north wing and knocked on Morgan's door. From within came Morgan's voice, strangely clear and melodious. "Come in."

The room was almost dark; there was only the moonlight and a single candle on a table patterned with cards. The tapestry of Atlantis, drowned in shadow, stirred slightly with the draft from the door. Morgan, in her white robes and necklace of twisted gold, stood by the table, looking down at the cards.

"Lock the door," she said with a quick upward glance, "and sit down. Don't speak unless I tell you."

Linette obeyed. This new voice, more musical and solemn than her ordinary voice, made Morgan again strange to her; it was the voice of a priestess in the water-pure joy of some ritual before a loved diety. She thought of the Arthurian Morgan, priestess and incarnate representative of the triple Goddess; this Morgan, too, seemed like that.

"You see the cards," said Morgan, gesturing with a delicate gravity over the patterns. "The four suits are the four elements—coins, earth; staffs, air; cups, water; and swords, fire. You see how the coins, staffs, and swords—earth, air, and fire—are placed in an inverted triangle, with the aces at the corners and the Fool upside down in the center. This is called the Triangle of the Sun's Weird; it belongs to the Sun's opposite, Gronw, the Lord of Darkness. If the Fool and the triangle were right side up, it would be the Triangle of the Sun. The Fool is the card of the Sun, the principle of light; the divine folly is its challenging of the gigantic darkness."

Linette sat listening with intense concentration. This was unlike any seance she had ever heard of; it was beautiful, magical, mythic. The name Gronw troubled her vaguely for an instant; she had heard that somewhere recently. But she lost the remembrance as she listened to the words.

"Now I put three queens into the triangle. The Queen of Cups is for you; I am designating it as your card. The Queen of Swords is mine. These go in the upper part of the triangle. And the Queen of Staffs, the Queen of the Air, goes here below the Fool, because the spirit I am calling is known as the Queen of the Air. In her time she had the greatest command of the powers of the air, such of them as were children of darkness."

Linette wanted to know more about this Queen of the Air, but remembered that she had to be silent. Now that the moment had come, she felt uneasy at the thought of the powers of air and darkness. But Morgan, without continuing, blew out the candle, leaving only the cold moonlight. She seemed to forget Linette's presence; she moved counterclockwise round and round the table, chanting in a low voice. Linette felt the cold move along her spine, and she could not distinguish the words of the song.

Morgan stood opposite the window and lifted her face toward the moon. "Mother of all; Arianrhod, Blodeuwedd, Cerridwen; you who were called Druan Gwen: it is I, Morgan your priestess, who call on you—I, the servant of the accomplishment of your will. Not for myself do I ask this, but for your exterior glory. By your power as Cerridwen, command your slave Gronw to send to me my sister, the Queen of the Air."

She closed the curtains, shutting out the moonlight, and turned toward the table. With her glance a great wind sprang up from the center of the cards, though it scattered none of them. It passed, and a slender green flame that burnt nothing stood up from the card of the Queen of the Air. Its circle of pale light illuminated the cards and Morgan's white shape and Linette's half-frightened, fascinated face.

"Sister," spoke the voice out of the flame, "you have so far kept your bargain."

"As in this, so in the rest." She addressed Linette, "Ask her any questions you will."

"Who are you?" breathed Linette, hardly able to speak.

"I am the queen. Once I was queen on an island in the cold seas; now I am queen of a vaster realm, and I dwell in the House of the Dark and do not repent that I turned away from the Sun. In my earthly life and in this life I have done great things; many have died cursing me because of my power. It is not wise to wrong me; those who wrong me learn the terror of my vengeance."

Linette felt dislike and fear rise in her, mingled like sounds, increasing like notes rising to a higher and higher pitch. The queen's presence was around her like an intense darkness, a dreadful darkness that filled her with cold; her old sensings of overpowering dark chimed sharply with it, as if across time she had foreknown the queen's coming. She wanted to cry out to Morgan to dismiss the queen, but her mouth moved without sound.

"You are afraid," said the voice, with a cold and heartless beauty. "I am a stronger spirit than you; you cannot endure me or withstand me. Know my name, then: I am Morgause, half-sister of Arthur, who ensnared the king to ruin. I made of my son Mordred an instrument of destruction. Because of me many have come down to death, and many to dwell in the dark mansions. Few have escaped me ever; and you shall not, you who tremble as if you looked at a sharp sword in the hands of your enemy."

Linette, shuddering, knew that the suffocating darkness around her was a presence of evil, so intense that she felt she could not breathe. She tried to take her eyes away from the pale flame, but could not.

There was a ringing in her ears, a darkening across her mind so that she thought she was fainting.

"You cannot withstand me. I will cast out your weak spirit from your body; and the spirit that moves the body once yours will not be you but I, Morgause, who was Queen of Orkney."

Linette felt a dreadful power lay hold on her mind, beating against her being like dark wings. Her self, the living Linette, was being over-powered and buried by this other, this devouring other; she felt her body passing out of her own control. In helpless horror and outrage she felt her body rise up rigid, heard her own voice saying, "Sister, it is almost done. She still struggles, but that will not be long."

"How can you destroy the Cup if you are in this body?"

"I will leave it when the time comes, though she will never come back to it. Meanwhile I will use it to seize the Sword for you, the power of which will help us. The Sword for you; the destruction of the Cup for me."

Linette felt herself awash in darkness, compressed to a living spark of consciousness struggling blindly not to be put out. Nor would she surrender possession of her body. For an instant, in a fierce upblaze of assertion, she broke through the Queen's hold. She screamed out in her own voice, a high wordless cry for help from anywhere, such a shriek of terror and near-despair that it rang through all the castle.

Four thousand miles away, Cristant Aberglas sat up suddenly in the pre-dawn chill, with her hair streaming around her, and gazed startled into the unexplaining darkness.

Julian and Anthony, surprised from their second's silence, sprang up and stared out the window at the faintly-lit tower. "That was Linette," said Julian in an almost breathless voice. "Come."

They ran down the stairs of the keep, along the arched walk, up the north stairs. They could hear Rhodri banging on the door and shouting, "Linette! Linette, are you in there?"

"She is," cried Julian down the corridor. "One of you, break open the door!"

"I will," cried Rhodri. He took a running start and hurled himself against the door. The lock gave, the door crashed against the inside wall; the force of his rush carried him staggering headlong into the room. Anthony and then Julian, arriving behind him, drove in without stopping. For an instant they glimpsed the frozen apparition of Morgan, white as her robes, lit by a ghastly green light that seemed to cling around Linette; Linette stood rigid in it, opposite her, with her back to the door.

Then Linette spun with incredible speed and rushed on them, crying out in a strange language, her voice transfigured by rage itself to a dreadful beauty like a hawk's cry. She flew at Julian, but seemed to rebound as from an invisible barrier. For a second she stood as if stunned, her face swept clean of all human expression; she cried out in a voice like song, "Trust in amber while you can! I will grow stronger, and it will not protect you. Nor will you want it, after the destruction!"

"Linette—" began Anthony, and stirred toward her. She cried out without words, that sword-like hawk-cry, and was on him with talons not used like human nails, that seemed to him like stabbings of fire. He seized her wrists and by all his strength got her hands away from his face.

"Fool!" she cried. "You think you'll see the Cup! But I will destroy it and you and all this place as far as the fire reaches—five leagues' poisoning and burning of the earth, pool of death spreading outward! By the power of the Sword, the dark fire will be loosened!"

"Morgan," rang Julian's voice above the other, "you are responsible for this!"

It cut across the brazen hawk-cry like a falling sword. "No," shrieked Linette against it like a snarl of curlews, "not she but I, Morgause of Orkney! Down, down, vixen—resist, will you? Sister, I need more time!"

Julian stood rigid at her full height, her eyes fixed on Linette like piercings of light. She traced a cross in the air, speaking in a ringing voice, *"Ego te exorciso, in nomine Patris, et Filii—"*

Linette's voice shrieked to Morgan in syllables like the war cry of eagles.

"—et Spiritus Sancti. Ex ea exi, spiritus impura, in nomine Domini nostri Jesu Christi Filii Mariae—"

Linette gave one further cry, no longer in the hawk-voice, and collapsed against Anthony. The green light around her flicked out and left only darkness.

"Get some lights," said Julian in a suddenly drained voice. The others could hear her groping in the darkness, feeling for the draperies.

"I'll light the candle," came Morgan's voice, shaken. Moonlight poured cold into the room; and at the same moment the match-flame sprang up and clung to the wick, showing the white faces of all of them and the dark blood streaking Anthony's cheeks. He was holding up the full weight of Linette, who hung in his arms, her face and shut eyelids like wax.

"Is she alive?" came Rhodri's taut voice.

"Yes. Is there a couch in here?"

"Against the wall," said Julian.

They placed Linette on it, and in a moment she opened her eyes and immediately closed them again before the candlelight. "Is she gone?"

"Yes," said Julian. "She's gone."

Linette stirred, then sank back. "Ah—my head hurts. Rhodri, help me."

"Both of you," said Julian, "take her to her room."

When they had gone, she turned to Morgan. "Why didn't you open the door?"

"I didn't dare. She was between me and it."

"How did this happen?"

"We were holding a seance, and suddenly she screamed and began acting like that."

"I'd rather you didn't hold seances under my roof; you see what can happen. I don't like people seizing on my guests or screaming at me in sixth-century Gaelic. Please don't do this in the future. Good night, Miss Cornwall."

And she went out, leaving Morgan with the vivid comprehension that Julian did not believe her.

8. Stones of the Sun

"Aren't you going to ask Morgan Cornwall to leave?" Anthony asked Julian.

They were waiting for breakfast in the sunlit dining room. Linette and Rhodri were in the garden, and Morgan as usual had not come down. It was Friday morning, fresh and clear, a little cool for July.

"No," said Julian. "I'd rather know where she is."

"But isn't Linette in danger? Suppose she tries that again."

"Linette's danger is Morgause, not Morgan; and I think she can hold if her will doesn't weaken. I'm afraid she'll have to risk it. We're all in danger, more than we can comprehend."

Julian, as she spoke, was looking at the yellow roses in a bowl on the table; but her mouth and voice were suddenly like stone. Anthony, hearing that tone, felt a sudden cold, as if comprehension had bypassed his mind and gone straight to the bone. "The Queen."

"The Queen," said Julian in the same voice. "You heard her last night. She wants Linette; she wants Excalibur, but that's for Morgan; she wants to destroy the Cup. That's her consuming hunger; Linette is a tidbit to her."

Anthony still did not comprehend; his mind seemed to spin at the sound of Julian talking like that about her niece. The voice went on, stony and unbelievable. "And also another side effect. 'Five leagues' poisoning and burning of the earth, pool of death spreading outward.' "
He saw Julian's hand then, clasping and unclasping with a movement like something dying.

His mind seemed to explode. "But she can't—!"

"Oh, she has powers. You saw some of them; and if she says she can poison and burn, I expect she can. We must assume so; we dare not ignore this."

"What do we do?" His own voice, though he did not know it, had gone low and dead like Julian's.

"I don't know yet. Five leagues—that's not only Silverthorne, but the whole city and countryside, perhaps the other shore of the bay."

"Could we get the people to leave?"

"Saying what? 'Get out before a sixth-century sorceress destroys you along with the Grail'?" Julian shook her head. "And do you want to accept that, the destruction of everything?"

Anthony looked out the window at the sunlit courtyard of Silverthorne. The east wall was still full of shadow, but the peacocks pacing on the grass glinted turquoise and amethyst; as he watched, one spread its tail like the sudden unfolding of a fantastic flower. Aramelissa came through the gateway, with a basket of roses in her hand. In the morning silence he could hear the light movement of leaves outside and the breaking of the sea.

"No," he said. "You know that, anyhow." The stony sound had gone out of his voice; he could not really believe that Silverthorne could be destroyed. But that was irrational; of course it could, and not only Silverthorne. He looked at Julian's face, and his mind made another effort to close with the reality. "What, then?" he said.

Julian's voice was low, and she looked at him with a grave and steady gaze. "I think possibly it may depend on you."

"What do you mean?"

"I don't know why I think so—a kind of inspiration perhaps. You want to seek the Grail; Morgause wants to destroy it. I don't think she really could, though she could destroy us in the attempt. But why should these two desires confront each other, now and here? It seems like more than coincidence—like a kind of convergence. The one as the answer to the other. I can't guess any more than that, but suddenly this quest of yours is no longer for yourself alone."

"Yes, I see," said Anthony slowly, with a look as if he could not quite breathe. "Or rather, I don't see; but I feel somehow that you do. But if that's true, there's no time for delay. I can't just 'put myself at its disposal'; there must be some quicker way."

"Morgan would know, if there is," said Julian. "I'd try; she might say something to you which she wouldn't say to me now. In fact, I think you'd better stay here till this is over; you can use the Eagle Tower, where you slept last night."

"You're right, I think. I'll try Morgan. She might even tell—I hope by accident."

*   *   *

"I can't really describe it, Rhodri," said Linette. "It was horrible—it was like drowning without losing consciousness, under all the dark water in the world. I don't like to think about it, even now."

They were sitting on a stone bench in the rose garden, facing towards the morning sea.

"I'm sorry she scratched Anthony last night," Linette commented after a moment. "He was rather good, wasn't he; the first I remember, after getting out of the dark, is him holding me up, just before I fainted."

"He stood his ground rather well," said Rhodri, "when she came flying at him. But last night was last night, and we have work to do today."

"Morgan wants the Sword; did you know that?"

"No; I thought it was Morgause."

"They were talking about it before you came. Morgan wants it; Morgause only wants to use it, I think against the Grail."

"Does it occur to you," said Rhodri, with a tone of exasperated resignation, "that this is getting more and more fantastic? That if somebody had foretold this to us last week, we'd have thought they were mad?" He took a deep breath. "All right. I think I know why Morgan wants it. I was reading in that book, the *Llyfr Caer Mair*, last night, before the trouble and again after it. This is what I found out.

"First, your second sight was real. The Princess Christant really was young, and she really was succeeded by her brother. His name was David, and he wrote the last part of the book.

"Second, the tradition of the Pendragons was true. Madoc did bring Excalibur out of Britain, to keep it from being misused by the brother who finally defeated or killed all the others in the quarrel for the throne. And he did put it in a secret place connected somehow with the crypt of St. Michael, which was being built before he left; the place was called Annedd Cledd, the House of the Sword.

"His brother wanted it for a reason. It was connected in preChristian times with the kingship, and the pagan element that still secretly persisted believed that its owner was the true king. Well, in the twelfth century there was a certain upsurge of this paganism, a certain infiltration of it into the reigning classes; William Rufus, a king of England, was mixed up in it, among others; and so was this brother of Madoc's, whose name was also David. So of course he wanted the Sword to strengthen his political position and gain him a better title to the throne.

"Madoc wouldn't give it to him, and David was too busy with other fighting to take it. Then after he'd won, some kind of compromise was effected; Madoc was allowed to go into exile with his followers, taking

the Sword, which could consequently no longer create trouble in David's realm even if it couldn't help him either. David was interested in
the crown more than the cult.

"But Morgan is a priestess of that cult, apparently. So now we
know."

They stared at the sea. The sunlight dazzled across the wave-tops
and enriched the grass of Silverthorne.

"Did you read any more?" asked Linette.

"Yes, but I'll tell you later. We should eat breakfast and start work.
You won't mind the dark, will you, since Morgause is gone?"

He heard Linette stir abruptly on the stone bench and draw a small,
sharp breath. "Rhodri, she isn't gone. She shadows me; I feel her somehow, lying in wait for me, biding her time. She'll spring on me again;
I know it."

"Keep away from Morgan," said Rhodri; "you can't have a seance
without a medium. Meanwhile, look at the time; let's go to breakfast."

In the strong sunlight of late morning, Morgan sat on the broad rim
of the lion fountain and stared blindly into the pool. The glare on the
water dazzled her; she shut her eyes and felt the light pressing red-gold
against her eyelids and the burning strength of the sun penetrating her
hair and her white robe. For a moment she seemed to free herself of
the weight which overwhelmed her; her mind dropped away from conscious thought and lay lightly on the surface of sleep, like a leaf on the
face of the pool.

"Your Majesty." The voice startled her back into the world; she
opened her eyes and saw Anthony standing on the other side of the
fountain.

"Why do you call me 'Majesty'?" she asked, stirring slowly with
the weariness of one wakened too soon from sleep.

"Because you are the Queen of Gor."

She shook her head. "Gor is buried in Great Britain and belongs to
another. I am queen of nothing." Looking at him through the dazzle of
the light, she took in the unhealed scratches on his face. "What do you
want from me? You should hate me."

"Why should I hate you?" She sensed in his voice some puzzling
pity, and it would have irritated her if she had not been so tired.

"Because of your Linette," she said, lowering her gaze back to the
glittering water. "She would have died, and Morgause would have lived
in her body. That sounds cruel, doesn't it? But I have seen too much

death, and it doesn't matter any more. A short life is best anyway, too short for bitterness."

Anthony looked down at the bright hair glinting off light till it seemed a vortex of brilliance without color. He thought of Linette, but Linette was safe and he put the thought quickly aside. A more urgent task had to be done now. Yet at the same time Morgan's bent head and the weary attitude of her hand upturned on the stone moved him profoundly. "Is your life bitterness, then?"

"I am tired," she said. There was a long silence; the sun dazzled on the water, and the peacocks paced gaudily across the lawn. Anthony sat quietly on the opposite rim and saw that Morgan's eyes were closed.

"I remember Venta Belgarum," she said; and her voice came low and as if from a great distance. "Winchester of the kings. I remember the grass growing among the paving stones. I remember how it looked on fine afternoons, the Roman buildings falling a little into decay but with a kind of splendor, the tall columns all white in the sunlight. Now, from so far, I see how fragile it looked, as if a dark sea would come in suddenly and drown it."

She frowned suddenly, as if struck by a swift pain. "Tintagel. There was a cave there, straight under the castle rock. At high tide the sea poured through it from both ends, but at low tide we could walk through from beach to beach. Morgause was the oldest, and she was hard and reckless like a boy. I remember the day she wouldn't come out of the cave when the tide was rising; she stood on a high rock and watched the waves dash in and shatter on the rocks; she was drenched through with the spray but she was laughing. Elaine and I ran and told father; he had to make his way in and get her, or she would have drowned."

Anthony felt as if someone had hit him hard. That spray-drenched child laughing at the smash of waves on rocks—a love of force, of destruction perhaps—and yet a real child, who had been loved then, yet who could want to destroy Linette.

Morgan echoed his half-formed thought. "Maybe it would have been better if she had drowned. I say it because I have loved her; and what she now is, is beyond the reach of love, deliberately and unimaginably—I think what happened to our family did it to her, began it at least. And yet we were all old enough to remember it; and Elaine too was forcibly married, and I later—

"I remember Gor. The palace was a spiral earthwork, with a stone tower on the height looking out over the wild country. A poor country, scraped bare by the wars; and yet there was gold for necklace and arm-ring, there was wool for robe or plaid; there were skilled workers in bronze or iron, and there were warriors and hunters who were among the best of Britain. My husband Uriens was not worthy to be king of that country. A straw-haired half-Saxon too eager for war, a drinker and a runner after women— Me he was afraid of, after that first night of drunken bravado, the night before the marriage, so that I dared not refuse him in the church—"

She was silent, biting her lips. "But he gave me Owain, and for that I can thank him. Owain, my son, my delight; he was like my father's people, like Morgause—tall, dark, with strong, fine hands. Intelligent and gentle he was too, like my father, like my mother. It seemed there was nothing of Uriens in him. And yet he loved his father. Once I tried to kill Uriens, with his own sword; but Owain wouldn't let me.

"But at the time of the rising of the Kings against Arthur, by the mercy of Arianrhod he was still a child. Morgause's husband was killed then. We went down to Arthur's court after that; it was then that I came to know Venta and Castra Legionis and the other cities of the south. But they took Owain away from me, to train him for war. That was when I came to know Arthur, and I hated him because I thought he had caused my unhappiness; but I shouldn't have, for he was a man unparalleled, a very Llew come again— Did I tell you that to the old religion the king was Llew, incarnate in human form, just as I was Arianrhod? Did I say that I myself had handed him Excalibur, in the king-making for the people of the old rites, when he came to the holy island? It was not the customary sacred sword of Uther and the ancient kings; none, even the oldest priestesses, had ever seen it before; we were reluctant to use it in the ritual. But when I touched it, I knew that the customary one was a trinket and that this one was truly the Sword of Llew. A power went out from it, and a fire slept in it, as if from the vital force of the sun.

"And at this time, in Venta, he gave it into my keeping. That was right, because I was the priestess; only now, it seemed to me, because I was not a virgin I was not Arianrhod any more, but Blodeuwedd. You know the story, how Blodeuwedd must abandon Llew and give Gronw her favor? They will tell you this was because Gronw was her lover, but the truth is that this was her duty. She had to be priestess of Llew's sacrifice; except for that, the fruitfulness of the earth would cease. That was what they said in the holy places. And yet they also said, on the holy island, that the human swordsman or spearman was Gronw only at the moment when he drove home the blade; that Llew's power entered into him and he in his turn became Llew. But there were other holy places where they said differently.

"I gave him back a false Excalibur instead of the true one; and I gave the Sword of Llew to a chosen successor, Accolon, a young warrior who loved me and whom, indeed, I liked for his ardor. And, to my shame be it said, my anger entered into this; and I think that was why it went wrong. For Arthur killed Accolon in the battle; and at one stroke I missed my enemy and lost my friend and failed, I thought, the Lady of Light.

"But I thought later that it was her will I should fail, because of my anger. Her deeds must be done in purity of heart and for love. Arthur had gotten back the Sword, and I returned to Gor for fear of his justice. For a long time my bitterness continued; the worst I did was to send Arthur a poisoned mantle, and I can say in my defense only that I was nearly mad with anger and grief. Did I say they had taken Owain away from me? I was alone there.

"Uriens had not come back to Gor, and I was ruler. I restored the worship of the Goddess to its old strength there. But I had no place in the rituals: I could not be Arianrhod, I had failed as Blodeuwedd, and I was too young for Cerridwen, the queen of wisdom, whose hair is white as the stars. I was near thirty, and my life was full of grief, and I wished for my death.

"In the holy grove one twilight I stood and prayed before Druan's image; I prayed for my release, and the young moon hanging in the west shone on the image's face. Then the sight of my mind was changed; I saw not the image before me but the great Goddess, Cerridwen the all-wise, cloaked in blue and with hair like the stars. Her eyes looked into mine and spoke to me without words. And what I understood was, 'You have served only my shadow, and not served it well; but you will not die till you serve and know my true self.' And I did not grow any older after that, and my anger left me; even when Owain was killed by accident, by his own cousin Gawain, I did not blame Gawain or Arthur or anyone.

"And in the end Mordred rose against Arthur. And the word of the Goddess came to me again: 'Go down into the south where you will find Arthur dying, and take him to the island of Avalon.' I rode south, and I found him after the last battle; but he had had the Sword thrown into the sea. I did not dare think of that; it was my business to obey. I took him back to the ancient holy island, and I saw the ruined shrine with nettles growing on the broken altars, and Arthur the last child of Ygerna was dying. And as I stood there in my tears the Otherworld flowed around us like a sea, as I had known how to make it do when I was young; and the ruin was no longer there, but the apple-laden groves and the country of the undying. This too flowed away; and I cannot remember what came, except that it is both bright and dark in my mind; but when it passed, I lay in the grass among the ruins of Glastonbury

Isle, and it was night, and the Sword of Llew stood by me, stuck upright
in the earth and fiery-bright against the darkness. When I came back to
the lands of men, I found that a year had passed; and I gave the Sword
to the new king, Constantine son of Cador. And he clung unswervingly
to the new faith, so that I never touched it again."

She was silent; her face seemed troubled as if she were trying to
remember some elusive thing. Anthony had forgotten his errand; he
leaned forward, shocked with tenderness and pity. As he watched, something fell into the pool, troubling the water; and he realized that Morgan
was weeping.

"It is too long. I want it to end. I can't remember, and I am devoured
with longing. How can I best serve, except by getting the Sword back
for the true mysteries? If I could hold it again, I might remember and
the end might come. Morgause's wishes trouble me, yet what other way
is open to me? I wish I too might end in this destruction."

She seemed to have forgotten Anthony completely; her head was
bent so low that her face was hidden, and a lock of bright hair fell
forward and lay on the surface of the water unheeded.

"Does the destruction have to be?" asked Anthony in a low voice
in which compassion mixed with a sense of awesome crisis. "Is there
any way of stopping her?"

Morgan answered almost uncomprehendingly, as if out of some
depth where she could hardly hear him. "I do not know."

Aramelissa, shelling peas in the kitchen a few yards from the lion
fountain, heard the stir of Morgan's dress against the grass as she went
away, and breathed more easily. She had overheard the conversation
casually at first, then tensely, hardly daring to move. Now she stirred,
dropped a handful of peas into the bowl on her lap, and threw the
purple-green hull into a bag.

So this *soi-disant* Miss Cornwall was Morgan le Fay. That was
astonishing, but not beyond the realm of possibility.

Still, the theology of it was puzzling. Milton had said something,
hadn't he, about the pagan gods being actually demons?

> Who with Saturn old
> Fled over Adria to the Hesperian fields
> And o'er the Celtic roamed the utmost Isles.

But could demons prolong someone's life for fourteen centuries?
But all that was speculation. She resolved to pry a full account of

last night out of somebody; meanwhile it was clear only that mysterious powers were at work and to no good purpose. Destruction? It was fortunate, Aramelissa thought, that her daughter and daughter's family had gone away for a week. There was no need to worry about them. That left the problem of Julian and how to get her to a place of safety.

She frowned, and broke a pea hull into neat, small pieces. It was no use; there was no way of getting Julian to leave. Something else would have to be done. One could only watch and see what happened.

"She doesn't know," said Anthony, with a gesture as of laying a pile of documents on the table. "So—now what do we do?"

"Do?" said Julian without raising her head. "There is nothing."

"What about the Grail?"

"That isn't something you do."

They were silent. Anthony aimlessly flipped over the pages of the Welsh dictionary on the table and did not even glance at the *Llyfr Caer Mair* which Julian had been translating. Outside all was still except for the faint sound of water running in the kitchen, which cut across the windless murmur of the sea. His mind balked and would not grasp the imminent event or move toward finding an act. The woods of Silverthorne and the white walls and the sky hung before his eyes like a painted screen.

"We are left where we started," said Julian slowly at last. "Faced with a quest we don't know how to begin."

"And what if we do find the Grail, or let it find us? What will it do?"

"I have no idea."

"And what would it be like?"

"I don't know."

The silence flowed back. Then Anthony said, "It is real, isn't it? The Grail, I mean."

"Morgause believes in it. She should know. You and I could be caught in some sweet madness, but not Morgause, because she hates it."

"I don't understand any of this. I don't know what I'm supposed to do. I don't even know how to begin."

"At least," said Julian, staring at the radiant walls as if she had not heard him, "if we're mad, we'll never know."

Anthony went out without further words. After a moment she heard his feet in the vaulted gateway and guessed that he had gone out to the woods to walk and think what to do. Slowly she let her eyes move across the table where written papers lay scattered like leaves. The *Llyfr Caer Mair* lay where she had left it, its enamelled ornaments glinting dully against the dark binding. No, she thought, that must not happen again—not the collapsing inferno of towers, not the trees withering in flame, not David's outcry of lamentation: "Better to have fed the birds of the air than to have heard the roar of this burning!" For a second, Caer Mair blazed before her mind, black in an agony of fire, its corpses twisted in the lurid glare; then it was gone suddenly; the silence poured in like a tide, and the forest flowed over the ruined stones. A memory of some poem came to her—New York, was it, where arrowed hunters stalked deer in the green ruins? No, the deer were irrelevant; Morgause had said burning and poisoning too. There would not be any deer.

She was powerless even for tears. A blank despair knotted in her like sickness, and she bowed her head forward onto her clenched fists. But in the dark of closed eyes a grey current of stillness flowed through its old channels in her being; the despair came unknotted, and her hands opened on the table in a gesture whether of giving or receiving.

"How strange it is in here," said Linette, hardly above a breath.

They were moving almost noiselessly down the passage, but the slight sound of their steps raised a faint resonance out of the darkness; she felt that even that was too great, and a dread shook her of sudden reverberating echoes breaking out of the darkness, forcing on them too overwhelming a recognition of the narrowness of the abyss of time. It was as if they stood on the brink of an invisible canyon, unthinkably deep but only hands'-breadth wide, across which strangers watched them with immortal eyes. Not Morgause now troubled her, but an obscure awe, as if a too quick shifting of the lantern-light across the presence of the darkness might suddenly catch that other eye-gleam.

They stood a moment in front of the tombs, looking at the carved letters. Linette felt the memory of yesterday's sight fold around her mind like the smoke of torches, untouchable and obscure; a panic like a cold needle touched her, and she almost seized Rhodri's arm and said, Let's not go on. But she held herself in check; she could see Rhodri's face in the lantern-light, lit up from within by an absorbing passion like that of a great painter self-forgetting in his art. For a second she guessed what this quest must mean to him, quite apart from the Pendragonship: the utter if momentary fulfillment of his being. At this moment neither she nor he existed for him; there was only that truth which he loved with a complete, selfless love.

She shook her head, wishing she had something that meant as much.

But the shaking would not shake away the stony depression that weighed her down as if the very air were granite.

Once more the silent journey threaded the dark. The sense of presences had receded now; the circle of light seemed like a candle lost in vast wastes between galaxies, in an immense, timeless cold of uncreation. Even the walls of white stone seemed part of that emptiness, old and cold and not real, like stellar mists that might suddenly divide and show distant nebulae through the rifts. Linette drew closer to Rhodri; he was the only warmth or life in that chill, dreamlike void. He put his arm around her and drew her to him, and they went on.

Suddenly he stopped, stopping her with him, whispering, "Give me the light." He held it at arm's length; at the fringes of the brightness a dark something resolved itself into a rectangle of ironbound timber closing the corridor. They came up to it; Rhodri touched it with hesitant fingertips before he spoke.

"A door," he said softly, "a door seven, maybe eight hundred years old. Oak, with great scrollwork hinges and bars and a lock like a bank. Do you know that this door should be falling apart? That the iron should have rusted away?"

Linette did not answer, only looked at the door with its black iron. Excitement was clearing away her depression like wind-stirred mist; she heard the breathlessness in Rhodri's voice and saw the intensity in his face, and something in her flared with an answering fire.

Rhodri pushed the door, first lightly, then hard; the lock made a sound in its socket. He dropped to his knees to examine the lock and thrust the lantern wordlessly into Linette's hands. While she held it close over his shoulder, he took from his pocket a little leather case full of tools and a minute bottle of oil, and began to work at the lock. The minutes seemed to lengthen like hours as he worked delicately with the stubborn, ancient iron. Then with a slow, grating sound the lock yielded; he pressed the door and felt it move under his hand. As if to prolong the suspense, he put all the little tools carefully back in the case before he rose; the lantern trembled a little in Linette's hand, half with fear, half with anticipated delight. Excalibur, she thought, with a brightness as of fire in her mind. Excalibur.

Rhodri took her hand, as if to draw her into his triumph, and pushed on the door. It stirred slowly and reluctantly on the massive hinges and swung stiffly inward with a sound of iron. The walls were suddenly lost out of the circle of light, and there was a dark smell as of something long closed. They moved breathlessly in, and Linette cast the lantern-light around till they had seen four white stone walls lined with dark shapes.

"It isn't here," she said, disappointed.

"Something is," said Rhodri, with the excitement still in his voice. "Chests."

Linette realized what the dark shapes were, and her voice once more kindled. "I thought they were tombs."

Rhodri shook his head; his eyes were vivid in the lantern-light. "Ten to one this is the secret treasury of the House of Cadwallen."

He knelt by one of the great ironbound coffers. "Lockwork again; I might as well be a professional burglar. Shall I do all the locks before we look in any?"

"Do. I can't stand waiting from chest to chest." She could hardly breathe for suspense, guessing his hope that the Sword might be locked there.

He moved from one to another; there were four, one at each wall. "The chests are that way too," he said in a voice almost soundless with awe. "Not rusted, not rotted. Nothing decays down here."

Neither of them spoke their thoughts, but the imagined brightness of Excalibur seemed to shine like the lantern.

At last all the locks had been dealt with. Rhodri and Linette returned to the first of the great oak coffers. "Are you ready?" said Rhodri in a low, breathless voice, as if success or failure depended on this one thing.

"Yes."

He lifted the lid. No fiery light blazed forth; the lantern beams spilled onto heaps of cold brightness.

"Silver money!" exclaimed Rhodri on the low intake of breath. "And it isn't even tarnished."

Linette took up a double handful and let it spill through her hands like sand. The cold, moonlight glitter of it amazed her till she forgot what it was worth; she wanted to play with it as a child plays with bright stones. She took up separate coins and stared at the old letterings and strange kings.

They went along the wall to the second chest. It too contained silver, but mixed with the money were silver candlesticks and bracelets and necklaces and cups and rings. The third chest was full of gold: coins, rings, chains, and chalices, circlets and coronets and gold-hilted swords, enamelled or incised or embossed or plain. Rhodri picked up something which lay on top and looked at it closely in the light. It was a pendant apparently, but utterly different from anything else in the chest, rounded and symmetrical and full of a harsh life—pre-Columbian of some kind, even Linette knew. It troubled her mind vaguely with a sense of some dark meaning; the light on the gold brought suddenly the image of Caer Mair in flames.

Rhodri put it down without speaking and opened the fourth chest. Out blazed cold, bright fires like flame and ice—ruby and sapphire, garnet and carnelian and pearl, beryl and carbuncle and amethyst, amber and emerald, diamond and lapis lazuli, opal and chrysolite and moonstone, some set in gold and some loose like pebbles.

"Oh," breathed Linette and could say nothing else. Rhodri made no sound except to draw in his breath sharply. Neither moved for a minute, only crouched by the chest gazing at the multicolored tangle of light.

Lightly, almost caressingly, Linette put her hand out to a long necklace of amber and let it run through her fingers like water.

Rhodri, without a word, took a pale necklace of gold and amethyst and fastened it around her neck. He made her get up; and she stood in solemn and dazzled joy, the lantern still in her hand, while he decked her like a queen with the treasures of Gwynedd. He crowned her black hair with a coronet fiery with garnets and rubies, put massive gold bracelets set with sapphires on her arms, clasped a belt of joined gold disks set with garnets around her waist. He loaded every finger of her hands with rings; he fastened so many brooches on her dress that it shone like jewelled armor. She stood brilliant-eyed, glittering like a barbaric goddess in a shrine. The thought fleetingly touched her of Schliemann decking his wife with what he called the jewels of Helen; oh, it would be like that, and Rhodri would be famous, and they would go on from glorious discovery to discovery all their lives long.

"Look," said Rhodri sharply, with his hands in the chest, "here's another box in this corner. Carved all over—seems to be clasped with silver."

Forgetting the jewels themselves in intense excitement, he set the lantern on a closed chest and bent over it, working delicately at the box with the little tools. He did not see the color ebb slowly out of Linette's face, and her eyes grow wide and dark with horror. She stood rigid as stone, hardly able to move for the weight of the gold. Her mouth moved as if she wanted to cry out, but no sound came. Then the terror was driven out of her eyes by a hard, fierce blaze; her mouth ceased striving and took on an expression between scorn and a cruel smile as of triumph.

Rhodri, with his back to her, opened the carved box. Within lay a mass of soft, fine-bleached wool; he felt through it and brought out a hard shape in a case of white damask tied with gold. The silk, after eight hundred years, was still fresh and unmarred. He loosed the gold strings and drew out a smooth flask of crystal, as long as his hand and as large around as a small coin. Its stopper was of wrought gold sealed with white wax. Inside was what looked like water, clear as if new-drawn from a spring, but with a soft phosphorescence whose light lay in his hand.

"Linette, it has to be the Water of Vision," he said in an awed, breathless voice. "One of the treasures of Gwynedd." When Linette did not answer, he said more sharply, in sudden alarm, "Linette?—"

He looked over his shoulder and caught a glimpse of the white face and the hard, blazing eyes. Then her long, white hand reached over him and picked up the lantern, and smashed it against the stones.

There was nothing but the small, pale glow of the crystal. He saw her hand reaching toward it and through the shattered horror of his mind knew she would smash it too. Blindly he seized her wrist with his free hand and thrust the crystal down into the wool. It still gave some light; he saw her other hand going for it and caught that too. There was no sound this time; he struggled with the Queen of Orkney in total silence. The two hardly moved in the near-dark, though each was striving with determined savagery to break the other's force.

Linette, thought Rhodri confusedly, Linette's gone, this strength can't be hers—

The remembrance of Julian's pendant crossed his mind like lightning. *Trust in amber while you can.* He held the queen's two hands with one hand, reached back with the other for the amber necklace, and thrust it against the queen's strong fingers.

With a shudder, the fingers relaxed. Then, groping with weakness, they caught hold of the amber and clung to it.

"Rhodri, help me," came Linette's voice, shaken and dreadful. "She's still trying—this isn't strong enough—"

He caught up the box with the crystal, shoved the box in his pocket but kept the crystal out to light the way. Its tiny light showed almost nothing, only a wraith of white stone; but he held it like a lantern as they hurried back through the passages. His free arm was around Linette; he could feel her light, rapid breath and the tension of her body in which every nerve seemed to give off shocks like electricity. She held tight to the amber, struggling in her mind with the diabolic darkness that poured around her like overwhelming water.

Rhodri did not pause in the cellar or even in the kitchen. He brought Linette out onto the back porch, where the hot late-afternoon sun fell dustily on the fading boards and kindled the large thin leaves to a green fire. Linette collapsed shakily onto the steps with her back to a post; the amber beads spilled into her lap like lengths of clover-chain. The slanting light on her jewels made them blaze like little suns themselves, so that she seemed protected by an armor of light. She felt the dread power withdraw even its shadow from her, leaving her quiet and drained of strength, her mind empty as a white-walled room filled only with sunlight. Idly as a child she watched Rhodri restore the delicate crystal to the safety of case and wool and box.

"Rhodri," she said in a while, "I'm sorry."

"It wasn't you; it was her, the Queen of the Air."

"I tried, but she was too strong. It was worse than last night. I felt it coming, weighing on me, though I didn't know what it was." She looked down suddenly, and her hands tightened. "If it goes on getting worse, she'll win and that'll be the end. I'm not so much afraid of being shoved out by force; but if I surrender, I'm afraid she'll keep me."

"Keep you how?"

"I don't know. Her slave, her prisoner—something."

"Does the amber help?"

"It weakens her, but it doesn't hold her off anymore. Last night Aunt Julian's pendant was enough, and that was less amber than this."

"Rubies are also supposed to be proof against sorcery; were they?"

"Not that I knew. But I wasn't touching them; they were above my head."

"Listen," said Rhodri after a moment, "I left my tools down there. Will you be all right in the sunlight while I go get them? And I'd like to put things in order a bit."

"Yes, but don't stay long; it's getting late. Shall I keep the box?"

"No, it's all right in my pocket. I'll be back before dark."

He went, and Linette waited. She sat still, her eyes half-closed, thinking of nothing, letting her mind and will float on the surface of the sunlight. The inevitable headache lay like a weight above her brows, but she was too tired to care. The sun dropped rapidly toward the west; she opened her eyes and saw the long tree-shadows fade into the shadow of the world. She sat small and exposed under the apocalyptic glory of the sunset whose fires were reflected in the darkening river. The riverbanks were already in night. Beneath the sinking brightness of the sky she felt her fear rise with the darkness of the riverbanks, slowly spreading in cold pools, creeping silently up the slope and around the steps. She took off the crown and pressed her hands to the rubies; she wound the string of amber round and round her arm. The sun-colored stones seemed to strengthen her, though they were almost colorless in the fading light.

Rhodri appeared suddenly, with a lighted lantern in one hand. The sight of his face shocked her; the skin seemed stretched tight on the bone, and not only with exhaustion; and its color was grey-white, out of which his dark gaze came like stone. She opened her mouth to question, but no sound came.

"I'll tell you as we go," he said brusquely. "Let's get to some light."

As they ground their way over the oyster shells, with the headlights picking out the trunks of trees, Linette held tight to the sun-colored jewels. Rhodri's anguish communicated itself to her as fear, not of Morgause this time, but of something she did not know.

"I found another lantern," said Rhodri in the same almost harsh voice. "I got my tools and was about to go. Then it came over me that we'd come to the end of the passage and not found the Sword. I thought there might be another way out of the treasure chamber, to where it was. I tried the floor for an echo that might mean a lower crypt; there wasn't any. I tried the walls too. One place did sound a little different from the rest, so I took out a stone; but what do you think?

"Earth and rock, that was all. Red clay and sandstone. There was a place scooped out, nothing in it that I could see; I don't know why. I put back the stone and left."

His voice had faded into a hard despair. Linette sat motionless, forgetting even the jewels, as he spoke again with a stony finality.

"Excalibur isn't in the treasury; we felt to the bottom of everything. It isn't in the passage; we couldn't have missed it. It can't be in the tombs, it was hidden long before; and if it ever was in the scooped place, it isn't now. God knows where or whether it ever was. But we haven't found it, and we've come to the end of our road."

It was night in Caernarvon when Rhodri was struggling with Morgause. Cristant lay in bed in the house by the old wall, her mind drifting on the borders of sleep. Suddenly an image took shape in her thoughts, the face of a dark-haired girl wearing a crown set with red stones. Fear came into the face, a horror so dreadful that Cristant herself sat up and shook her head, trying to drive the image out of her mind. But it would not go, though her eyes were wide open and straining into the dark; and then something came into the face that mastered terror and turned into hate so intense that Cristant seemed to shrivel before it. The mouth curved into a smile more like an animal's snarl, and the eyes subtly changed as if a different spirit looked from behind them. Cristant felt a suffocating darkness touch her mind, though she knew it was not herself the darkness wanted. She braced herself to suffer whatever her terrible clairvoyance might demand of her; the transfixing gaze seemed to pierce her, and she shut her eyes. Then the face flicked out like a match, and she sank back trembling upon her pillow.

*　　*　　*

Linette and Rhodri hurried through the dusk of the courtyard toward the lights of the dining room. They arrived with a dull sense of relief and exhaustion, but their mood was unlightened even by the prospect of telling Julian about the treasure. Linette mechanically smoothed her hair and set the crown on her head, but its brilliance gave her no delight; shreds of darkness clung around her mind and shadowed the gems.

Anthony was standing by a window, looking desperate and miserable. They did not notice him till he turned. At the sight of Linette's dark hair and clear pallor amid the light-struck blaze of jewels, his face seemed momentarily to kindle; but at once the joy was replaced by a bitter and dark concern.

"What happened?" he asked, striding rapidly over to them.

"What do you think?" said Linette, dropping into a chair. "You haven't found the Grail and we haven't found Excalibur."

"What's this about the Grail?" asked Rhodri.

"The Cup Morgause wants to destroy," said Anthony. "Julian believes—I don't know what Julian believes, except that somehow the achievement of the quest will stop Morgause. But I don't know where to begin; I'm not even sure what achieving it means. I've been walking in the woods all day thinking about it, but I still don't know." His glance returned to Linette, to the flame of jewels contradicting her despondent gaze. "Something more than that's happened to you, though."

"Morgause tried again with Linette," said Rhodri, "just after we'd found the jewels of Caer Mair." He too looked at the fiery interplay of light on the stones, and his mouth tightened. "I ought to be happy that we found the treasure; I was happy at first. More than just its splendor— the evidence of a unique civilization. That ought to be enough for anyone. But I can't forget that I found the end of the passage and no Excalibur."

"But you know Excalibur's there somewhere," said Anthony, "or those two wouldn't be so bent on getting it. Especially Morgan. I talked to her; she seems completely sure." The memory of Morgan's anguish came back to him, and he hoped he would not have to tell of it.

"I'd forgotten about that," said Rhodri. "It could be that we've missed something, though I can't imagine what. The same argument is true for you, isn't it?—since Morgause is so sure of the Grail. I wonder why she thinks Excalibur would help her against it."

"Maybe Excalibur is like the Grail," said Anthony, "a point of convergence, an object of power. Maybe Morgause thinks she can use it simply as abstract power, divorced from any association of good or evil, like a piece of artillery; that she can train it on the Grail, power against power, and annihilate it—probably annihilate both. In which case Morgan is getting cheated, because she thinks Morgause is going to let her keep it."

"Sword against Cup," said Rhodri, knitting his brows in intense thought. "And so Julian thinks, evidently, that they can be used for one another as well as against? That there's some sort of connection between them?"

"She seems to think of the power of the Grail as being greater than the power of Excalibur—as if the strength of the Grail would somehow neutralize Morgause's attempt and keep the destructive fire from coming out. But if the connection exists, it occurs to me—we might help one another. One of us finding one thing might help the other find the other."

"You know what happens if we fail, don't you?" said Rhodri with lowered gaze, his voice full of earnestness. "I don't understand this very well myself; but this business of Excalibur isn't as small as it looks. In some way it's involved with the long striving of man against the powers of darkness."

"And the Grail—there's something worse than the five leagues' poisoning and burning. If Morgause destroyed the Grail—no, what I'm thinking is impossible—but if it weren't."

"You mean the world as a Waste Land," said Rhodri in a low voice, "like in the myths?"

"The utter Waste, the abyss. I have seen the edge."

They were silent for a moment. Then Rhodri gestured impatiently as if to break the spell. "It all sounds mad, doesn't it? Especially since we're moving among things we don't understand."

"But which we have to deal with anyway," said Anthony. "I can begin by telling you the story of the Sword according to Morgan."

Julian found them like that, grouped in the candlelight, intent on the story; she looked with wonder at the blaze of strange jewels in the light, but did not interrupt, being busy with her own conjectures.

Supper was brought in before the tale of the Sword ended. Then Rhodri had to recount, in full detail, the story of the jewels and Morgause.

"I hope to see this treasure," said Julian at last, her eyes shining. "Not only for the story and the splendor of their civilization—but I have always felt a mystery in jewels, something of fire and color and light, something everlasting. The old poets did well to say that paradise was built out of them."

"Please, not tonight," said Linette with a troubled look. "I feel the darkness at the back of my mind—I don't want anyone to go there now."

"No," said Julian, with an unreadable brightness in her eyes, "I wasn't going tonight. My place is here till the quests are over, for I too have my part in the quest, though I only partly guess it yet. So far I have been searching in the *Llyfr Caer Mair*."

She drew a long breath, surveying their intent faces. "I haven't found out where Annedd Cledd was—only that Madoc placed the Sword there before he left. Bran, who wrote the book, is very guarded about that part. But he does tell a story which is rather strange and seems involved with it. It seems that at the time of the voyage he was only an apprentice bard; the Chief Poet was his teacher, Kynon. And Kynon loved a woman named Ancret, a priestess of the old gods. Originally he was trying to learn about the ancient mysteries from her, because he wanted to write a new kind of poetry; and when he sailed with Madoc, he brought Ancret with him. All went quietly during the original building of Caer Mair. But Madoc sailed away to get more colonists and left his sister Goeral in charge. Bran was in love with Goeral, that's very clear; he inserts a poem in the narrative, all about 'the bright braids of her hair' and so on; it seems both she and Madoc had red hair of a very fine color. But now Ancret took the opportunity to set up a circle of stones in the forest, among oak trees, there to worship her goddess Druan Gwen. Some of the people of Caer Mair followed her—notably Rhiryd, Madoc's brother; Kynon protested, but by now Ancret had turned from him to Rhiryd. On the day of the Midsummer rites Kynon went to demand her back from Rhiryd; but Rhiryd killed him. It was done within the framework of the ritual, Kynon as Llew and Rhiryd as Gronw. And then, according to Bran, a shadow of darkness came upon Caer Mair.

"Goeral stood out against this darkness and against the influence of Ancret. The situation developed a political aspect; Rhiryd wanted to be ruler of Caer Mair and felt it was his right, since he was the only prince of the House of Owain who was present and perfect in body. There was another brother, Cadwallen, in Caer Mair; but he had been a hostage of the English king, and had been blinded in revenge for some Welsh victory. The ancient law was that the ruler could have no defect of mind or body; you remember the war of Owain's sons started because the eldest was Iorwerth Broken-Nose. The situation darkened as the year passed into winter.

"In the end Goeral did something. It is not clear what; Bran doesn't want to talk about it. All he says is, 'In Annedd Cledd the glorious princess sought the will of the powers of light; and in Annedd Cledd she laid aside her mortal life, as a sacrifice for her people, because of the great evil of the shadow. And there she still lies at the entrance of the inner chamber; it would seem she slept, if she did not lie so still. She is to wake at the drawing of the Sword.' "

"A strange passage," said Rhodri.

"Yes; that's why it sticks in my mind. Ancret considered herself defeated; she walked away into the forest and never returned. But the cult and the politics went on. It got very complicated; even Bran, who was now Chief Poet, was mixed up in it for a time. He was responsible for setting up a countercult, more or less Christianized, centered around Goeral and Annedd Cledd. He made Cadwallen ruler, as you might guess; and the chief princess of the House of Cadwallen bore the title Druan Gwen, in Bran's sense, a symbolic figure of the earth or the human spirit. Druan Gwen had three aspects, maiden, bride, and ancient queen of wisdom; and there were three crowns belonging to the cult, one for each aspect. There was a crown of silver and pearl, which remained forever on Goeral's brow in Annedd Cledd, though a princess wore one like it; there was a crown of ruby and garnet, which the princess wore when she was married and afterward till she grew old; and there was a crown of silver with deep incised patterns and a single sapphire, which she wore in her old age. I rather think you've found the ruby and garnet one."

"I wish I could find Excalibur," said Rhodri.

"No, listen," said Julian. "It has to be there. Bran says Annedd Cledd was built; he says Goeral lies at the entrance of the inner chamber. Did you look for markings on the walls, or anything like that?"

"Not closely enough."

"Speaking of the Druan Gwen cult," said Anthony, "where's Morgan?"

"In the Atlantis Tower," said Julian. "She wanted to eat alone; I think she's trying to avoid Linette, after last night."

Linette went to sleep that night in a room full of lighted candles, so that there was no dark there; and her head and neck and arms and fingers were loaded with all the sun-colored jewels brought out of the hoard. But they did not save her from dark dreams that troubled her rest without allowing her to wake.

"Morgause, my sister, why have you done these things?"

The green flame flicked like a serpent's tongue over the cards. "Morgan, my sister, why have I done what things?"

"Last night you gave away secrets to Julian and that young man.

Today you broke the lantern and tried to break the crystal which is certainly some possession of Druan. You have put them on their guard—and why did you try to break the crystal?"

"Sister, you know nothing of the mysteries of the Shadow of Druan; if you did, you would not accuse me. The powers of our enemies have weakened us too much. We know we will dominate the earth at last, but centuries yet must pass before the Shadow of Arianrhod is embodied in a woman and bears the Shadow of Llew. Meanwhile the destroying of one of the alien mysteries by means of another will be a great victory for us and will strengthen us. But now we must work with less strength; and when we seek to possess another's body, our spirit must battle with that spirit. The struggle causes these violent effects."

"Why do you call Excalibur one of the 'alien mysteries'?"

"I mean only that our enemies attribute a meaning to it as they do to the Cup."

"And the crystal? I know you have little concern for the Lady of Light, but you should not interfere with my mysteries."

"I tell you we batter the soul like a madness; we are not wholly responsible for what we do. But consider that the girl is weakening from the horror; even now, because I am near, her mind is open to black dreams. And soon now, after I conquer, victory will be in our hands. I can imitate her every movement, phrase, and turn of voice; not even the Pendragon will know it is not she."

"For this time I will accept your reasons. But I am half inclined to try my strength without you."

"And risk failure now? Tomorrow should end our quest. They can hardly be long in finding the hidden doorway. But they must not find the Sword before I control the girl."

"I can lay a spell at the door and divert them into the Hidden Land. You will have time."

9. The Hidden Country

Morgan, as usual, was not at breakfast. Neither was Anthony; he
had decided to set out on his quest, and had gone before daybreak. At
the table no one said much; Linette had slept badly, Rhodri was vainly
retracing the plan of the passage to see where he had gone wrong, and
Julian was groping among the complexities of her knowledge for an
answer to the riddle of the Grail.

In the sunlit kitchen of the old house, Linette stood still while
Rhodri decked her once more with the sun-colored jewels and set the
bright crown on her head. He considered it more carefully now; it was
light and finely-made, with narrow, blunt points like the crowns of Char-
tres, and set so closely with garnets that the gold appeared almost as a
tracery around them. The rubies were clustered in a group of five at the
front, and the whole thing kindled in the light and cast glittering reflections on Linette's hair. Rhodri looked at it and thought of the civilization
that had made it. The jewelwork was Celtic; the shape suggested France
at the blending-point of two eras. What unheard-of cultural synthesis
had shaped Madoc's Caer Mair? And then the thought mingled in his
mind with the soft darkness of Linette's hair.

They had no definite plan except to record and examine the treasure.
Rhodri had brought the necessary equipment; he seemed savagely me-
thodical today, as if by carefully keeping all the rules he could batter
the inscrutable powers into giving him success. But as they made their
way slowly down the passage, the immediacy of the past pressed once
more around them, the sense of vasts of time thinning to a tenuous veil.
To those walls the twelfth century and the twentieth were alike irrele-

vant; time was annihilated there, and Linette would not have been startled to think that she and Christant's burial procession walked there invisible to one another in the same motion.

On the threshold of the treasure chamber she shivered briefly at the memory of Morgause but went boldly in. The chests still stood open, though the shards of the lantern had been cleared from the floor. They began carefully to disentangle the splendors of the jewel chest and lay them in large, deep trays.

"Now, how did this get in here?" said Rhodri, lifting something out of the glittering mass. "It ought to be in the gold chest—or ought it?"

He held it close to the lantern. Linette saw that it was a broad, intricately patterned bracelet or arm-ring, made of bright reddish gold without stones. Its style was different from that of the other pieces, a single spiral woven and coiled and ending in a dragon's head.

"They didn't wear arm-rings in the twelfth century," said Rhodri. "There's some special reason not only why it's in this chest, but why it's here at all. I could swear it belonged to Madoc and was an ancient emblem of the Pendragons." He slid it onto his arm above the elbow. "Well, sun-colored things; I might as well have one too."

"That reminds me," said Linette, "you never did show me the hollow place."

"I will now," he said. He felt a turning-over of desolation as he spoke of it, but he wanted Linette to see it. A conviction had come on him that he should search the tombs after all, since there was nowhere else; but he would have to reconcile Linette somehow to the idea of opening them. He had a tentative theory that Excalibur had once been in the treasury, that it and the body of Goeral had been moved elsewhere; and where else was there to look? But what could make Linette willing to see the remains of the Princess Christant?

Maybe the realization of bitter necessity would do it. He pried out the loose stone, and Linette thrust the lantern through the hole and looked in.

Immediately she drew back shuddering, pale as the stone. "There is something in there. Bones."

Rhodri took the lantern and peered in. "Well, why didn't I see them before? Too disappointed, I suppose, because no Excalibur. And there's not much left of them, is there? I see the skull, though." He looked at them with detachment, noting the obvious conclusion that the preserving spell did not reach outside the passage. "I'm sorry they startled you. I wonder what they're doing there—not human sacrifice in the House of Cadwallen's territory."

"He was a traitor," said Linette; "and they walled him up alive."

Rhodri turned sharply at the tone of her voice; he saw her eyes fixed on the stones with a blind gaze. All the life in her face seemed concentrated in her eyes; and their sight was turned inward or elsewhere, leaving her face like something sculptured in candlewax. Fear touched him, since he guessed now that her clairvoyance meant the nearness of Morgause.

"He had betrayed the Sword to the children of shadow, the strangers from the south; and he led them into the passages of Annedd Cledd. But they were taken as they passed the westward corridor. The strangers fell by the swords of the Britons, but the traitor was taken alive and condemned to die behind stone. Yet through the last hole Prince David pierced him with a spear, part mercy, part quittance for his father Kyneurin and for Bran. And they closed the north passage with stone against the searching of the strangers."

She was silent, and the fixed gaze passed. Part of Rhodri's mind noticed that; the rest was blazing like a midsummer bonfire. He realized, almost mechanically, that she had clarified an obscure passage in the *Llyfr Cuer Mair*; the very phrase "to die behind stone" was there. But that was a detail, gone as soon as thought of, consumed in the skyward conflagration.

" 'As they passed the westward corridor,' " he repeated, hardly able to speak. " 'Closed the north passage with stone'—Linette, Linette!"

"Oh, yes, yes," cried Linette, catching his hands in an exaltation that flamed from his own. "I saw it. Where the passage turns west, where we thought there was a dead end!"

In moments they had brought tools from the cellar and stood breathless before the blank wall at the turn. Rhodri struck the stones hard with the pick-handle; there was a faint hollow sound.

"Only this one wall," he said in a voice unsteady with excitement. "Look how the blocks are set in, so that the passage just seems to turn. Linette—this has to be it—"

He dropped abruptly and set to work; she thought he could not trust his voice to say any more. His breath came in small, sharp spurts as he struggled with a stone. Then grindingly it came out, longer and longer, thicker and heavier than any ordinary stone. He knelt motionless beside it, as if he could not dare to look; the individuality of his face was almost washed out by the conflict of hope and dread.

Linette crouched beside him and thrust the lantern through the hole. "It's true, Rhodri," she whispered. "There's another corridor."

*   *   *

Julian, in the cool, many-windowed library of Silverthorne, frowned thoughtfully for a moment at the *Llyfr Caer Mair*, then put down her pen and rose in search of a reference book. As she took it down, she glanced out the open window and saw Morgan crossing the courtyard to the Atlantis Tower.

She'll help Morgause; I know it, thought Julian in a piercing visitation of insight. But if she can't be alone—

She leaned out of the window. "Oh, Miss Cornwall!"

Morgan looked up and came closer to the keep, so that they could talk without calling. "Good morning, Miss Silverthorne."

"You're coming from breakfast, I suppose."

"Oh, yes. My book is keeping me up late, so I sleep late."

"How is it going?"

"Very well. I'm nearly half done."

"But you need to take a little time away from it. Why don't you come up and talk for a while. I'll have Aramelissa bring us some tea."

"Why, how kind of you, I know you must be busy yourself."

Neither lady was deceived by these charming formalities. Morgan knew that Julian wanted to keep her under surveillance, and Julian knew that Morgan knew it. But Morgan did not quite see her way to breaking off diplomatic relations with Julian, so she came up to the library as if she had all the time in the world.

"There," said Rhodri, setting the stone on the floor, "that's the last one we have to take out. Just mind your head when you go through."

"What do you think, Rhodri?" whispered Linette in a tense voice. "Will it be stuck in a stone and anvil? Or will it be all fire, the way Morgan saw it at Glastonbury?"

"We'll have to see. I've got the tools; you hold onto the lantern. Give me your hand; come on."

"Holy God! Where are we? Where's the passage?"

"*When* are we? Rhodri, don't let go of my hand."

She was still holding the lantern, and he was still carrying the tools. But they were standing outdoors in a grassy place, under a sky full of stars.

Rhodri looked up and around, at the sky and the trees. "How did we get here? Are we alive, do you think?"

"Yes." said Linette, "because I can feel your hand." She followed his gaze. "At least the stars are the same."

The familiar constellations of early evening hung over scattered pine trees—the Dipper, the Northern Crown, the Dragon, the Swan. But they seemed extraordinarily large and bright. Venus barely showed in the west; in the east the full moon was rising with an improbable white brilliance.

"It ought to be daytime," said Linette. "My watch says ten."

"It can't be ten at night; the moon looks more like seven. Is your watch running?"

"No—listen, Rhodri, we've walked in our sleep and come out at some opening."

Rhodri shook his head. "Can't be. The lantern would be burnt out."

"You tell me, then!" Her hand tightened on his.

"No, get hold of yourself," said Rhodri. "It's incredible but a fact: we walked out of that passage into some other place."

"Where, then?"

"The Otherworld, probably, along with unicorns and cockatrices and whatever else is here. You remember Morgan's story, that she could enter it at will?"

"Yes." Reassured by a rational explanation, however bizarre, Linette released his hand and looked more carefully around her. "Really, though—this looks like the ground we ought to be on; there's the river."

"It's the Otherworld river, then," said Rhodri grimly. "The thing is, how do we get back?"

"What do you mean?"

"I mean Excalibur won't be here; it's in Annedd Cledd in our own world. You don't think Morgan would help us, do you?"

Something in his tone made Linette turn her head and look at him. He seemed suddenly different from the Rhodri of the other side of the doorway; or rather that familiar Rhodri had become, as it were, transparent. She saw now what she had half-glimpsed when he struggled with Morgause: all his intelligence and ability was brought to a heightened flame which burned through him as through glass. The world they had left, not this one, was truly alien to him; this one was his natural element. She knew she was looking at the Rhodri who was the Pendragon.

"Stand where you are," he said. "I'll look for the doorway."

He felt all around them in the half-dark, seeking an invisible entranceway; he worked outward in circles till he had explored all the area for some way around where Linette stood.

"No use," he said finally; "they've got rid of it somehow. We'll have to find another way back. But we could leave the tools here to mark the spot."

He examined the tools to see if any would be useful as weapons, but they all seemed too awkward. So he cut down a smallish pine sapling, got the branches off, and wedged one of the instruments from the case—to Linette's uninstructed eyes it looked like the business end of an ice pick, bright and wickedly pointed—into the lighter end. She first thought that the result was a gig, like those used for crabbing; but by the way he picked it up, she saw it was meant for a spear.

"Which way do we go?" she asked.

"We might as well continue northward. That way, we might find ourselves nearer our goal if we stray back into our own world—not that that's likely." His teeth showed in a grim suggestion of a smile. "We won't get back easily. Morgan will have seen to that."

They walked, hand in hand, for a long time, while the moon climbed slowly higher up the sky. The country was parklike, without underbrush; pine straw and short grass covered the ground, with pink fireweed showing here and there. Linette noticed with surprise that the quality of the moonlight was subtly different; she could actually see the color of the flowers. The river, light-streaked, dropped behind the curve of its shore; but they could catch, on the edge of hearing, the small sound of the sea.

They met no one. Now and again they heard somewhere in the semi-dark the sudden liquid voice of some bird; and once they caught, far off, the sound of hoofs and glimpsed a white beast passing among the trees. Linette wondered whether it was a unicorn.

Presently they came to a bit of slightly higher ground where an oak tree was growing among the pines. It was old and tremendous; the fantastic knotted roof of branches closed out the stars. Immense boughs drooped to the ground.

"If we can get up in that," said Rhodri, "I expect we can get some idea where we are. Those branches should be an easy way up, if they're sound. I'll go first, since I'm heavier."

They mounted easily almost to the top of the tree and looked out through a gap in the leaves. "Oh," breathed Linette, unable to say anything else.

In the bright moonlight, pine-darkened hills sloped down to a wooded plain and a moon-pale river that ran into the sea. By the joining of sea and river stood a wall-enclosed city; the lower part of the wall was white stone, but the upper part seemed to consist of living trees. Within it were also many trees, with sharp pinnacles rising above them like white glass or ice; and trees and spires were caught in a glitter of lights as in a jewelled net.

"Mobile would have been there in our world," said Linette, "though it would spread out to here."

"Hush," whispered Rhodri sharply. "Something's coming. Cover the lantern."

Linette crouched close to the bark, burying the lantern with her body and hand. Rhodri slipped noiselessly lower down the tree and held his spear ready.

Peering through the small leaves he saw a tall woman-shape moving among the pines; her long robes seemed to drift after her like grey, wind-driven cloud. Her face in the moonlight was ancient yet smooth, ageless, with a stern beauty that made him think suddenly of high, distant peaks. Her hair was pale and shining like spun silver, and the light on it seemed to be more than the moon.

She paused under the oak, her hair still glimmering in the shadow, and looked up. "Strangers," she said in a clear, strong voice, "you need fear no harm from me. I am not one of the Haldir."

At the sound of that archaic music Linette felt a sudden desire to speak, but she thought of the voice of the flame and was silent.

"I saw your light from afar," came the old, beautiful voice, "and I have keen eyes by night or day. You come from the world of human-kind."

Rhodri saw it was no use hiding. He dropped to the ground and stood sternly before the grey woman, trying not to show that he was a little awed. "Who are you, and what business do you have with us?"

She smiled. "Not so fiercely, Pendragon. I am chief of the Wind-wanderers in this land; strangers and enemies call me the Grey Witch of the Hills. But my true name is Celebrin, Silverweb; and you are safe in my company, for the Haldir avoid me."

Linette by now had come down the tree and stood beside Rhodri. "You say 'Witch,' " she said thoughtfully, emboldened by Celebrin's words. "But you seem very different from the other witches I know."

"You mean the Queen of the Air, I suppose? Oh, yes, we know her here; and I can see by your eyes that she has been interfering with you. But none in our world deal directly with the lords of darkness, except the Haldir and the Ruiners; and I myself am in allegiance to Lauriel. As for my business with you, I have none, unless it be to answer your questions and give you what guidance I can."

"Lady Celebrin—" Rhodri took a breath, trying to sort his questions. "Who are the Haldir you keep mentioning? How did you know I was the Pendragon? What is that city by the river?"

Celebrin laughed. "Not all at once! To begin with the easiest—I knew Madoc's arm-ring when I saw it. Bran the Chief Poet described it to me, in the days when he came to this land."

"You are long-lived here," said Linette, surprised at her own confidence in Celebrin. "But you do not seem weary—I know a lady who was born in the sixth century—"

"I know of her, though we have never met. Formerly there was more communion between your world and ours; that is how I know your language, though I think I do not quite speak it as you do. Once there were many places where the boundaries of our worlds joined, where people could pass from one to another; but of late years they are grown very few. I think they will grow fewer, because your world drifts farther and farther from the ancient harmonies—" She paused as if breaking off a thought.

"As for the Haldir, whom some call the Bronze People—you would not care to meet them. They are the same race as Lauriel's people, but I have told you they deal with the darkness—is that not enough for you to know? You will recognize them by the bronze they wear.

"The city is Eldis, the citadel of Lauriel's people, the Eldir. Lauriel, the Golden, is a name of the Queen of these lands, because of her hair which is compared to living sunlight. And she will welcome you gladly and give you whatever help is in her power."

Rhodri straightened. "We would no doubt be honored, but there is no time. We must get back to our own world without delay."

Celebrin looked at him keenly for a moment without answering. "Do not despise Lauriel's help," she said finally. "Go to her; ask her for it. And waste no time. There are evil forces preparing in this world, though I do not yet know why. It is not only the Haldir now; one of the Ruiners has been seen."

For a moment she was silent, looking off into the dark as if with foreboding. "Iron and the jewels of the sun are of no use against the Ruiners. If I had foreseen this meeting, I could have brought you silverweb cloaks for your protection; for the Haldir fear my hair and the light of it and my power that is in it. Though I cut it to my shoulders at every sunset, by the next sunset it is out the door of my house; and my daily task is to weave cloth of it, which the Haldir and the lesser forces of darkness will not come near. But against the Ruiners, even that has no power."

She shook her head, and her hair scattered glimmers of light around her. "Well, even a bronze sword is better than none. Lauriel's warriors fought the Haldir here, twenty years ago; there should still be some tokens of the battle."

She walked to and fro in the moonlight, her eyes fixed on the ground; then she knelt quickly and searched with her fingers under the roots of the grass. As Rhodri and Linette came beside her, she drew from under the grass a long, straight sword, leaf-green from lying in the earth.

"The edge is dull now," she said; "and there is no scabbard. But it should serve you till you come to Eldis, if all goes well."

She looked deep into Rhodri's eyes as she gave it to him. "I see your errand, Pendragon; and you must indeed return to your own world to finish it. But be warned. The powers that are gathering may be aimed against you. And I see worse than that. A shadow is over you and over this lady; you and she have given some opening to the workings of the enemy. If you have committed any falsity, or any failing of trust, take care! I think you will never return to your world till you have paid dearly for it; and if you refuse the payment, you will fail in your task. Remember Arthur your ancestor, who paid bitterly for his pleasure with Morgause; even so, many things were lost that might have been saved."

"What are you saying?" asked Rhodri, stung. "I have not committed any falsity."

"I will be glad if I am proved wrong," said Celebrin. "I would come with you if I could, but I must keep watch along Lauriel's borders. Go to Eldis, and lose no time! I feel the presence of danger like a darkening of the air around us."

They parted, Celebrin southward toward the curve of the river, Linette and Rhodri northward toward Eldis. Linette's memory lingered on the radiance of Celebrin; it was more than the glimmer of her hair, it was an invisible shining as true as the invisible darkness that clung around Morgause. Is my mind, she thought, opening to perceive good as well as evil? It would perhaps be worth this struggle if it did.

Rhodri frowned a little, pondering Celebrin's half-accusation. But what had he done? Of course, nothing; his behavior had been highly honorable. Arthur and Morgause—yes, that had had its bitter fruit in Mordred. But he himself had not meddled with Linette's chastity, and he felt a little insulted that Celebrin had supposed it—though no doubt it was a natural supposition.

But his annoyance cleared quickly; the journey was too beautiful to waste on feeling insulted. He paused after a moment and dismantled the spear, throwing away the shaft and putting the instrument back unharmed in its case. There the tools all gleamed again, in a silver row against the velvet lining; he thought how beautiful and efficient they were, and how he had found the treasury of Caer Mair. If Excalibur failed to turn up, he could publish his discovery and have openly the glory of his achievement . . . He frowned, wondering if Celebrin could have meant instead his entertaining of such a thought. But anyway he would not entertain it. He quickened his step and began whistling an old Welsh tune he had learned as a child; he had forgotten most of the words, but remembered that they had been written by Madoc's brother Prince Hywel. Now and then he tried a sweep at a tall weed with his sword; sometimes he took the top off the weed, and sometimes not. Linette, looking at him with a touch of amusement, could see that he was enjoying the situation immensely.

"I had fencing at school, you know," he said, with an experimental thrust at a sapling. "Although this isn't quite the kind of sword for it. Still and all—" He finished the sentence by cutting down a spike of tufted grass.

"How far is it to Eldis, exactly?" said Linette after a while.

"It looked about three miles, from the tree. I'd say we've done half that."

They went on; but he had stopped whistling, and carried his sword not playfully now, but lightly and firmly as if in readiness for an ambush. Linette thought he had felt her own sense of unease. The preternatural moonlight laid an untroubled stillness on the woods, but in her own mind stirred a vague foreboding of something sinister and unseen. "Rhodri," she asked a little hesitantly, "what did Celebrin think you'd done?"

"I've no idea," said Rhodri shortly. "But we'd best not talk; there may be Haldir about."

Still they went on. Presently Linette asked in a low voice, "Rhodri, how much kerosene was in the lantern?"

"It was full. Six hours."

"It's been burning more than four already. What if it goes out before we get to Eldis?"

"Nothing. We have the moonlight."

"Do you think we should put it out?"

"I don't know."

Suddenly he froze, silent, his head up as if listening. Linette listened too, straining to catch sounds through the dark. She could hear the leaves stirring faintly, and the sea beating far off with a dull, muffled sound. Then through these, hardly audible, crept a rustle of distant voices and movement among the trees. Through a bright space of moonlight some way ahead passed a knot of tall shapes in armor that did not seem the color of steel. They carried round shields and long spears that glinted dull-gold where they caught the light. The shimmering armor was formed into tunics of ring-mail that came to the knees, and on the head of each warrior a conical helmet gleamed the same dull gold. Linette's hand, ice-cold, was startled by the touch of Rhodri's as he drew her sharply back into the shadow.

Scattered pines stood around them, with here and there a scrub oak; there was nothing to climb. Not far off a wild elder tree was growing, with the scent of its creamy flowers heavy-sweet on the air. Linette had already hidden the lantern with a fold of her dress. Rhodri drew her silently into the deep shadows behind the elder, then motioned her to creep into the hollow between the manifold trunk and the long-leafed, ground-sweeping branches. He crawled in after her, crouched tense, his sword ready. The ground under them was cool and dry; the sweetness of the elder flowers lay like a weight on the close darkness.

The voices of the Haldir came nearer, cold, melodious voices that reminded Linette sharply of the voice of the flame. Like Celebrin they spoke in an archaic English whose accent sounded strange in her ears.

"Morandir should have returned long ago," was the first sentence that came clear. "I fear some misfortune."

"More of Lauriel's warriors, maybe, than he could match. I could wish we were safe back at Mithremyn."

"I wish we were back at Ando and had never left," came another voice. "We have our own enemies without challenging Lauriel."

A fourth voice broke sternly in. "Let me remind you that the men of Ando and the men of Mithremyn owe allegiance to the same Queen and the same commander. The orders of the Lord Angoré are to seek out the Queen's enemies, not to quarrel among ourselves or shirk battle. If Morandir has failed in the Other Place, that is his responsibility; this patrol is yours."

"They say old Ironheart might go himself, if Morandir fails," said the Andoan who had spoken. "I wish he and the Queen both would go where they came from. They are none of our kind."

"Ill will it be for you," said the more commanding voice, "if either of them hears of your words. And the alliances of Mithremyn are not your affair. But no more of this. We may attract Lauriel's people or lose those we were sent to catch."

Linette, curled in the dark, had at the first mention of the Queen felt the return of a remembered fear. The darkness had begun to oppress her mind; she clung to the jewels, but the force of the dark beat against their barrier. The iron handle of the lantern was weaker still, had never been any protection; all her barricades seemed to tremble before the dreadful night that bore down on her, starless and suffocating as lightless water, drowning her in a cold chaos of uncreation and death. She fought wildly for life, to keep the last imperilled spark that was Linette from going out. But even as she struggled, there came an instant when she knew her body was no longer subject to her will. Her mind grew almost still, waiting in horror for what would next happen.

The Queen sat upright, rustling the elder boughs. The lantern, no longer hidden, filled the hollow with yellow light that flared through the openings of the leaves like volcanic fires. Rhodri seized the lantern and lay around it, shielding it with arms and body. One of the Haldir cried out sharply, "What was that light?"

"A phantom of expectation, Umbar," answered the commanding voice. "There is no light."

"There is none now, Captain; but there was."

"There is light," cried a clear voice; "but light against light shall dash into darkness!"

The Haldir rushed toward the elder tree. Rhodri burst out, sword ready, his face white in the glare of the lantern. The Queen had risen, taking the lantern in her hand; she had put her fallen crown back on, and the jewels in it flamed like coals of fire. Her eyes burned with a fierce dark brilliance; her mouth curved in cruel exultation. The Haldir stood in a half-circle before her, just out of reach of Rhodri's blade. They lowered their heads in silent homage to the Queen, then levelled their dozen spears silently against Rhodri; the bronze points glittered in the lanternlight.

"Take him alive," commanded the Captain. "He is the Queen's prisoner."

Instantly the spears turned wrong-way-round like staves. The Haldir crowded around Rhodri, trying to beat him down with the spear-shafts. He held up his left arm to protect his head, and tried to lunge through them towards the Captain. A warrior seized his sword-arm, but he broke loose and swung. The blade crashed hard on the Captain's shield and snapped. Rhodri struck furiously with the broken piece, and the shield was not quick enough; the sword nicked through the Captain's armor, and blood appeared on the bright mail.

"Fools!" cried the Captain, in a white-hot anger. "Can twelve of you not master one man?" He dropped spear and shield and dived at Rhodri, bearing him down. Other Haldir dropped onto the tangle of them, freeing the Captain and kneeling on Rhodri; someone caught his arm from behind and wrenched away the broken sword. He writhed and fought with reckless violence, but they were too many. For moments he was at the bottom of a swarming mass of men; then he was pulled to his feet, with his hands bound cruelly tight behind him.

"Royal Lady," said the Captain to the Queen, "shall we do more?"

"No, Captain," she answered with a lift of her head. "I will do my own pleasure concerning my prisoner." But Rhodri, looking anxiously at her, realized it was not the Queen who spoke. For the moment, Linette had won.

Yet his mind steadied to a cool realization of their danger. What could Linette do, even so? And how long before the real Queen came back, and how long before someone realized this was not Morgause?

"By your leave, Lady," said the Captain, "I will secure him better." His fury had turned cold and ice-hard; the sting of his hurt, slight as it was, made him want to insult and humiliate Rhodri. He tied another rope to Rhodri's neck and wound the loose end around his hand, as if it were the leash of a dog.

"Royal Lady," he said when he had finished, "you will accompany us to the secret stronghold?"

"I will, Captain."

They set out quickly and silently toward the river. "We have a boat hidden for crossing," said the Captain. "We must go a roundabout way to Mithremyn, Lady, unless you have some better intention."

"I have not," said Linette. She had no idea what she would do at Mithremyn, and no desire to hasten their arrival; but on a long journey, she might think of a plan.

At that moment one of the Haldir called out sharply. The others froze where they stood, and a great rushing noise poured out of the sky. Now, thought Linette, and looked toward Rhodri; but he was staring at the sky, and suddenly the moonlight was darkened out by something nearer and heavier than a cloud. Linette's horrified gaze for a second could not take it in; there were wings, leathery and bigger than sails; and suddenly the wings drew in and the thing descended heavily on the cover of pine needles.

"The Lord Angoré," said the Andoan with a sharp intake of breath.

Something, a tall shape, was visible now behind the huge pterodactyl-like head. It dismounted and approached the silent band, manlike in form, but of fabulous height so that its head was level with the saplings. Linette felt that at will it could overtower the trees. Blackness cloaked it like starless night; through a fold of the black gleamed the cold brightness of steel mail. A steel helmet glittered on its brows; and around its head shone a chill light, showing features noble and hard like carved diamond, and eyes like polar ice. A breath of dead winter came with it, annihilating the warmth of the summer night. The Haldir themselves had drawn back. Linette, true to her part, stood her ground, but felt herself freeze to the bone with bitter cold. Rhodri also stood still, tangled phrases running wild through his mind: faded splendor wan, stood like a tower, dauntless courage and considerate pride—surely not the Dark Lord himself, coming like death, the Prince of the powers of the air, whose breath was ruin?

"I come at the command of the Queen." The voice was like a terrible river pouring down heights, inexorable and of a dreadful untamed splendor. "Deliver to me your prisoners."

"Great lord," came the Captain's voice, "there is only one prisoner. The Queen herself is here."

The cold eyes pierced Linette; she felt them go like knives into the hidden places of her mind, and her thoughts paralyzed and tottered like falling towers. This was death, then—

"Here is no Queen," came the voice in a cold scorn. "This is the tool and instrument of her Majesty's pleasures. Let her be bound like her companion."

The eyes released her; but she stood numbed and devastated while the Haldir tied her hands behind her, taking care not to touch the lantern or the jewels she wore. Her own eyes were wide with the sole knowledge of doom: death was not yet, but it could not be long in coming.

Rhodri stood frozen upright beside her, with bleakness in his heart. Celebrin's obscure words had been truth: he had utterly failed. He, Linette, Britain, Excalibur, the Grail—all were falling down into the dark.

"Captain Morithil, you shall take this beast and bring the Queen's prisoners to the hidden stronghold. Your men must march across country as they came. There is no news of Morandir?"

"None, great lord."

"Then I myself will deal with the last of the Queen's enemies. Let the Darkness conquer!"

Morithil repeated, as if it were a sign or salute, "Let the Darkness conquer!"

And instantly the Lord Angoré was not there.

"You have heard the new orders," said Morithil. "Let the prisoners be put on the beast."

Rhodri and Linette were compelled at spearpoint toward the pterodactyl-thing and unceremoniously helped on. The beast had neither fur nor plumage, only a cold purplish-black hide and vast leathery wings; its head was like something long dead and hideous, with no semblance of life but the irrational chill malice of the eyes. Linette shuddered at touching it, as if it were a snake. She and Rhodri sat forward, almost on its neck; Captain Morithil mounted behind them.

"I will unbind you when we are in the air," he said, "so that you can hold on. I must bring you alive to Caer Sidi."

With a sound like sails in a high wind, the beast left the ground. Linette and Rhodri were borne helpless into the rushing night, toward their unknown punishment.

10. The Wild Shores

Anthony had set out before dawn from Silverthorne. It was still cool; the sky had just begun to turn from white to gold. He lifted his eyes once to the roof-line of the stable, knowing that Julian would have lent him Solario; but after all, it was better not to take the horse, since he did not know where he was going.

It was still almost dark in the Silverthorne lane, and not much brighter on the main road. He shut the gate and hesitated a moment, wondering if he had made the right choice. To put oneself at the disposal of the Grail . . . He had made no elaborate provision, only stuck some bread in his pocket and fastened a hunting knife to his belt; anything more seemed contrary to the spirit of the quest. Standing there in the grey light, with his white shirt and his uncovered blond hair, he did not look like a man embarked on an improbable adventure; he seemed only an inconspicuous walker on a summer morning.

He looked up and down the road, weighing his choice. Northward the road ran to the city; southward it plunged through wood and open land, and finally down to the ceaseless rise and fall of the Gulf of Mexico.

Better go southward, into wilder and less familiar country, more like the forests and wastes of the romances. And the Castle of Carbonek, where people had seen the Grail, had stood by a sea.

In the cool, colorless dawn he set out south along the roadside. When he reached the river, the first long golden light broke out across bay and river mouth and the broad span of bridge, awakening the green of trees and the unexpected whiteness of seagulls. He crossed over past Grand View Park, outside the boundaries of the city now; and the road struck inland, out of sight of the sea.

For some time he walked on, past pine woods and scattered buildings. The July day grew warm as the sun climbed; he stopped in the scant pine-shade now and then and looked up through the bright needles at the flawless sky. He crossed the north fork of Deer River by a small bridge, soon the middle fork, and after some while the south fork. As he walked, he mapped out his journey in his mind. He was walking the length of Hollinger's Island, from Dog River to Fowl River. After Fowl River he would be on Mon Louis Island. The road led to Alabama Port there, and he must make another choice—either to go straight on, to Cedar Point and across the great bridge over Grant's Pass and the Pass aux Herons to Dauphin Island; or to turn west through Coden and Bayou la Batre, and thus northward through the many roads of the county or west along the shore of the Sound. If he went to Dauphin Island, he could get a boat across to Fort Morgan on the other side of the bay. Well, he need not decide yet, there was time to think. But if he failed in the quest, he realized with a renewed shock, he would not be travelling these roads again.

By ten, he had come as far as St. Philip's Church. At that moment, miles away, Linette and Rhodri were about to enter another country.

As he approached St. Philip's, he was trying again to unriddle the riddle, to translate myth into fact. He thought of Rhodri's dark suggestion last night—the world as a Waste Land, the destruction of nature. This he had not thought of in advance, only of the Waste Land of the mind, an abyss which he sensed rather than understood. Morgause, after all, had spoken of five leagues, not a world.

But suppose the thing were possible. A spiritual Waste Land could tend to produce a natural one: not the mythic land of sand and thorns, but a worse desolation, a tangle of steel covering continents, skies lost in the poisonous smoke, all forests gone. Nevertheless he did not see how the loss of a cup, however priceless, could make a Waste Land of the spirit; surely the dark apprehension that it might was irrational.

His thread of reflections was broken as he came into the clearing before St. Philip's. He lifted his eyes to the red brick walls, almost painfully plain, yet concealing he knew what mystery. Ought he, perhaps, to go in and ask to contemplate the chalice? All chalices were essentially the Grail, vessels of the one sacrifice. The idea seemed brilliantly simple; and yet he knew, instantly, that things could not be so simple, or so easy.

But the thought brought him to a standstill as it continued to unwind. The idea had been off the mark; a chalice without its sacrament was only a beautiful cup, not a thing of power. Then the arch-chalice, the Grail, had importance not because of its ancient history but because—because what? His mind spun; it had touched some knowledge so elusive he could not get hold of it. What if the destruction of the Grail meant the destruction of all the grails?—not a loss of cups, but the breaking of that unity which held the worlds together, as if from the solar system you removed the sun—No, surely it was not possible; Morgause could not win such a victory as that; the rulers of the universe would not let her—

He broke away from the spot at a rapid pace, as if to leave behind that sudden vision. But he soon slowed again; the day had caught fire, and the July sun beat strongly down upon the land. He was hot and getting tired; his eyes were dazzled and his thoughts began wandering from one thing to another without pattern.

In the growing dullness and fatigue of his mind, he did not notice the car and the man and woman till he was almost upon them.

The tableau at first seemed self-explanatory. The woman stood to one side; the car, small but rather new-looking, was raised on a jack while the man changed a flat tire. Clearly, however, the people were too unlike to be travelling together. The lady was tall and slender, with a rather restrained face and long, pale hair gathered in a knot at the back of her neck. Her clothes proclaimed the foreigner: a tidy blue-and-white-striped suit and a white hat with a pale-blue scarf trailing from it. Anthony guessed that she was about thirty, and the man slightly older. The man seemed to belong with a green farm truck parked farther down the road; he was shorter and broader, dressed in denin and a red-and-white checked shirt. His hair was black, cut longish; his face, ruddy and coarse, had nevertheless a kind of animal vitality.

Anthony would have offered his assistance, but the man had finished and put the jack away. By now Anthony was within hearing distance, but they were turned away and did not see him.

"Thank you very much, sir," said the lady in a precise British accent. "How much do I owe you?"

"An' what would a lady like you say she owes me?" His voice was deep but somehow unpleasant.

"Perhaps five dollars?" She sensed the unpleasantness; her voice had a nervous note, as if she were anxious to go.

"An' why would I think of taking money from you? There's something I'd like better."

She answered more nervously still, and a bit sharply, "I don't understand you, sir."

"Jus' a little bit of your company. A few hours won't make much difference, wherever you're goin'. I know an empty house down the road a bit—fine place, people gone for the summer. An' I've got some liquor in my truck—we could have a good time."

"I don't doubt the liquor," she said, drawing back with an air of scorn. "I can smell it, even at this time of day." But her voice wavered a little, bewildered and edged with fear.

By now Anthony was nearly alongside them. The man laid his hand on the lady's arm; she snatched away from him as from a roach.

"You there!" said Anthony. "Let her alone!"

They both turned. "Who d'you think you are?" said the man angrily. "Sir Lancelot?"

Unbidden, the thought flashed through Anthony's mind: Lancelot saw the Grail. But there was no time to think that. He advanced with as masterful an air as he could summon. "Are you going to let her alone and get out of here?"

"I fixed her tire, and she ain't paid me yet!"

"After what you've said, she doesn't need to. Get out!"

"Suppose I don't." And he made a movement to take hold of the lady's arm.

Anthony knocked him down.

But he was not down long. He rose halfway and tripped Anthony; and down they both went, fighting in the weeds of the roadside. The lady looked on, frightened and at a loss. She would have called for help, but there was none to call. The situation was totally out of her experience.

The man was brawnier and heavier than Anthony, but he was also older and stouter and less quick. Soon he began to tire and lose his breath. Suddenly he broke away from Anthony and scrambled up some distance off. "You damn' young fool, can't take a joke! Knockin' folks down by the side of the road! I'll have the police on you!"

And he sprang into his truck and drove at a wild speed down the road.

Anthony, who had also risen, stared after the vanishing truck with hot indignation. "I hope he does get the police! When they hear why, he'll get more than knocked down!"

The lady, looking at him, felt pity mix with her gratitude. His shirt was torn at the shoulder and dirty from the earth of the roadside, and a cut above his eyebrow was bleeding.

"It was good of you to help me," she said. "I'm sorry you were hurt."

Anthony became for the first time conscious of the cut, then of the dirt and the torn shirt. He laughed ruefully. "Oh, don't worry about it."

"Can I give you a lift someplace?"

"No, it's all right. But can you make the explanations, if any have to be made? You'll be safe enough in the car. But I can't stay, you see; I'm on a quest. I'd like to stay longer and talk, but I can't. Good-bye."

And with that he crossed the road and plunged into the woods on the other side. The lady stared after him for a moment, and waited half an hour for police who never appeared, and then went on her way. But even after she had returned home from her holiday, she used to think sometimes of the strange young man, and wonder whether he were a little mad and whether he had succeeded in his quest.

"Actually, no," said Julian; "I don't find my life too narrow here. I am out of the immediate turmoil of civilization, in a place where new things come slowly; but there are old things here, beautiful things, the sea and the sky and the trees. When new things come, I can see them in perspective and know what they are. And, as the proverb says, 'All places are distant from heaven alike.' You understand this yourself, or you would live in London instead of Torquay."

"I suppose you are right," said Morgan, not much caring. She wished Julian would cease talking and let her get back to her spells. The crossing between the two worlds was not finished; for nine hours Rhodri and Linette must remain in the timeless void between the worlds, of which they could have no knowledge or memory. At the end of that time they would emerge on the borders of Eldis, and word had already gone to the council-halls of Mithremyn. They could be forgotten for the moment. But the antennae of her mind trembled with a sense of new danger; and she guessed instinctively that it involved the fairspoken young man, the scholar, to whom she had told her history. Morgause had said he was looking for the Cup. What if he found it; what if he let loose its power against herself and Morgause? She had heard of the burning anger of the Sun Lord. There was reason to find out what Anthony was doing.

Julian sensed her unrest and eagerness to get away. But she must not get away. "Perspective," she said thoughtfully. "At school, they taught us that: draw a road over the hills, that grows small and smaller as it winds through the passes, and vanishes over the horizon as if it fell off the world. Did you ever see a picture like that—a strange, evocative thing, with a grey sky?"

"I saw the road itself," said Morgan. "It is life." She paused. "All roads go somewhere. But that road, when you are on it, seems to go on forever; you come to a crest and look down, and see nothing but more windings and more hills."

"It has to get somewhere at last," said Julian. "Your words remind me of some poem; I wonder if I can find it."

She rose and went to a bookshelf. Morgan knew and seized her moment. She reached for Julian's silver inkwell and poured a pool of black ink into the palm of her hand.

She bent over it, concentrating her eyes and mind on the darkly shining surface. Her skill in the seeing-arts was old; she did not have to wait long. The blackness receded to the edges; tiny bright figures appeared like reflections, sharp and far off. A pale woman held converse with a man by a stopped car. Anthony appeared. Angry words came over the fine antennae of Morgan's thought: You there! Let her alone! . . . Who d'you think you are? Sir Lancelot? . . . The men fought; one fled. The other spoke a moment with the woman and disappeared into the woods across the road.

Morgan released the pool from her thought, and it relapsed into blackness. She poured it back into the inkwell and cleaned her hand, more or less, with a handkerchief. Julian was still across the room, with a book open in her hands.

Morgan shut her eyes and sent her thought searching through dark wastes for the Queen of the Air. Morgause, Morgause, her mind called; and soon she was aware of Morgause's thought reaching out to touch hers.

Morgause, sister, the quester is a danger. Send to him your servant, the shadow of the Shadow of Druan, whom I may not behold. Let her stop him; and if she falls, summon what other powers you may command.

"It's not much after all," said Julian, turning with a book in her hand. "Only a Spanish quatrain:

> "Night falls;
> The dark road is savage.
> I do not ask you to go.
> I do not ask you to stay."

Anthony dropped to the ground at the foot of a pine tree and sat still for a few minutes, gradually catching his breath. He did not know exactly where he was; he had run an irregular, zigzag course, to make himself harder to find. He did not at present want either the inquiries of the law or the possible vengeance of the man and his friends; he preferred to forget the irrelevant adventure as soon as possible.

But there was nothing to be gained by reflecting on its pointlessness. He had halted close to a small, deep-chiselled stream; and presently he leaned over it, where a spring welled out of the clay bank, and had a drink and washed his face. The water stung in the cut, but the bleeding had stopped; he decided, after examining it by feel, that it was rather insignificant. He got rid of as much of the dirt as he could, to make himself less conspicuous if he met anyone; but he could do nothing about the torn sleeve.

He judged by the sun that it was nearly noon. In the pine woods, away from the sea, the heat hung heavy and motionless. He thought he might follow the coast now; it would be cooler there, quieter, and more conducive to meditation. Following the bank of the stream, he walked eastward.

It was definitely noon when he came out of the trees. The pines ended abruptly; the solid, grassy earth sheared off and dropped a foot, to a narrow verge of yellowish sand.

> Come unto these yellow sands
> And there take hands,

he thought irrelevantly. The lines sounded like a child's game; he had played, somewhere along this coast, all the summers of his childhood. Everything was as he remembered—the grey, dragonish twists of drift-wood cast up on the sand; the scuttling fiddler crabs that burst out when he disturbed a log; the clear, warm shallows at low tide, with sandbars appearing like islands, and ripple patterns etched on the sea floor. Small drifts of seaweed edged the last high tidemark; writhen logs lay in the low water like the bones of sea serpents, mixed in some places with beams of broken barges. It was a scene at once lonely and familiar. On a windy day, under a grey sky, it would have filled him with a strange excitement. Now, under the steady blaze of the July sun, it was desolate but serene.

He ate some of his bread under the last fringe of trees. A small wind stirred the pine needles, and the sun glistened in them as if they were made of glass. Anthony considered his route—north to Mobile, now, or south to the Gulf? He decided to keep on southward, for the same reason as before. True, Fowl River lay that way; but he could go briefly inland to the bridge and then cut back to the coast.

He pocketed the rest of the bread and set out southward along the shore. Now and then a pier jutted out, or a house showed through a screen of trees; but in the burning, motionless noon no one appeared on porch or pier or shore. The breeze had completely died; the heat oppressed like a weight, and the whole coast seemed abandoned to him and an excessive plague of flies. He brushed away the insects, and with the side of his hand scraped away the sweat from his forehead and mouth and eyes. Already his throat was dry: and from the heat and the incessant glare on the water, his mind was weighed down with the heaviness and dullness that would be prelude to a headache.

After a while, he raised his eyes painfully and saw clouds building up in the north and west, immense, purple-black clouds like distant mountains. Rain would come and cool off the molten weather; soon, he thought, he should start keeping a watch for shelter.

The clouds rolled out like seas and swallowed up the merciless sun. Anthony felt a numbed relief; the sun's unmitigated glory could be too much for mortals, as royal Jupiter's was for the princess Semele, who was withered by excess of brightness. That may be why we live on earth, he thought, to prepare us for the glory. We have to get used to the light by degrees, or we would be blinded by it like people coming out of a cave into the full noon.

A drop of rain fell heavily on his shoulder. He looked up; more drops fell cool on his upturned face. There was a roll of thunder, loud and close; he realized abruptly that he was the tallest thing on the shore, a good mark for lightning. The rain was beginning to fall faster; he saw it would soon be a downpour. But he was in a lonely part of the coast, and there was no shelter in sight.

He took refuge among the pines, but they gave no protection. The rain poured through them, as if they were pillars in a roofless hall— rain like a waterfall, immense drops so close they were hardly drops but an undivided stream, as if the bottom had fallen away from vast superterrestrial seas. In seconds Anthony was soaked as if he had fallen into the bay; he was blinded with water as if he were still under the sea. He ran through the woods, hoping for some roof or dense thicket to shut out the torrent. Every fold of the land had become a rapid stream, rushing with muddy waters towards the sea.

He glimpsed through the wall of rain a pale light back among the trees, and plunged toward it. With the water in his eyes, he could not tell what it was. He was quite close to it, and then he was in, and there was no more rain.

He rubbed the water out of his eyes and stood still. He was in a garden walled round with a high hedge of roses, enormous dark-red roses that weighted the air with a heavy fragrance. The rain was still falling as fast as ever, and he could see lightning; but the rain fell away from the garden as from an invisible roof, and he could hear neither it nor the thunder. He grew colder than the rain could have made him, knowing that this garden could not belong to the world of the pine wood.

The place was large as a cathedral, walled with roses and roofed with rain as with silver and glass. It was half-dark—darker, he thought, than the stormy wood outside. There were trees of a kind he had never seen before, with smooth trunks like black marble and strange, curving branches clothed with red leaves. And the leaves, it seemed to him, were not red with autumn; it was their native color, instead of green. The trees stood in a perfect circle and seemed too symmetrical in shape, as if they grew obedient to some force of mind. Lamps hung from their boughs to light the dusk of the garden, gold and silver lamps fantastically wrought and encrusted with gems. There was no grass or ground to be seen; underfoot was a carpet of short-growing crimson flowers, shaped like starflowers and springy like moss, with no green leaf showing. They gave out a strong, sweet scent, a little like gardenias but more subtle and powerful. In the center of the garden rose a pyramid of circular steps of some shining black stone, perfectly smooth and without carving, except that from the lowest step a fountain of water poured thinly out of an opening carved like a leopard's mouth, and lost itself under the short flowers. On the low, flat height of the pyramid stood a black stone chair like a throne, also shining and smooth as glass; and on it sat an image like a woman. She was dressed in black, of some heavy, shining material that clung to her body and left her arms and shoulders bare. It had an Eastern look, wrapped-round and darkly lustrous and fastened by an immense brooch of red gold. The hair, weighted with a barbaric crown of red gold, hung in great masses of black behind her, luxuriant and billowing, like that of some Sumerian queen entombed before the flood. The image itself he thought was ivory or alabaster, because of the glimmering whiteness of arms and shoulders and face. But the face, now that he saw it, held his gaze like a candle. It was perfect as a strange flower; the eyes, dark and large and brilliant-seeming, gazed wide open into invisibility; the mouth, blood-red, showed against the alabaster like the veining of an orchid. The features were noble and proud, like a queen's in some Assyrian of Babylonian sculpture. Yet there was something disquieting in their carved expression, something barbaric and cruel in the curve of the mouth, as if too-long gazing might freeze the gazer's own veins into stone. She sat like an image of Astarie enthroned in a shrine, ageless as the deserts and strong as time; Anthony felt that any hammer striking to break that image must shatter like glass.

She moved her head. Anthony stood rigid, watching an image rise from its chair; he felt her dark gaze upon him and knew that, whatever she was, she was not stone.

With a swift leopardlike grace she came down the pyramid and stood on the short flowers. "So you have come." Her voice was low, languorous, and melodious, with a rich, hot brightness; it woke in his mind, like an echo, the tones of Linette's voice, which seemed thin, brittle, and sharp beside it. "What do you desire of me?"

"Great lady," began Anthony, and could say no more words. Her eyes held him in a brilliant, considering gaze; he became conscious of how wet and dirty he was, and felt like a beaten barbarian slave in the presence of an empress. He wanted to apologize for appearing so miserably in her sight; he wanted to praise her as the splendor of the universe; he wanted suddenly to fall to his knees in homage or worship. Her face overcame him like a spell; it seemed cold as starlight yet of a terrible burning beauty; it seemed to look down from an exalted height on the joys and toils of men, as on a play of puppets or shadows. Few only, and those uncommon, did it regard for a moment as worthy of notice; its desires and hatreds were like a consuming fire, elemental as meteors. Such a woman's love might destroy like the embrace of flames; and yet it seemed she could make it worth the death.

She came close to him; he could smell the sweet, heavy-hanging perfume of her hair, and grew weak before her beauty and power. Linette's image came to him; she seemed wraithlike, frail as cobweb and ephemeral as the snowdrops of forgotten springs. His mind seemed to go round and round in a deepening dusk, as if this woman's strength and pride and passion, and the burning tigerlike gorgeousness that was in her, were a dark whirlpool of air that spun him like a straw. He felt desire and despair flare strong in him; they seemed a blaze all around him, burning his memory of the past into ashes.

He had lowered his head. Her voice came close to him, so that he could feel her warm breath; he grew dizzy with the closeness and the perfume of her hair. "I am older than all your race; I am called Stabay and Bodb and Lilith. Many are those who have loved me and died. Despair, then; I have chosen you for mine."

The image of Linette seemed far off and faint, a ghost-shape confused somehow with a golden cup. Lilith's face and body and voice were overpowering him; his strength seemed to leave him, and he sank to his knees with his hands on the flowers. The subtle scent rose from the flowers; confused visions of strange passions like corridors of flame curled through his reeling mind, with the consuming glory of fire. No doubt her love would devour him, but it was a death emperors would seek. A fold of her lustrous black raiment brushed against his face, and it had the same fragrance as her hair. He seemed to breathe darkness like air; it coiled through his mind like clouds of a heavy incense, so that he could not think or remember. In a moment he would embrace her and give himself over to her desire.

But something in his mind still struggled, holding out against the spell. There was something he had to remember. His will hung poised at the edge of a sea of darkness: plunge in, or listen to this faint outcry at the back of the memory? The pause itself strengthened the remembering; painfully he turned his mind toward it, as if straining to see through the deep night. Brightly lit as with firelight, one image became distinct against the dark: a girl, black-haired, crowned with gold and with red jewels; her dress glittered like jewelled armor, and it seemed that in her hands she held a cup of gold. He thought confusedly of the Grail-Bearer in the old romances; then it came clearly to him that this was Linette glittering in the flamelight of Silverthorne and linked in his memory with the object of his quest.

He knew that his eyes were closed, and opened them. Bodb's black gown trailed lustrous along the flowers; her power filled the twilight like a crimson mist. He dared not look up at her, lest he be caught again and irretrievably, like the prey of a leopard. With an effort he stood upright on the crimson flowers, keeping his eyes fixed on their short blooms. "Great lady," he said, steadying his voice against a sense of mounting peril, "choose another lover. I am not staying."

"Fool," came the voice full of growing anger, "will you leave me for her, who will fade and fail?"

With an unhuman strength her white hand took hold of his chin and lifted it. He looked straight in her face, saw in its whiteness the eyes burning with an undying hunger, naked with torment and the eternal fixity of the soul. Into him her gaze licked, trying the roots of his mind for a crack where her flames could take hold.

Violently he broke away and plunged across the red lawn, past the lamp-hung trees, out through the gap in the hedge. The rain dashed down on him with a cold shock, as if wakening him from a trance. He ran headlong, tripped on a root, fell face-down in a deep runnel of rainwater. Raising his dripping head, he looked back and saw the hedge of roses turn into a curtain of flame and disappear, and heard a long cry of rage and hunger fade down the wind.

"What time is it?" asked Morgan.

"Past one. I'll ask Aramelissa to bring us some lunch, I think."

"I didn't know it was that late," said Morgan. "Surely I'm wearing out my welcome."

"Not at all," said Julian, smiling. "I want to talk to you as long as I can."

You do, thought Morgan; and I know why. But aloud she said, "I'll be delighted to stay as long as you want me."

The day had clouded over, and now rain began suddenly to fall in a solid white torrent. Thunder broke like a distant crash of stone.

"It's raining in," said Julian after a few minutes, as a gust sent a loud spatter across a sill. "I'll shut the windows."

"No, don't bother," said Morgan, rising. "Let me do it."

She reached out into the rain to get hold of the casements. The wind rushed in her face and stirred her hair, and she shut her eyes and thought of the stone tower of Gor long ago.

Something stirred in the deep places of her mind, the sense of another presence moving there like a night wind in haunted mountains. She concentrated all the force of her thought upon it, to learn what it wanted.

Morgan, Morgan. The quester has escaped us. The Dark One has failed, as she has failed with others before.

Then we must try other means, answered Morgan. I fear this Anthony.

There are other powers, stronger than the shadow of the Shadow. We have half the Otherworld at our call. What of the cold king, the iron lord, the destroyer?

No, we may need him with the others. Send a lesser power for now; we can call Ironheart later if need be.

You must come and help me. Otherwise I will not help you.

I will not quarrel with this lady unless I must. I will come when I can.

I will send against the quester. Let the Darkness conquer.

"Are you having trouble with the casement?" asked Julian, rising from the table. "Here, I'll help you."

With the long cry still ringing in his mind, Anthony got up and took his bearings among the dripping pines. The rain had grown less; the lightning was spending itself away eastward over Baldwin County. In that direction the trees thinned to the seashore; he came back to the water's edge and realized that he had been running northwards, the way he had come. His mind hung poised for a moment like a pair of scales, wondering whether he ought to turn south again; his plan had been that, but now something else had taken a hand in the matter. Chance or destiny had driven him north from the hedged garden; let chance or destiny guide him then. And as he formed the choice, the depths of his mind clenched suddenly on it with an obscure sense of finality.

The rain stopped as he walked along the shore; the afternoon sun came out a little softened, but bright and hot. He sat down on a grey log to rest and dry out, and to meditate awhile on his adventure.

Because of his dissertation he knew the Grail story in Malory rather well. He remembered episodes where some of the Grail questers—Perceval and Bors, in fact—met with beautiful inhuman ladies who tried to trap them with enchantments. The Perceval passage in particular stuck in his mind; he could see the very shape of the page as he tried to recall the words. There was something about how, after she had failed with Perceval, the lady had rushed onto her ship and gone sailing off in an awesome roar and yell of wind—and "all the water burnt after her."

Apparently, then, one could expect to meet Lilith. He was clearly committed to the quest now; he had crossed some boundary from the purely natural world into this other. He wondered when he had done it—perhaps plunging into the woods after his rescue of the woman. On reflection, that adventure seemed less pointless after all; it had some flavor of the abrupt encounters in Malory, and formed a suitable entrance into the quest.

He began to walk again, between the water and the grey tangles of driftwood. After a while he came to places he had not passed on his way south; houses and piers became more frequent, and sometimes there were people who stared at him as if they thought him a dubious character. He laughed derisively to himself; the fight, the rain, and the muddy fall had plainly not improved his looks. But the questers of old, after a few weeks of wandering, must have lost a good deal of their glitter too. He had a sudden mental image of Sir Bors riding wearily through a ramshackle village, with a clamor of children and dogs at his heels.

With the clouds gone, the afternoon grew oppressive; he felt unreasonably tired and sat down to rest several times at the edge of the trees. Once, reaching into his pocket for something to eat, he found that the rainwater had ruined the bread. He threw it at the water's edge for the gulls and went on.

The sun was lowering now, and the tide had turned. He was glad the glare was gone; his head and eyes ached dully, and he knew that in a while he would probably feel sick with the pain. The shadow of the pines fell across the narrow beach now, and he had passed all the piers. Down at the water's edge a little way off, where sunlight gleamed through a gap in the trees, a small boy was building huge fortifications around a sandcastle to shut out the rising tide.

I am a fortifier of sandcastles, thought Anthony, with a sharp sense of the fragility of all he loved. With constant effort, could I get the walls high enough?

"Hello there," he said, coming beside the boy. "That's quite a fortification you have there."

"It's a castle," said the boy, looking up with a preoccupied glance that focused into interest; "I don't want it to wash away." He stared at Anthony with disconcerting directness. "You look shipwrecked. Did you meet any pirates?"

"In a manner of speaking," said Anthony.

"My father says Jean Lafitte buried treasure all along here. Are you looking for it?"

"No," said Anthony. "I'm looking for a gold cup."

"Like the holy Grail?"

"What?" Anthony was so startled by the question that he would have dropped anything he had been carrying.

"It's a gold cup," explained the boy patiently. "It's in a picture in the King Arthur book; it has light around it, and the knights are sitting at the table. But I like the Sir Bedivere picture better, because it looks like the place up there." He gestured vaguely northward.

"Well, I hope your castle stays built," said Anthony. "I have to go and find that cup." And with a nod of good-bye he trudged on along the sand.

The sun sank lower; there was no more glitter even on the most distant water. He waded a silted-up canal, whose water was unexpectedly cold at the bottom; the sudden chill on his burning feet made him shiver. He dipped his hands in the water and wet his face; for a moment, with the coolness, he thought his headache would go away. He went on, and the long shadow of the pines seemed to lie across the world.

The last houses had fallen behind. The sun was setting, and he was alone in a wholly desolate part of the coast. The lonely light fell with a reddish tinge on the grey flow of tide and the driftwood-strewn sand. The wrecks of trees looked strange and sad in that light; and so did the barnacle-whitened stumps of dead trees that still stood upright in the water, showing where living pines had flourished long ago, on land that was now under the sea. He thought with a peculiar regret of good land being eaten away, year by year and century by century, by the barren salt sea. The lost land of Lyonesse, and Ys of the bells, and Atlantis, and the forest of Spinnaie—all drowned, with their castles and their towers and their Roman roads; and if the bells of Ys rang under the sea, no ear of man could hear them. And neither pine nor green grass nor wild fireflower would ever grow again on this drowned land; awhile longer, children would pick barnacles off the stumps and men would moor boats to them; and then they would be worn away, and no one would remember that land had been there.

He awoke from his reflections and found himself alone on a darkening shore, with the light fading out of the sky. On one side, the dark waves lapped at the sand with small noises; on the other, dark-green reaches of salt marsh stretched as far as the eye could see. He remembered a picture in a book he had had as a child, the same, maybe, that the boy had spoken of. In just such a desolate place of salt marsh and sea, Sir Bedivere had hurled Arthur's sword away.

With that sense of twilit desolation the whole weight of his weariness seemed to fall on him. He sat down on a piece of wrecked timber, with an aching feeling through his whole body that seemed only less shrill than the pain in his head. He shut his eyes for a moment's relief, swayed, and caught his balance with a startled sense of waking. Why he was so deeply tired, he could not quite gather; it was as if he had been walking all afternoon through a dense, resistant element like water.

Leaning down to the waves' edge, he splashed his face with the cold water; but there was nothing to drink. The thought reminded him of his hunger. He wished he had not thrown the bread away; even waterlogged, it would have stopped the contracted feeling in his stomach.

It was almost dark when he went on; the last of the sunset had faded, and the moon had not risen. He had not gone far when he saw a dark expanse cutting across the sand; he did not know what it was. But as he came close, he did know, and laughed suddenly and bitterly with a kind of despair. He had forgotten Deer River. It flowed at his feet, all its forks joined in one dark mouth, into the sea.

There was no bridge or ferry, nothing but the dark marsh stretching inland, he did not know how far. But he had impatiently thrust off his momentary despair. There was nothing to do but either swim the river, or retrace his steps and find his way back through the woods, or struggle inland through the swamps to the bridges. He resisted the idea of going back, and losing himself in benighted woods amid rattlesnakes and other such creatures did not appeal to him; and wading through an unknown swamp, with snares of quicksand, water moccasins, and heaven knew what else was an even less pleasant prospect.

He was still trying to reconcile himself to the obvious when he saw another figure standing a little way off, near the side of the river. "Hello there!" he called. "Got a boat?"

The figure turned slowly; he saw it outlined against the sky and knew that in all probability it did not have a boat, or anything else belonging to the common earth. It seemed to be a man—but, by the shape against the paler sky, a man helmed and wearing a shirt of ring-mail and leaning on a sword.

Anthony thought of the dark woman and was silent. Then he thought of Sir Perceval coming with the ship to take Bors on the sea journey. "Sir," he called again, "are you sent to be my guide?"

"Yes," came a voice out of the dark. "I am sent to guide you on the road you must go."

Anthony hesitated; it occurred to him that he would like to see this guide. He groped in his pocket for matches; the box felt dry and they would probably light. Holding the box ready, he came up warily to his guide.

The man stood motionless, waiting for him. "I see you would prove me. Strike your light, then; look on me, and say whether you will trust me or no."

Anthony struck a match; and in the brief flare before it went out, he saw a face pale, noble-featured, and somewhat stern, black hair worn long to the shoulders, and ring-mail that glinted dull gold. A streak of the same dull gold had run for an instant along the sword.

"I will trust you," said Anthony. He had glimpsed the man's eyes, which were grey and full of thought; there was no spell in them.

"Look, then" said the guide, with a wide gesture northward across the land.

Anthony looked; and he seemed to look down from a high place, across miles of woods and grass and remote hills. The shape of the land was familiar; but unicorns moved shining among the trees, and in other places men in bronze armor passed stealthily through the woodland. A sourceless light showed everything distinctly, like a firelight showing each separate blade of grass against the dark. And everything, however far, stood sharp-edged and plain as if seen through the wrong end of a spyglass, but very small.

His gaze was drawn to the brightest part of the land, at the river mouth far up the bay. White and many-spired, pinnacled with crystal and jewelled with myriad lights like diamond, walled with living trees on a rampart of stone, a city shimmered there like carved starlight and cast the radiance of its towers over the waves.

"That is starry Eldis," came the voice of the guide behind him, "which is in the hands of our enemies. That is where we must go."

"The Cup is there, then?"

"No. But we must capture Eldis, perhaps tonight; and you must lead us."

This seemed strange to Anthony, though he half-remembered similar adventures in the old quests. He asked, "Why must we capture it?"

"Because it is held against us by the queen Lauriel, a most potent sorceress; and because of her, we can get no power over this land. But you shall lead us to victory, and drive out Lauriel, and rule as king in starry Eldis."

This plan of conquest and kingship seemed irrelevant to Anthony, clashing sharply with the urgency of his quest. And yet, was it irrelevant? He remembered that Galahad had been made king in Sarras; yet surely that was after the quest. "Need it be tonight?" he said. "You know my quest; if I fail in it, Mobile and the people I love may be destroyed."

"It must be tonight," said the guide. "Your world is not important to us."

A slow, cold blaze lit in Anthony's mind like an aurora borealis, heatless but pouring over all a preternatural illumination. "You are no more sent from the powers of light than was Lilith," he said slowly. "You want to draw me away from the quest."

"Yes," said the guide; and the rising moon shone on his face so that it seemed full of a stony splendor like a sorcerer's. "I, Morandir, am sent to draw you out of your own world into this other. Why not? You are free to go where you will and dwell where you will. What is Mobile to you? Let another seek for the Grail, if it must be sought, and save Mobile if it must be saved. You see that Eldis is a fairer city."

Anthony looked; its beauty shimmered before him, the net of light, the crystalline towers under the moon. He did not remember Linette or Julian or his parents; he forgot Silverthorne and the pillared houses and the great boughs of oak trees. Images of trivial and ugly things jostled in his memory: a cheap grocery store with an open front, a dirty street, grey tumble-down shacks, a waste field full of wrecked cars. All of Mobile and his own world seemed drab and worthless, a grey, grimed place under a dull sky, its colors faded, its once great beauty fallen into decay. But before him the Otherworld shone in its enchantments under the moon, and the spires of Eldis glittered like a galaxy. Names like diamonds poured through his mind, phrases like crystal and silver—*the kingship of Ormus and of Ind; shone like starlight, decked with the spoils of provinces; to ride in triumph through Persepolis.* And yet all those orient and jewelled wonders of poetry could not compare with this unearthly power and splendor. The conquests of Alexander paled beside it. And at the thought, the vision opened out before his mind; he saw his fame and great name spread like a rich golden light over all the lands of Otherworld—Anthony the Great, Olympian Anthony—what price that? Only to cast away all memory of the grey and half-dead, only to leave it to quick, merciful fire. He saw himself enthroned after that in a great paved square, under the starred sky, while among the torches the bronze-armored warriors shouted, "Long live the Emperor Anthony!" He was too deeply in Morandir's power even to be aware of it, as it wove itself subtly around him like invisible threads.

"You will find it a hard battle," came Morandir's voice; "and even in victory you will not sit secure. For Lauriel is no faint-heart, but a Queen forethoughted and terrible, mightier than Cyrus or Xerxes or Tamburlaine. We know her; we have fought her these many centuries. Great has been our labor and pain."

Anthony looked into Morandir's face and saw him as a warrior of many battles, tried and steadfast, valiant in forgotten wars. The wisdom of centuries shone in his eyes, and with it a resolute defiance that nothing could conquer. To command such men; to be greater than they, more skilled in war, more magnanimous in victory and more unyielding in defeat; to lead them in the fierce exultation of battle, to conquer by undying deeds so great a prize—it seemed a resounding legend out of Bronze Age epic, like the battles before high-walled Ilion. Neither sorcery nor the swords of Eldis, not the power of gods could stop him; starry Eldis would fall to him, and he would reign crowned with immortal fame in the throne of its kings. Let Lauriel do her mightiest; her power would break impotent as waves round the steps of his throne.

"And in the end," said Morandir in a voice of proud grief like Aeneas' harpers singing of Hector dead before Troy walls, "it will go hard with us, and we shall be driven forth with pain and despair out of the citadel we shall have held for our centuries of joy. Our power will be cast in the dust; and we shall fall by the bitter swords of our enemies, never to live again; and we shall be prisoned in the dark fires everlastingly, never to know daylight again or the bright sky. For we have dared to set ourselves against the Prince of Light."

And Anthony's heart was wrung with sorrow and pity for the warriors he would lead to such ruin, and for himself, damned with them to eternal pain; and yet it seemed worth the outcome, to defy the King of the Universe, the all-powerful Emperor in His tent of stars, who with a word could destroy all. To rebel against the eternal Monarch, the invulnerable invincible Lord of the Sky, who wore the sun as His diamond upon His brow and wielded the lightning—to dare His worst, and endure His hardest stroke, and scorn hell with its pains—that, that was the only game worth playing, the only strength worth daring: to have as foe the One who was mightiest of all.

"Give me a sword," he said, like one drunken with high words in the clamor of a hall. "I dare defy Lauriel and Lauriel's master, the invincible Lord whose kingdom I will yet trouble if only for a moment—" He put out his hand to the bronze sword which Morandir silently gave him; and as he touched it, the cold of the metal cut through the intoxication of the spell like cold water. Clarity lay across his mind like the narrow moonlight along the sword-blade, touching the surface of it with something that troubled the magic. The sword lay across his two hands; white light along cold metal—what, what was it? Something he had read somewhere, a poem: there was a dark hall hung with purple, and a bed where a wounded knight lay, and a woman wept beside him; there was writing on a stone—

It eluded him; he could not remember what the poem was. But now the magic was broken; he heard again Julian's voice in the library of Silverthorne, urging on him the immediacy of the quest. The courtyard outside the window, sunlight, the walking peacocks, the white and green—he raised his head and saw bright Eldis burning coldly like starlight, all the clearer and more intense because he knew what his choice must be.

There Morandir also stood, with the moonlight frozen on his helm; he did not move, but Anthony felt the atmosphere vibrate with danger as with unseen lightning.

"No," he said, handing the sword back to Morandir. "I know the work I have to do; and the Prince of Light is not like that, and starry Eldis is not mine."

"You have a choice," said Morandir, holding the sword lightly by the hilt, his eyes gone relentless and still under the shadow of his brows. "You shall take the sword one way or the other—in your hands as a conqueror, or through your body."

"I will not take it at all," said Anthony; his hand went to his belt, and the hunting knife flashed out under the moon. "Take yourself out of my way; I have a river to cross." He knew, with a remote cold rationality, that his knife was no match for the long bronze sword; but so close to swordpoint he felt only a tense lightness and the determination to strike fast and sure.

He saw the change of expression in Morandir's eyes, saw the heavy bronze sword swing up lightly as a stick, caught the flash as it reached the height. Then he had sprung in, seized it just under the hilt as it fell, and jabbed with the hunting knife at Morandir's hand.

The sword dropped with a soft splash into the marsh; and Morandir stood like one turned to stone, staring at the small gash on his hand. Anthony had backed off a little, breathing hard, unaware that his own hand was bleeding from catching the sharp sword-blade. He gripped the hunting knife, waiting for Morandir to make a move to pick up the sword.

But Morandir did not move; his eyes, wide open, were staring pools of horror. Something began to happen, hideous and unthought-of as the events of nightmare, holding Anthony's eyes so that he could not look away. The skin of Morandir's hand began to draw back from the edges of the wound, as if it were melting like ice, leaving the raw flesh exposed. And that too began to draw away, and the white bone showed horribly in the moonlight. Morandir's lips moved, as if he wanted to say something; but no sound came. His whole hand now was no more than a skeleton, while the living eyes still stared in unspeakable horror. The melting was creeping up his arm; the bone showed as high as the elbow. Under the ring-mail the shape of his body changed, as the frightful transformation worked there. It was spreading to his other arm and his legs, while the untouched face watched like a mask except for the dreadfully alive eyes. The right arm was no more than bare bone; and the bone too began to crumble slowly into dust. The slow change was reaching his face; Anthony tried to stop looking, and could not. Morandir could not see it; but the agonized eyes strained to, while the hair turned to dust and the helmet fell down and rolled across the sand. His legs were crumbling bone; he swayed and fell clattering, and finally died. The eyes were the last to go, and remained shockingly alive to the last.

Anthony too fell down on the sand, covering his face with his hands lest he see those straining eyes in the dust of the skull. He still saw them, etched as with fire on the blackness under his eyelids. Then mercifully the image was overthrown and drowned by a great wave of darkness.

11. Caer Sidi

The candles were lighted now in the library at Silverthorne. Julian wondered how much longer she need go on, and how much longer she could think of things to say. She thought, with a flicker of weary humor, of filibusters in the Senate; but surely none of them had ever been as desperate as this.

"Elaine was the only one of us who could flower in Venta," Morgan was saying. "She and her Roman name, the name of an empress— Helena, they called her; and her hair like pale gold, where mine was fire and Morgause's was darkness. I can see her now in the high chamber that she had, with the marble walls, and the blue sky outside the window; I can see the curve of her wrist as she reached for an alabaster cup she had; I can see the flowered linen of her dress and the gold pins in her hair. And no doubt even the gold of the pins is crushed long ago in I know not what grave."

She paused wearily; these memories so long buried disturbed her now, and Elaine seemed almost as immediately near as Julian. I grow old, she thought; it is not the withering of the face that means age, but this, when the long dead are present to us like the living. A sense of foreboding brushed her mind like a feather, but she shook it off. It was time now that she brought this to an end.

The courteous disuse of magic had been finished since midday; but till now she had not quite dared to turn her arts on Julian, though she knew the amber pendant was useless against the mysteries of Arianrhod. Now she shut her eyes and lowered her head and willed with all her power and the Goddess's that Julian would begin to tire. She heard Julian's voice passing over her like an alien music, something about Horace, *montium custos nemorumque Virgo, diva triformis*, but paid no heed, concentrating the force of her mind on Julian's.

Julian felt the pressure like a sudden and heavy weight pressing strongly upon her. Speech seemed like wading in deep water, as she had done as a child; for an instant there rose to her mind an irrelevant vision, herself and Malcolm playing in the bright shallows amid sandbars and drifted sea-logs, the resistance of the water to their feet as they waded toward shore. With a start as of waking, she became aware of the intentness of Morgan's eyes on her, those deep eyes the color of violets, ancient and beautiful like unfathomable wells. Of course Morgan wanted her to be silent and let her go.

She picked up the thread, repeated the Latin phrases in English, letting her tired spirit rest on the words as on the waves of a flowing tide. " 'Virgin guardian of the mountains and the groves, three-formed goddess.' Wasn't she the Muse too, the original of the classical nine?"

"In Britain even in my time—I think everywhere earlier."

"And kept the cauldron of salvation, I mean inspiration." Julian shook her head a little to clear it—must talk sense, not mix up words. "There you get an idea carried on into the Middle Ages; the Welsh poets used to talk about Mary as Muse. So did Chaucer, for that matter, though I don't suppose he made the connection. So classical in his lore, don't you know." She rose—must move to wake up—and got the big blue-and-gold text. "He talks about your Goddess quite independently of that. Emelye says it in the Knight's Tale:

> O chaste goddess of the woodes greene,
> To whom both heaven and earth and sea is seene,
> Queen of the regne of Pluto dark and lowe—"

Aramelissa, coming in with the supper, looked at them both with her sharp old eyes. She had heard every word in the kitchen just below and sensed Julian's desperate tactics of delay. The necessity, apparently, was to keep Morgan away from the tools of her art and the dark quiet of the Atlantis Tower.

Morgan could not eat much, nor could Julian; both were too taut and at odds, and Morgan's mind was concentrated on the tiring of Julian. When they had finished, Julian went on talking about Chaucer and then about the ballad of Thomas the Rhymer.

She is strong, thought Morgan, looking at her with a reluctant admiration. This could last all night. And a sense of growing urgency tugged at her mind; Linette and Rhodri should be in the Otherworld now. Julian was not going to tire enough to stop; the break must be made, and quickly.

Morgan rose. "Well, Miss Silverthorne, I've had a most enjoyable day. But it's getting rather late; I ought to go."

"Oh, stay awhile!" said Julian, with all a hostess's cordial insistence.

"No, not another minute. I really need to get back to my work. Thank you, and good night." And she started towards the door; but Julian was there first, and shut it, and set her back against it.

"Miss Cornwall, I am sorry to have to detain you; but you are not going out of this room."

The stirring came again in the depths of Morgan's mind, and she felt the presence of Morgause's thought. Forgetting Julian, she stood rigid, listening with all the faculties of her soul.

Sister, sister, we have lost the quester once more. Morandir was sent against him and is dead. Help me.

I will. You had better look to the others; the nine hours are passed.

They have spoken with her of the silver weaving.

Attend to them. I will leave this place at once.

Once more she turned her gaze outward; Julian, pale and unmoved, was watching her with a grey, penetrating glance. Overpower her will, came Morgan's thought; make her move or faint. She fixed her eyes on Julian's.

Julian raised her head, as if a thread had been drawn taut. She found herself unable to look away. She forgot that the violet limpidities were eyes; she seemed to be looking into deep pools, no, one pool, very deep, very old, under the shadow of trees immeasurably ancient and vast, in the heart of forests that were ages old before Britain was an island, ever dying, ever renewed. Aeons of dead leaves lay on the forest floor. And in the pool shapes moved, human or unhuman, in glittering armor or glimmering robes, druids and Romans, sun-heroes like fire on the hill-tops, pale queens with drifting dark hair. She felt drawn towards the pool, as if it said, Come closer, look deeper, see the faces of the gods who ruled the young earth.

Yet there was some reason why she must not go nearer, why she must stand where she was. She could not remember, except that her weight was holding something back or down. She felt a restlessness of the ground under her; she was on the trapdoor of Hades; if she moved, the dark king would burst forth in his iron chariot. Door, that was it. Mustn't open the door. She stood still and fixed her mind on the pool; it divided into eyes, merged again, was once more a pool. But the drifting shapes had changed; something else was happening.

Morgan felt her own eyes caught and held. The grey gaze seemed to pierce into her thoughts like steel. The eyes that held hers became like uncolored light, the cold light of dawn, peering into dark forests and dark caves. It would search out her secrets; it would lay bare her hidden thoughts. For the first time in centuries she felt the chill, light touch of fear. She must get away before this unknown power was her ruin.

She backed away from Julian, breaking that thread of gaze. She gathered all her powers of mind and will and enchantment in a terrible concentration. She could see nothing, hear nothing; immeasurable darkness pressed against her soul, and she felt an anguish as of annihilation.

Julian, watching her, saw her grow death-pale, her eyes closed, her face strained with some agony of spirit. And then, simply and suddenly, Morgan was not in the room.

Julian leaned against the door, reeling for an instant under the horror of madness. No, she told herself wildly, it isn't beyond thought—we shall all travel with the mind after time's end—not unthinkable for her to anticipate her powers.

She grasped at a chair and collapsed into it, with shut eyes. Where does she get her powers? she thought dizzily. Not heaven surely; from hell then? And if so, does she know it?

Morgan opened her eyes and stood, shuddering in body and soul, on the grass of the courtyard. Only twice before had she done this, and the experience was terrible. Her body was not sufficiently subtle to travel with her thought without extreme agony as of dissolution. But it was over now; she must move, must act. No one must go from Silverthorne for help. She went out of Silverthorne gate, her nerves still shrilling and jarring like marred electricity; the three cars, Julian's, Aramelissa's, Anthony's, loomed on the ghostly gravel in the moonlight. She drew from her belt the Goddess's ritual knife, small and sharp and silver, and pierced a tire on each.

Then she moved quickly through the dark edge of the woods, where the bushes along the path caught at her dress, toward the stable that glimmered white under the moon. She undid the latch, feeling for it in the shadow of the roof, and pushed the door open. The stable-smell stirred in the night air, and a horse whinnied softly in the dark. She turned the wooden fastening of the stall door and whispered, "Solario, come!" The black horse followed her into the moonlight, his splendid head up, his ears pricked as if listening. Morgan remembered, as if drawing something out of a great depth, that horses were sacred to the Sun. Had Julian known that, naming him Solario?

She fixed the horse with a commanding gaze. "Go. Cross the river. Don't come back before day."

A shudder passed through the horse, and he laid back his ears; the great dark eyes stared wildly. Then he turned abruptly and plunged out of the clearing into the woods on the other side.

Morgan turned quickly back to the castle, passed through the gate, threaded the passages toward the Atlantis Tower. There should have been no light but the moonlight from the high, open windows; but turning a corner she saw candlelight by the tower door. And in the circle of candlelight stood Aramelissa with a broom in her hand, sweeping near the threshold.

Morgan brushed past her and put her hand to the knob, but the door did not yield. She realized that it was locked, that she had not locked it, that she had no key.

She turned a few steps back down the hall and faced the sweeping woman. "Aramelissa, give me that key."

Aramelissa put a narrow brown hand into her apron pocket and drew out a brass key that glinted in the candlelight; she held it high for Morgan to see. Her old gaze fell across Morgan's with a look of pride and shadowy triumph. With a single gesture she threw the key out the open window, into the moon-spattered darkness of the courtyard.

So that anguish of enchantment must be done again. Aramelissa stood like a pillar, waiting for the blast of Morgan's magic; she saw Morgan turn pale and dreadful, as if she herself were suffering that blast. And then Morgan was no longer there.

Once her hands were free and she was sure of not falling, Linette's horror began to leave her. The Queen of the Air was gone, and so was Lord Angoré; and the pterodactyl beast, hideous as it was, apparently was not going to kill them forthwith. As for Captain Morithil, she had fooled him once; it might be possible to fool him again. She straightened, holding the lantern in front of her. Plans must wait until the situation defined itself at Caer Sidi; in the meantime, the best thing was to let her mind rest in the wind of the flight.

She half-guessed it was the moonlit darkness that brought her this peace; even in the Otherworld it was the same soft dark of all the summers she had known, when she had chased fireflies in old gardens as a child. Even the sensation of flying was not utterly strange; she had known something like it on the ferris wheel at Mardi Gras and the flying sailboats at Lake Pontchartrain, in a whirl of brightness and rushing night. The memory of that past gaiety brought her a poignant sense of her own world and the sweetness of life; and she lifted her head, resolving more firmly not to give them up without a struggle.

Rhodri had no such memories. The half-tropic night was wholly alien to him, far from the cool, sweet evenings of summer in Wales. The difference made him think of those evenings with a terrible sharpness of grief. It did not matter that he himself would not see them again—but where would they be when servants of darkness had cut down the trees and covered the mountains with iron? He bowed his head with bitterness and shame. He had a dark sense of what to expect from the Haldir—cruel enchantments of fire and ice, hideous metamorphoses, death soon if they were merciful. None of that mattered except for Linette—ah, on whom had he not brought ruin?—he himself deserved it, would embrace it whatever the pain. He cursed himself for unmaking the spear. He had guessed from the sword his enemies' dread of iron; why, in his anxiety over his tool, had he exchanged steel for bronze when he could have kept both? And now that folly had cost everything. The dearness of Britain tore at him in images swift as dreams—the hills below Cader Idris at twilight, friends at Cambridge laughing in the common room, his mother's fireside with the china ornaments on the mantel, a walking tour in Cumberland, Cristant at the window. The thought of Cristant startled him for an instant—he had almost forgotten; then the lashed sea of his remorse poured on over him. With Excalibur lost, how would Britain be helped in the evil day? Bitter visions rose before him—the land's beauty choked under cement and iron; all grace of life gone; a people exterminated or without souls. Endless stony buildings stretched away to a dusk-red sky; a girl came into a paved court, her hair in short tight graceless curls, her green suit of some nameless shiny material tight as another skin, with stiff, fantastic excrescences that destroyed even the lines of her body. She stood there, waiting a sterilized lust, with blank eyes that knew nothing of love, honour, or thought; and she was Cristant's child. He turned from the vision in shame and horror. Ah, what use as Pendragon was he? His body ached and hurt from the Haldir's blows. He clung to the pain; it seemed elusive and too slight, when he ought for his folly to be in such searing agony that there would be no room in his mind for any kind of thought. Images of fire, wounds, torture rose before him; it was not right that the Pendragon should go unscathed when Britain was doomed.

Linette, with the wind rushing past her face in the moonlight, was almost happy. She felt like a bow drawn back, ready for anything, her mind full of a fierce, bright-edged laughter. She looked down past the beating wings; Eldis glittered like a royal diadem far behind. Below, the wooded plain rose in pine-dense hills; she thought of the smell of the pine needles in the warm dark and could almost hear the small animal-sounds under the light rustle of the wind. She recognized what would have been Wolf Ridge and Spring Hill and the other western rises, streaked with streams like threads of dark silver. In the hollow between two hills a string of lakes lay like spilled moon, where in the other world she and Rhodri had heard distant music like the harps of unearthly dances.

The purplish beast was flying in wide circles now, descending toward the grassy land around the lakes. The small, steep hills near the west end of the lake grew larger; and the vast beast settled heavily on the rising ground between water and hills.

Linette sprang lightly off, poised to dart for the thickets at the end of the lake. Rhodri, blind with his thoughts, dismounted slowly and did not look around. Captain Morithil climbed down warily, with his spear ready; the dried blood made a dark streak on his armor.

Linette edged close to Rhodri, ready to swing the lantern in Morithil's face, grab Rhodri's hand, and run. She lifted her eyes to the terrain—the still sky, the motionless water, the hills. And as she looked, her purpose sank and died, and a cold, daunting horror rose in her like the opening of frigid springs. The general shape of the land, she knew; but a subtle and sinister distortion twisted and changed all things as in a nightmare. The mounds seemed unnaturally steep and high, like barrows of the unquiet dead. A circle of water gleamed round the foot of one; it ought to have been rainwater not drained off; it was not. It shone with a wicked depth and blackness; she shrank from the sight of it as from something foul to touch. All her shuddering senses seemed to cry out that this was not the place where she had walked with Rhodri; it was the Otherworld, where nothing was too fantastic to be true.

The thing that was too fantastic began to happen. The hill shuddered; a crack opened in it, from which poured a violent red light like fire. It gave the ring of water a molten look and threw sharp shadows behind Linette and Morithil and Rhodri. Then, very slowly, something narrow and reddish-gold extended out of the crack, level with the ground where they stood. It touched the near shore and lay still, bright and thin, a few inches above the dark water. Linette saw that it was a bronze sword-blade, giant-long but no wider than the sword Rhodri had broken, and cruelly sharp at the edges.

"Cross," said Captain Morithil. And with a slow, cold horror she realized that the sword was a bridge, and that she and Rhodri had to cross it and go into the hill.

"I can't," she said in a dry voice, shrinking a little from the firelit blade. She thought again of hitting Morithil with the lantern, but felt it as useless; in this world the ground might sink under one's feet, or one might run without moving as in a nightmare. As if paralyzed, she watched the spear-point lower at her; it glittered in the fierce light.

"I'll go first," said Rhodri, his voice sounding strange in his ears. He had not thought he could despair more; yet he realized that till now he had still hoped. Now an utter cold horror choked him; he knew of this sword-bridge from old tales, and a sharp confused memory came to him of a wrangle among scholars and an older story beneath the overlay of romance, the bridge into an Otherworld country not of Morgan but of Persephone, the queen of the dead.

He set one foot on the blade, was startled when it gave a little; he had forgotten that he was not yet a shadow. At least it was flat up, not edge up as in the tales; one might barely cross it without falling or being cut. At that moment a voice cried hollowly within the hill, "Three freights of Fairface were they that went with Arthur."

And Morithil answered as if it were a token, "Seven alone returned from Caer Sidi."

Rhodri knew the words, an echo of an old, wild poem of the harrying of Hades. Three shiploads of Arthur's men went to the Dark Country to capture the Lord of Hades' cauldron—after that, the tale was so broken and tangled with age that its meaning and its very narrative were lost. No more was clear but the disastrous refrain that broke through again and again—seven alone returned from Caer one name or another, but it was all the same place, the dark kingdom, the country of the dead. Caer Sidi, the stronghold of the old gods, down in the underearth darkness—it was there, and nowhere else, that the sword-bridge led.

He felt a sharp jab, the spear-point pricking through his shirt. "Move." He stepped out onto the sword-bridge, balancing like a tightrope walker; he could feel the blade buckling under his weight. The air above the water was deathly cold. By the time he reached the middle, the blade had bent down to the dark water, so that the bitter-cold surface lapped against his shoes. He balanced desperately; he had a horror of falling into that freezing depth. He reached firm ground in the archway of the crack, but he would not look in; he turned his gaze once more on the land of the living.

The blade had sprung straight again. Linette stood rigid on the far shore, her head thrown back, her face white under the black hair and the blazing crown. "Come on!" he called in a dry, unreal voice. "Don't think about it, just do it!" She set a hesitant foot on the bridge, then with a burst of resolution came over fast, not looking down. The blade bent less under her weight and did not touch the water. Rhodri caught her in his arms, and there on the steps of Hades held her close. She had her back turned toward the land of the living, her head bent and her eyes closed; she did not see Morithil crossing boldly over the bridge, did not see it remain completely straight under his feet. But Rhodri saw, and tightened his embrace around her, and wished with all his heart that he had never seen her to bring her into this.

Once more he felt the savage jab of Morithil's spear. "Linger not in the doorways of Caer Sidi, prisoners of the Queen." Rhodri met the bitter grey gaze and thought what a satisfaction it would be to shove Morithil into the lightless depths.

"Come, lass," he said to Linette. He could feel her body trembling against his; but when she opened her eyes, they were blank and bright with the nerve of despair. She put her hand lifelessly into his; her fingers moved restlessly like dry grass.

They turned their faces away from the land of the living. Before them on the floor lay the great bronze hilt of the swordbridge, bright as molten rock in the flaring red light. They stood in a square chamber of reddish rock; before them, opposite the crack, was a doorway formed of three great grey stones like the arches of Stonehenge, immense and rough-hewn, immeasurably old. The opening itself was not large, no higher than the door of a tomb; it held black darkness, and out of it poured an icy air that seemed to freeze heart and bone. On each side of the door a fire sprang tall and ragged out of the stone, not broad but red and high, torn by the bitter air from the cold portals, rising towards the stone roof like horns of light. A great hand, white as bone, came out of the doorway and drew the sword back, so that its whole length lay shining along the floor. The hand withdrew; the hill shuddered, and the crack crashed to with a sound like the fall of immensities of earth's rock thrown from a burning mountain.

Morithil cried behind them, "Three freights of Fairface were they that went with Arthur."

And a voice answered out of the darkness, "Seven alone returned from Caer Sidi."

Linette and Rhodri, holding hands like lost children, passed the horns of light and went under the arch of stone. As they passed under, the cold pierced them like knives of ice, intense cold that seemed to numb their very blood and yet bit like fire. The floor beneath their feet sloped steeply down, and their steps sounded hollow, as in a vast place; the feeble light of the lantern showed a rough stone floor, but neither roof nor walls.

Down they went, deeper and deeper, as if they travelled in the infinite cold vastnesses between the stars. Even Morithil, following at their heels with his spear, seemed company in that hollowness of freezing dark. Linette, looking back once, saw that he too seemed dwarfed and pained by the abyss of darkness and cutting cold.

Vague visions flickered before Rhodri's mind, of Arthur and his men in bright ring-mail coming down the dark path into Caer Sidi of the many doors, where the dead had waited before the coming of Christ, where the evil dead still haunted the portals of hell. But Arthur had had Excalibur, that burned like thirty torches against the darkness and the cold. And nobody would have Excalibur now, only hollow darkness would have it till the earth crumbled. The gold arm-ring of the Pendragons clung to his flesh and burnt with cold; at the thought of it, his failure sickened him, as if he had swallowed the cold, foul water of sewers. He wished the ropes were still on, biting cruelly at his wrists; the rubbed red skin hardly hurt, and he ought to have been in pain. That would come soon, though; he shuddered, seeming to feel all over his body the stab of weapons.

The floor grew level, and a pale twilight began to touch the darkness. Their footsteps echoed suddenly and re-echoed, as if from a high roof and vast distant walls; a ghostly phosphorescence flowed as if under grey seas, revealing shapes that stood like rings of stones around another light that rose and sank and changed its hue.

Again Rhodri felt the jab of Morithil's spear urging him on. This is the beginning of it, he thought; when they walked out there, the phosphorescence would coil around them like smoke, would fasten on them, burning and venomous. He tightened his hand on Linette's, hoping it would comfort her; for a moment he put his arm around her, but the biting reminder of Morithil's spear this time made the blood come. He could feel the thin thread slide down his back, unless perhaps it was the cold sweat of fear. He still held Linette's hand; they walked into the glimmer like that, amid the grey stony shapes that stood with their faces toward the changing light; and the phosphorescence did not burn them.

A greyness was over everything, an ashen twilight that dimmed all colors; but Rhodri saw in the center of the rings of shapes a cauldron above a fire, and nine forms gathered around it. The fire had sunk to coals that glowed dull red; the cauldron was golden bronze, but its color looked dead and cold. The light came from what was in the cauldron; and as it sprang up he could see the nine women that gathered round it. All were robed in white that looked dim as mist; eight had the stature of mortal women, though with strange, fey faces that he glimpsed when they came near the cauldron, moving around it now in the ever-shifting patterns of dance. The ninth rose above them like the image of a goddess; she alone stood motionless, gazing into the cauldron. Her long, loose hair was stirred in the breath from the cauldron, and on her brow shone a great jewel like the moon. As the eight women moved around her, now one, now another would dip a silver cup into the cauldron and drink and lift her voice in a wild, beautiful chant like the piercing sweet cry of a solitary bird. The pale light from the cauldron rose and sank, now in one color, now in another; and each time it rose, it cast its glow strongly on the face of the goddess. The light would rise grey-white, and the jewel on her brow would be like the young moon; her hair would be golden-pale, and her face would be a maiden's face, innocent and fair. The light would sink and rise dull rose, and her jewel would be round like the full moon; and her hair would be dark and rich, and her face would be older and beautiful yet terrible with desire. Then the light would fall and would flow up grey-yellow like a stormy sunset; and her jewel would be like the waning moon, and her hair would be grey-white and wild; and her face would be a hag's, withered and witch-like, the eyes grey and dreadful with wordless knowledge. Then the light would alter, and she would be maiden again; and the circle of change would pass again like the changing moon.

Rhodri and Linette stood at the edge of the weaving circle of priest-esses, with the cold, wild chant in their ears and the frozen air about them like ice. No warmth came to them from the coals; but the light sprang up grey-rose and hovered like fixed lightning, and through it the goddess's eyes stared into theirs. Linette felt their gaze pierce into her, colder than ice knives, like a freezing poison that made the old pools of horror rise in the dark. Her spirit stood on a narrow ledge in a light-less underground cavern, as high as she could climb; she could hear the black invincible waters rising and lapping against the stones, fast like the tides in undersea caves. They swirled around her feet and ankles, relentless, rapid; soon they would reach her head and drown her. But Rhodri did not feel the tightening of her hand; his gaze was fixed in intense recognition on the goddess's face. Her eyes were a hot blue, not grey like Linette's; she was beautiful as Linette could never have dreamed of being; but the eyes that blazed with a naked hate, the pallor, the cruel mouth of scornful triumphant desire he had seen before, in the instant before the other lantern had been dashed out.

Her eyes stared into theirs, and Rhodri felt that he was sinking down and down as into a quicksand. Then the goddess was gone; he and Linette stood alone in a doorless chamber of rock, with no light but the enfeebled lantern still burning in Linette's hand.

Then he saw that they were not alone. The pale features vivid against the dark were Linette's, but on them was stamped that look of cruelty and triumph that had just been before his eyes.

"Linette, Linette, hold on!" he cried in horror. "Don't let her win over you! Linette!"

" 'Hold on'!" cried the queen with violent scorn. "Under the weight of the darkness? Down, you mindless chit, little stubborn fool! By hell, I'll crush you—and you too if you get in my way, you with your new-moon hair and sweet-princess ways—Elaine all over again, Saint Elaine, sweet pride of Venta! Elaine, Cristant, what difference is the name? I'll crush you too, you meddling sanctity!"

Rhodri had stopped listening a full second ago; he stood paralyzed and blind, his mouth and eyes like dark holes. "O my merciful God!" he said in an almost voiceless cry. "Cristant!"

Four thousand miles away, Cristant sat rigid in her bed in the small dark room, her hair falling in pale tangles over her white gown. Her eyes too were wide open, fixed on vacancy, her lips parted. She saw not vacancy but the narrow cell of rock, the weakening lantern, the white, passion-wrought faces. Rhodri's cry, Linette, hold on, was still echoing in her mind.

More than seeing, she felt her mind drawn to the other girl's; she sensed Linette's horror, the blind furious struggle against extinction, the hideous weight of the demonic rage. Then with a sickening start she knew that the Queen was aware of her, as if she had caught a sharp glance from a pair of eyes. This had not happened before, not even earlier in the night when she woke to the bright-lit scene of the Queen's betrayal of the Pendragon. She had seen all that, clear and sharp-edged as Morgan's vision in the ink pool—the Queen rising out of the elder bloom as through foam, the Pendragon beaten down by the spears. She had felt Linette's terror and the flare of the brief victory; then all had gone black.

She had sat awake in the dark since then; tomorrow was Sunday, she need not go to the shop. Her walls and furniture, saturated through all these years with the substance of her disciplined solitude, loomed shadowy in the moonlight from the windows. Ever since she had discovered her secret clairvoyance, she had lived thus, that she might be attuned and ready when the sight came. And she had, of this adventure, a sense that all had been a preparation for it.

Her mind opening to a glimpse of the cauldron, she had seen what followed. She had heard the queen shrieking about Elaine and about her; and now the suffocating darkness was pointed at her too, poised and about to thrust, a sharp knife-blade to pierce her out of life like a moth on a pin. She heard Rhodri cry out her name, saw him collapse onto his knees and bow his head into his hands.

*　　*　　*

Rhodri said no more, only knelt on the stone with his head bent almost to the floor. His mind seemed numb, unable to take in what he had done. Slowly he forced himself to look at it, analyzing the ignominy of it as if counting brick by brick a harsh wall. It was not that there had been any spoken bond between him and Cristant; but there had been that unspoken thing, and he had known it, had known too the depth and steadfastness of her nature. And he, the Pendragon, had broken this unspoken promise—had broken it not to some outsider, but to one who knew his secret and shared his task. Lightly, under Linette's magnetism, he had put her aside—had he hoped to conceal the thing from Cristant? A hidden treachery, then; but surely he had known she would have to know, and would feel the rejection like a kind of death. He had turned from her casually to another woman; and here stood the other woman, raging in the possession of the powers of darkness, likely at any moment to be thrust out of life and leave her body to the once-human Queen of the Air.

"Linette—" he said, without raising his head; and the laughter of the Queen answered him like a screaming of eagles.

Linette indeed. He himself had brought this on her by attracting Morgan here, who had called then on her terrible sister—useless to say he had not meant to, useless to say it was her own fault for attending the seance. Celebrin had said it truly—by his treachery he had given an opening to the powers of the enemy.

He looked up; the lantern, burning low, cast a weak light on the white, laughter-twisted face of Linette, of the Queen. Why was it not over, why would she not die and let it be done? He contemplated the time when it would be done, the quietened face all Morgause then, the voice pretending to be Linette's, urging that she was all right and that they should go on to the Sword. At least, he would not take her. He would say no; and she would kill him or leave him to die, it did not much matter. Two things might happen then. She might abandon the quest; and the secret of where Excalibur was would be lost with him, for no one else knew it was under Caer Mair. Cristant knew; but what could Cristant do, alone and shattered by grief? She would not even know whom to tell. And when the hour of desperate need came, no one would know where to look; and the ruin would come.

He looked up once more; his thoughts had taken no time, and nothing had changed. The Queen's laughter at him still rang in his ears.

Or, he thought, Morgause could go on alone, get hold of the Sword and use it to destroy the Grail. And then the ruin would come sooner. He saw the pleasant green country blasted like the landscape of the moon, Silverthorne seared rubble by a poisoned bay, no sign of Julian or Anthony. And Morgause walked away from it, carrying the Sword like a stick, in Linette's usurped body which, even as he looked, took on more and more the aspect of the dark goddess stooping over the cauldron, the face full of an unnatural beauty, the eyes turning a hot blue. And around the stain of the burning, all the green grass seemed to wither and shrink away. The barrenness spread; it spread across the sea, changing the color of the waters to a sickened grey-brown where the white bellies of the fish tossed and stank. It reached Britain, blighting grass and tree, turning the green one black; the vast dark grotesque buildings seemed to spring up in its wake, covering every inch of earth, the dead fields and the violated mountains. He saw again the stone courtyard and the curled girl, Cristant's child, her darkened mind questing in a loveless lust; there was no Cristant to guide her, for Cristant, grown solitary and prematurely old with anguish, had been locked in a madhouse, though bitterly sane. And over that deadened, bereft land an immense silent sky hung, blood-red and threatening. It won't be water, but fire next time.

The phrase from nowhere trembled in the Queen's laughter, as if struck by that sheet of flame. "Ha, ha, look at it then, look, you fool! Too late are we sorry, when we face the fruit of our deeds. But you shall laugh yet, laugh with me at the ruin of Britain, your revenge on the King of Time!—I haven't forgotten you, little fool. Die fighting, will you indeed? Crazy linnet flapping in the birdlime? Down with you, then. Don't you feel your death yet? Despair, surrender, little sand-wit! Yes, down, down with you! Do you feel my victory?—Yes, look, you wide-eyed hypocrite! Haven't you the child's wit to be jealous? Don't you know your dear Pendragon loves her instead of you? Hell take you, don't you see your revenge?—Down, crazy bird! Aren't you worn out yet? So, so, down!—Don't you dare try it, you pale fool! Princess Saint Elaine! You think I can't crush you in a moment, and return and crush her? Dare get in my way and I'll kill you and damn you! Cristant of Logres—ha, ha, ha, ha, ha!"

With a realization that sickened like a blow, Rhodri guessed what Cristant could do—and Cristant only, whom he had appallingly wronged. She must be able to hear this as well as see, or Morgause would not be screaming at her. The idea that she might care to be avenged on them, to leave them to their fate, seemed possible. But he would try. He rose heavily and stared into the Queen's eyes, as if he could thereby be more sure of making Cristant hear him.

"Cristant!" he cried. "If you can hear me, if you can do anything, help us! I don't ask it for me or for her, but I call to you as what Morgause called you, Cristant of Logres. If you can, draw the dark powers away from her, so that we can have a chance! I dare not ask anything of you in my own name, least of all this horror, this danger. But I ask it as the Pendragon: hold off Morgause for us, so we can perhaps not fail in the quest!"

Indeed, thought Cristant, why doesn't he call on me as himself? Is there no more than that between us, his being Pendragon and my being a daughter of Logres?

She had put her feet out of bed, so that they rested bare on the cold stones. She was wide awake; but there still was the vision, as real as the furniture in the moonlit room. She looked at it thoughtfully, suspended outside it like a spectator—shall I, or not? She could feel all their attention fixed on her like pairs of eyes—Morgause's, full of hungry rage, ready to destroy as coolly as a tiger and return to her first victim; Rhodri's, tortured and haggard; Linette's, faint like the attention of the dying.

And shall I be like that, she thought, weakened like that, and then die? What absolute cheek, to behave like that and then expect me to fish them out of trouble at my own expense. And if I die and she lives, he'll marry her.

Well, what about Logres, then? I am, after all, bound by certain promises to help the Pendragon.

But promises are terribly breakable, are they not? There's the evidence before me, about which I had better not think. And who's to say it would do any good? It's likely she will crush me, in a moment as she says, and go back and dispose of Miss Linette as if I'd never dared. A horrible way to die.

Yes, and then she'll no doubt dispose of Rhodri.

Cristant sat with her hands clenched on the edge of the mattress, as if to hold back the realization of bitter hurt and maintain the trained clarity of her mind. Hardly a second had passed in her reflections.

Well, Rhodri has asked for it, rather. Linette, indeed. A broken promise deserves a broken promise. What am I saying? No use dallying; all this while, the fight's going on, I suppose. Deserve it they may, but I don't suppose that lets me off. Logres may or may not be helped. One can but try.

She looked at the moonlight on the floor, as if in a prayer that what she willed would happen. She faced Morgause. Come, then.

Immediately the dark force broke over her, like an invincible wave, knocking her spirit off its balance and dragging it down as with a great pour of waters. The vision of Linette and Rhodri went out like a lightning; and she fought blindly in the whelming darkness like someone dragged down in an undertow, trying to get up for breath and light. She thought her soul was being cast out of her body; but she held her breath and did not drown, and was thrust upward again as by the turn of the undertow. As if treading water, she was aware once more of the cool semidark of the room, and the pale arches of the windows where the moon shone dimly through the thin curtains. But everything seemed heightened and too real, as in a fever. Then she felt herself rise out of bed in her embroidered white gown, and knew she had not willed to do so.

Impelled by the Queen, she went barefoot to the window and pushed aside the light pale curtains. The moonlight streamed onto her white face so that it seemed to reflect the moon as the moon reflected the sun. The roofs of Caernarvon spread below and about her like tumbled mounds of barrows; and far down, three stories far, the grey stones of the street reflected the lights and the moon.

Then she knew that she was going to leap down. That was why she was allowed to have her head above water; trapped Morgause did not want a long battle for dominance and had no use for her, but meant only to be rid of her and speed like thought back to Caer Sidi. Cristant, adrift like a lost swimmer in the dark void, understood with a strange detachment; once again she watched like a bystander as the Queen pushed the casement completely open and knelt up onto the sill.

The cool radiance poured over her hair now and into the room, making her like a statue of silver. The stones below seemed silver too, a pale river flowing between the dim houses. Over Caernarvon the moon was already westering, and stood over Anglesey round and white as a sand dollar, marked like the shell with the signs of a mysterious love.

Cristant sensed that something in the dark spirit of Morgause shuddered at that light and shrank away. Her own spirit fixed itself on the moonlight, thirstily as a shipwrecked swimmer desiring fresh water in a waste of brine. And she willed, with all her power, that Morgause should not move.

Morgause, caught for an instant in that intensity of will, was frozen motionless like ice while Cristant's heightened vision beheld for a splintered second not the moon but a woman in white, the wild maiden mother of poetry, her clear beautiful face turned with a lucent intensity toward the distant lord of light. Then Morgause, again dominant, broke violently away from the window, into the darker room outside the pools of moonlight.

Cristant was once again thrust far out, a minute spark of life afloat in the dark void between vast water and a sky without stars. The high lonely emptiness oppressed her, pressing in from all sides as if to turn her into nothingness. She floated, hoarding her strength, knowing that Morgause would try other means and that her death meant defeat for more than herself.

Morgause approached the dresser and passed her hand over the wood; thin green flames sprang up, pale as the poison with which she had poisoned Uther, playing without scorch across the smooth surface of the wood. By the greenish glow Cristant saw her own face in the mirror, pale and witchlike with the ghastly light from beneath, dreadful anyway because impressed with the demonic malice of Morgause. In the glass the Queen's gaze caught a wardrobe looming against the paler wall; she threw open the heavy door and caught the white undergarments off the hook, then the first dress she laid hands on, a thin blue wool. Quickly she dressed, not at all hindered by the modern fastenings, and left the gown in a tangle on the floor. In a drawer of the dresser she found a black velvet ribbon; she brushed the long hair and used the ribbon to tie it at the back of the neck. Something seemed to be missing; she realized the white bare feet on the dark floor and seized a pair of red shoes with little heels out of the wardrobe. Then she went out of the bedroom and down the stairs and let herself out into the moonlit street.

She crossed quickly to the dark side, where the deep shadow of the houses overhung the narrow sidewalks. To the west, down the vista of the street, the immense towers of Caernarvon Castle loomed dark over the roofs, blotting out part of the stars with their seven centuries of pride. Morgause lifted her head, smelling the sea in the air; the castle was a thing of yesterday to her, but in the mazes of this unknown city it made a mark for her steps. She began to walk rapidly westward, keeping as much as she could in the shadows, shuddering when she had to venture out into the cold pure brightness. There were few people about, for it was past three o'clock in the morning; now and again a car would pass, coming from the train station or from some late revel. All the houses were closed and dark. But to Cristant, with her heightened, almost feverish vision, a veil seemed to have been lifted. The castle stood forth with a terrible dark splendor, clothed in its past; she saw for an instant the English king's men on the walls, their armor glittering in the moonlight, and her own embattled people beneath, fierce against the hated invaders. Morgause was aware of the vision; for a split, compromising instant their two souls shuddered as one, with a nameless deep dread and sense of wrongs that would not be remedied. Then the battlements were again lonely under the cold moonlight.

A few cars passed, singly, their headlights spearing through the darkness; they were dark secret chariots conveying immortal spirits to a mysterious destiny. Of those that rode, most had a pale brightness, like the moon's halo in a mist; but a few were almost darkened, as if by thick clouds, and a few shone with a clear, untroubled light. She looked up to the houses of the street; their shapes were strange and jumbled, superimposed on other shapes of houses that had once stood there. Faces looked out of windows that no longer existed; shapes stood in lost archways or between vanished columns.

Morgause had come to an intersection that was drowned in shadow. She paused there, perfectly still like the stones of the house beside her. In the silence that followed the light, sharp tapping of her heels, Cristant could hear a faint sound that might be the sea and, louder, nearer, the rush of a car through the dark. Its beams pierced through the cavernous shadows of the side street, towards the crossing. She knew it was coming fast, but suddenly it seemed to take eternities to move any nearer. An ice-wind seemed to overtake her soul, paralyzing it; she felt her body gather like a tiger's about to spring.

The lights transfixed the intersection. Morgause sprang out like a cat; at the same moment Cristant's spirit broke through its paralysis, catching the triumphant queen off guard. The side of the car swept past, grazing the heels of her shoes; and she pitched forward onto her hands and knees on the pavement. But in her second of mastery, Cristant had leaped clear.

The car stopped with a shriek of brakes, and a man sprang out. Cristant never knew his everyday aspect, but to her sharpened gaze he shone like moonlight through a thin mist. He cried out, in a high, ragged voice, "Miss, are you hurt?" and came running toward her.

Morgause did not stay to answer. She scrambled up and darted into the dark side-street, slipped into an alley between two houses, and leaned against the wall, trying to suppress the loud sound of her breath. The man had caught one glimpse of her wild face and must have thought her half-crazed with despair or grief; but he could not find her in the dark, and at last went on.

Morgause listened in the dark to his footsteps dying away, and the slam of the door, and the rush of the car starting. She made her way back to the wider street that seemed to run straight for the castle, whose dark towers were still lit with the westering moon. Already she was past the walls of the medieval town; but Caernarvon still spread around her, a forest of high, peaked roofs, Renaissance and after, dark to all eyes but Cristant's except for the faint street lamps and the strong moonlight.

Suddenly the houses fell away; she stood in the wide open space before Caernarvon Castle. Its high walls and polygonal towers, with the moon almost behind them, cast an immense black shadow over the west edge of the town, and over Morgause who lifted her eyes to its dark battlements. Its cold power came over her like the touch of cool dark water, but it woke no memories; what was left of Roman Segontium lay inland behind her, its broken fragments washed in moonlight.

She went round the castle without looking at it again and came to the slate-covered quay. Below it the moonlit water flowed dark-grey, the river Seiont and the Strait of Menai. Morgause approached the very edge and looked down into the deep water, where it poured cold and with a slow sound toward the sea.

Cristant was almost too exhausted to go on fighting. The water looked cool and quiet in the moonlight, and her soul thirsted suddenly for its peace and oblivion; Morgause would see that the drowning did not take long. No one could say that she had not held Morgause off for a long time. Why struggle any more, when one could not hold on much longer anyway? There would be rest and darkness soon for Rhodri too; they would both be drowned deep in the river, the dark river that flowed forever and without noise through all the world.

But no, it must not be like that. Cristant tried to arouse herself from the oblivion and half-dream that wrapped like soft coverings round her mind. She could not picture to herself any more, in her extreme weariness, the ruin of Britain or the death of Rhodri. She looked at the cool pale moonlight on the water and willed, with a stubborn stonelike inertia, that Morgause should not jump.

But Morgause was stronger than she had been in the tower. Her will contradicted Cristant's, and they struggled in a motionless tug of war. Cristant, worn out already, felt the heavy pull dragging on her; in a moment she must go down like a sapling to which a wild horse had been tied. The image, from a cousin's mistake in reckless childhood, passed through her mind like irrelevant lightning and was gone—her cousin Gavin, wasn't that Gawain, the name of Morgause's own son whose mortal strength grew superhuman with the sun's course and sank with its decline?

The flash of thought struck across the darkness of Morgause's spirit like light from another world. Sunlight, green leaves, the red hair of Gawain—they startled her, and for a moment she forgot the battle. Her suddenly opened gaze lifted to the dark shore of Anglesey across the water. She had stood here, perhaps on this very spot, with her father once in the sunlight—

Like a bright torrent that whole world came crowding back upon her. They were at Tintagel by the Cornish sea; the sun shone bright on the rocky shore; she was kneeling by the water, making a little Tintagel out of the loose violet-colored pebbles. A pace away, Elaine paddled barefoot in the edge of the waves; Ygerna, white-dressed, stood at the rocky verge holding Elaine's soft baby hand; the hair of both flamed pale in the sunlight. Morgan, the littlest, gave a shrill cry of delight; Morgause turned and saw her lifted on high, screaming and laughing, over Avalloc's head; Avalloc's narrow, handsome face was turned up to her, full of laughter, the gold circlet gleaming across his dark hair— dark like her own, and she the eldest had been always at his heels, educated more like a prince than a princess. She was older; she was with him at Segontium, where he had gone to be sure of the defenses against the Saxons. They stood at the water's edge, where the waves sparkled under the sun; he explained to her, in terms she at twelve could understand, the defense of Cornwall against the raiders. "My eldest son," he had called her in jest; she might, he thought, be Princess of Cornwall one day, a great queen like Boadicea. He took off his circlet for a moment to try its fit on her own black hair.

And Uther had ruined it all, all that bright world—Uther Pendragon, the young High King in his stronghold in the Welsh mountains, son of the murdered Constantine. She and all of them had thought, when Avalloc and Ygerna rode off that day, that they were only summoned to plan alliance with him against the treacherous Vortigern, the Red Fox he was called, who had driven Uther out of his rightful lands.

But one night the noise of arrival woke her, the clatter of hooves and weapons under the walls; she caught a glimpse of Avalloc's face in the torchlight, strained and intense; but he left Ygerna and a garrison and raced away in the dark to another fortress. She learned in the morning that Uther was meant to think Ygerna was with Avalloc; and by afternoon the other castle was besieged.

It was hardly ten miles from there to Tintagel. Late one night Avalloc and two warriors of his household came to Tintagel gate, having slipped through the siege. She ran to meet him at the gate, her arms outstretched; but he strode past her without a word and took Ygerna in his arms. Morgause, not knowing what terrible guilt she had incurred to make him pass her like that, crouched crying for a while in a dark corner of the court, and fell asleep there, her black hair plastered in tangles across her wet face. She woke to the stamp of horses in the cold glimmer before dawn, saw him and his companions ride out, dark shapes against the paling sky, but dared not approach.

For a troubled hour or so she dozed in her own bed, her sleep tattered with nightmares, then was wakened by a great clamor in the hall. Ygerna, white so that her blue eyes seemed dark in her face, came and took her in her arms like a child and told her Avalloc had been killed last night a little past dark. She lay there, too dazed to cry, feeling the horror in the pressure of Ygerna's arms and the rapid beating of her heart.

Before noon Uther's trumpets sounded under the walls of Tintagel. Morgause looked down from the outer ramparts and saw him, a dark, narrow-boned man like Avalloc, and hated him.

But he had not come for battle. He and his embassy were let into the hall; the three girls, red-haired, fair, and dark, stood beside Ygerna as she sat dry-eyed in Avalloc's chair to receive them. His word was that the raiders had landed in force down the coast, that he needed to unite Cornwall behind him and provide a clear succession if he were killed. Thus he wanted to marry Ygerna at once. Ygerna's face went bright and terrible with anger; Morgause saw it and thought with fierce exultation. She'll call the warriors and they'll kill him now. But before Ygerna could answer him, he stepped nearer and said something close to her ear; Morgause saw her expression change, her mouth and eyes open like dark holes, the bright color of her anger struck white. It was all patched together in a few minutes; Uther's chaplain was called out of the knot of companions; then and there, in their black dresses of mourning, Ygerna was married to Uther, and Morgause to Lot of Orkney, and Elaine to Nentres of Garlot.

Lot left with the rest before midnight, riding with a great noise of horses to meet the raiders. Morgause, unmaidened, her soul aching with grief and outrage, crouched on the cold floor in the dark and prayed to the Lord of Darkness to help her avenge her father.

Ygerna too was to be avenged. For when she was deeply skilled in the dark arts, Morgause called back the whispered words of Uther to Ygerna, and knew who had come that night with the face of Avalloc.

And she had taken vengeance, handing Uther his death-sickness in a cup of wine. Beyond that she had gone too, turning Lot against Uther's son Arthur, conceived, so the dark powers said, on that nightmare night in Tintagel; seducing the boy Arthur; rearing Mordred in hatred to his father's ruin.

But why, after all? The thought struck her suddenly. Why had it not ended with Uther, death for death? All their faces crowded suddenly before her, masklike against blackness—yellow-haired Lot, dead in battle against Arthur; red-haired Gawain, the favored of the Sun Lord, dead in the battle at the last landing; brilliant, half-mad Agravaine with her own face, dead in the attack on Guenever's chamber; dull, pale-haired Gaheris and handsome Gareth, both with something of Ygerna's looks, both dead in the fight round the stake; Mordred, years youngest, slightly crooked in both body and spirit—Mordred whom she had devoured, keeping him alone with her when all the rest were gone; possessing him as she had wished to possess Linette, so that he lived only with her life; living in him still after Agravaine and Gaheris murdered her in her bed with one of her lovers, Agravaine master of the deed, driven to it by a jealousy he did not understand. Her spirit had guided the last sword-stroke at Arthur, keeping Mordred alive long enough for it, with Arthur's spear through his body.

But why? She stood transfixed at the water's edge, staring blankly toward the dark lift of Anglesey and the sinking moon. A cold wind out of deep regions seemed to blow through her. Had it been worth it, worth the sacrifice of all her kin and her own joy, to pursue a less and less satisfying revenge down the steeps of darkness? At what point had she begun turning to cruel deeds for their own sake? Perhaps when her own unhappiness taught her to hate others' peace. She had been already in the service of that dark religion that deepened slowly into dark magic; turning priestess and sorceress, she had made terror on the night hills, her soul growing more encrusted with power and corrosive malice as with rust or dried blood. In the end she had come even to this height of her ambition, to reign as a dark Persephone in the lost realms, partner of grim Hades and opposite and mockery of the Queen of Light.

And what had she gained thus but a wrung bitterness of heart, like a lump of corrupt matter in her breast, and a hideous emptiness as if she were a thin-worn shell almost rubbed through, barely keeping that dark mass from dissolution? But there would be no dissolution, no end, no oblivion. And would she perhaps grow worse till there was no shell of intellect or memory, only the foul stale corruption of her will? That had not happened to the Lord of Darkness, but he was old and strong; yet in the endless aeons, to what might not even he sink? And there would never be any end. Again for a split instant that bright morning was present to her; why had she not remained as she was then, the daughter of Avalloc most like Avalloc, gay and valiant, as they looked across the water to Anglesey?

But she drew her present being like a thick, dark mantle about her. Now she too was old, old and bold and strong. The blame of her misery lay not on her but on the Lord of Light; and on him would she endlessly wreak her revenge, ruining his devices and reiving his followers, herself a revenge because she had escaped his nets—she, the great Queen.

Her memories and her brief remorse had lasted the space of time it might take for a breath of wind to bend the trees beyond the strait. She remembered Cristant, and threw back her head and laughed harshly; better far to be Queen than a meek, weak prey. Now she would throw herself in the water and drown the fool and fly back like thought to Caer Sidi.

But in her moment of inattention she had lost control. Exhausted Cristant had had time to rally all her powers, like water in a well rising with rain; she willed her hand to move and it moved. She knew the chance would not last long; already she could feel Morgause's returned fury beating down, forcing her again toward the deeps. She walked quickly away from the water's edge, breaking almost into a run as the attack grew fiercer, around the castle and up the steep, and stood breathless at Caernarvon Castle gate. There was a bell there; she put her weight on it, pulling the chain till its small, wild clamor mixed in her mind with the infuriated gale of Morgause.

The gate opened; she barely saved herself from falling. One of the caretakers looked out, an old man with a flashlight; but to her heightened gaze he was a shape of pale light like starlight, and in his hand was a torch burning with a bright protecting fire.

"Sir," she said desperately, "I feel sick, and I can't get home. I think I may faint. Can't I stay in here a minute, till I'm better?"

"Oh, yes, miss. Do you mind coming in the caretaker's office, where you can sit down? And shall I call you a cab, or a doctor maybe?"

"No, no," said Cristant; "I'll be better in a bit. Let me sit by myself somewhere, where it's quiet." For Morgause would certainly not care whether the old man was present, and there was no knowing what consequences might follow.

The old man looked at her slowly; she was a lady certainly, her clothes told that; and from her face, all strained and white, there was indeed something wrong. Best be kind but careful. "I don't know what the Deputy Constable would say, but I'll let you sit in one of the towers if you like. The stairs are closed off, though; you'll have to stay in the lower story."

"Thank you," said Cristant, glad that there were to be no more high windows; she could feel Morgause ramming at her like a hurricane. "You're very kind."

He saw the anguish in her face and thought she was struggling to keep from collapse. Half supporting her, he brought her into the castle. The queen had tried to kill her by air, earth, and water, but not yet by fire.

Linette let herself down slowly to the floor and leaned with shut eyes against the wall. Rhodri looked closely at her; there was a blank quietness on her face, like the waxen look of funerals; but she was breathing, so not dead. Morgause must be raging now in Cristant like a black wind. His mouth seemed full of dust with shame and pity; he knelt beside Linette and held one of her hands in both his and bent low over it.

Her hand moved a little in his grasp; he looked up and saw her eyes, half open, fixed on him. "She did it," came Linette's voice, exhausted. "The queen's not gone; but it's not me now. She's going through me, like a high wind in a tunnel."

"Linette," said Rhodri brokenly, "I have to tell you something—"

"Not now." She shut her eyes again. "Let me rest."

"The lantern's going out," he said, dully, irrelevantly.

It had not gone out yet, but the flame was low and blue just over the socket. Its uneven flicker wavered and sank, threatening to go extinct any second. He guessed it must be near ten in the world somewhere above; here there was no time any more, and in a second there would be no more light. He leaned against the wall beside Linette, still holding her hand, and stared dully at the dying flame.

He had failed everybody. For an instant he saw the old Pendragon standing in a room full of books; he himself, a student from a remote country town, felt eclipsed and humble and proud. And now the trust placed in him had proved useless. They should have given it to someone stronger—Cristant, maybe. Cristant—he supposed she too would die now. But he could not feel any deep grief about it, or about the ruin of Britain; like Linette he was exhausted. His body ached with bruises, and his mind sank beneath the weight of too much happening.

Linette's hand stirred and tightened around his. "Don't," he said wretchedly. "Ah, don't."

She withdrew her hand from his. "Is it as bad as that?" she said in a low voice. "You never saw her but that one time."

"It was enough, though."

"How could you know each other well enough to make a binding promise?"

"You forget. There were letters. I knew she was like this—only I didn't know how much."

He shook his head. "And as for me—that first time, I felt she looked right into me. You remember she has the Other Sight."

"Such a little thing to cause all this failure. Is it fair, do you think?"

"I'm afraid so." He found it hard to speak. "So convenient if one could be just the irresponsible victim. But I had my chance. You see it every day—just a little falsity, and everything goes." He drew a breath. "Well, maybe not everything. Celebrin said something—Arthur and

Morgause. Maybe if I endure to the end, there'll be some remedy for my failure."

He turned toward Linette. "I'm sorry, though, that you have to endure it with me. It's not your fault."

"Isn't it?" said Linette. "You were true till you met me; and I was the one that spoke."

The scene came clearly to him. Yes, she had said it—*She will have forgotten you by now. Aren't I as beautiful as Cristant?* A slow anger started to burn in him; but no, there was no use in that. He was too tired for anger. And they were both going to die.

"You know, don't you?" he said. "That even if we had any chance to get out, it's all finished with us."

"I know," she said. "It wouldn't be decent, any other way."

They sat in silence then, staring at the wavering flame. Linette had moved a little closer to him, as if for protection against the final darkness; he could feel the warmth of her body not quite touching his. Her eyelids grew heavy as she looked at the flame; in her tired mind it tangled with the lost fiery Excalibur and with Morgan's Ace of Fire, Ace of Swords. If the Queen of Fire was Morgan's card, the Goddess, why was the castle of the old gods so dark and cold? But she could not think about hard questions any more; the flame, the only reality now, welled blue with flickers of yellow like some strange water.

Unexpectedly it went out. The wick glowed red-gold for a second, and then there was only darkness.

Rhodri put his arms around her and drew her to him. They sat like that for a long time, a little warmth to each other in the cold blackness. Linette had laid the heavy crown in her lap; Rhodri rested his aching eyelids against her soft invisible hair.

Perhaps they were dead, he thought, dead and judged. And this then was hell, this narrow dark room in which nothing else would happen forever. It seemed likely enough, in this place ruled by Morgause—not that her appearance as Goddess made much sense, for the many-named Lady had been worshipped perhaps before Britain was an island. But it was a strange hell then—more like a grave.

But, he thought, one could not repent in hell. And if it was not hell, alive or dead they might get out. His arms tightened around Linette as he thought it; stirred a little from her own entombed languor, she put one of her hands on his.

At the touch, his mind clasped fiercely on the opinion that they were alive. And furthermore, he decreed, they were going to get out and continue the quest.

"Sit back for a minute," he said. "I want to get up."

Linette moved, a little stiffly, as if coming out of a stonelike trance. Something in his tone seemed to make the wind of Morgause blow less coldly through her. She rubbed her chilled arms and listened to the small sounds of his standing up.

"We got in through the roof," he said in the dark above her. "There must be some opening."

"We can't see it, if there is."

"I have some matches in my pocket. Just a minute."

There was a second's pause; and then suddenly the close walls echoed with a tumult of sound such as could never have been heard in Caer Sidi in all the dark centuries of its being. Wildly, not bitterly but with a fierce joy, Rhodri was laughing.

"In my pocket!" he cried in laughter-broken breaths. "Put it in yesterday and forgot all about it! Treasures of Gwynnedd, in my pocket!"

"What?" asked Linette, straightening, escaping a little farther from the deadening malice of Morgause.

"It's the Water of Vision."

He opened the box; she could see the light welling out through the silk and the wool, dazzling even thus after the long darkness. He undid the wrappings; and the crystal shone strongly in his hand, making a red-gold translucence through his fingers. The white star-like radiance filled the rock chamber, even to the smooth ceiling where no opening could be seen.

Despite the disappointment at seeing no way out, Linette felt a kind of irrational joy. Strength seemed to pour into her from a source stronger than Morgause; the rush of the furious queen seemed no more terrible than a sharp draft in a winter doorway. Rhodri, too, putting the box back in his pocket, looked somehow happy, erect and taut as if for action.

But suddenly Linette was aware, with the sharpened senses of her soul, that something else was moving in Caer Sidi. Stirred from long sleep by the presence of the crystal, it was rushing upon them like a blackness filled with vast wings, conscious and full of a dreadful intelligence, servant of an evil older and stronger than Morgause. She felt the living rock shudder beneath her as in an earthquake.

Rhodri, feeling the shudder, guessed it too; his face was shadowed for an instant, then grew set with a hard incandescent intensity. He held the crystal high; it blazed out with a fierce white brilliance. Linette saw his face like lightning in the white blaze, as if he would will the walls down. "Powers of light that made this crystal," he shouted in a voice that seemed to mix now with a roaring in her ears, "put your strength in it to help us! Dark power, in the name of the powers of light, hold us no longer!"

His face for a moment seemed to twist, the lines of it to deepen like crevices before the blast of a scorching wind. Then, with a crash like the rending of lightning close at hand, one of the stone walls was torn with a wide crack from roof to floor. A dull red light beat through the crack and mixed with the white light of the crystal.

Heat as from an oven welled into the cold chamber. Linette felt revived by it, cheered, whatever might be in the place beyond. But Rhodri, looking at the light, shut his teeth like the jaw of a horse closing on the bit. It was not so easy as that to escape from Caer Sidi.

Linette had approached the crack and stood looking out; coming behind her, he saw her face turn toward his, masklike in the red glare.

"It's no good," she said. "Look."

He looked, the heat from the crack beating against his forehead and eyes as if he bent over a furnace. On the other side of the crack a long cavern ran, like a hall intersecting their path; opposite the crack a narrow rock passage plunged into darkness. But between, from edge to edge of the long cavern, lighting the jagged roof with its upcast glare, flowed a red river of molten rock. Rhodri felt his face parch in the savage heat; the very air was painful to breathe.

Linette stared blindly across the burning, into the black tunnel on the other side. She felt the second sight move in her mind, like walls dropping before her interior gaze. Traced against the dark, a golden incandescence brighter than the lava, burned the shape of an uplifted sword. Threads of fire ran up and down the blade and stood out like thin tongues, as on the sword in the Justice window of Providence chapel, not cruciform as Morgan had once seen it at Glastonbury, but militant and triumphant, like the blade of Michael the Defender, upholder of all justices. Her mind seemed hesitating on the brink of some insupportable knowledge. Then without time for fading it was gone, and only the red glow of the lava cut across the darkness.

"Rhodri," she said, "I saw Excalibur. A fiery golden thing, like what Mary Myers saw."

"I hope so," he said. "But we have to get out of here." He believed her, but the knowledge did not register; his mind was filled with the present necessity, and with a sickening fear.

"But now?" said Linette, staring into the furnace-red cavern. Her eyes were dark in the glare that beat against her face, and to him all expression seemed to be parched away from it by the knowledge of necessity. He felt time growing short for them—the red lava before, and dark undying powers massing and closing in behind.

"I read once," he said in a voice that seemed to him incredibly slow, half-articulate, "about an eruption of Vesuvius. A man was cut off from his companions; but he had on heavy boots, he ran right across the lava and got safe to the other side." He stretched out his arms toward her. "I'll carry you."

She strung the crown over her arm, obeying blindly like one hypnotized, and took the crystal. He picked her up, and she clung around his neck with a dizzy sense of displaced gravity. He had not realized how heavy she was, because of her height; almost mechanically he prayed, Don't let me drop her. Then, sick with dread, he stepped out through the crack onto the molten rock.

Linette, her eyes closed, felt the heat smite against her like the burning glow of an oven. Rhodri's body shrank together with a shudder of pain; she opened her eyes and saw his face shadowed and distorted, the sweat standing out on his forehead and running down in streams. His hands tightened on her so hard that it hurt; she said nothing, only clung to him and willed not to be heavy. His eyes looked blindly over her, fixed on the black blot of the passage and on the molten rock. The burden of Linette slowed him; the heat scorched through his shoes, the lava shifting under the weight like sand. Pain and the dread of falling filled his mind like the bite of fire, blotting out memory, searing so that all his life was concentrated in the consciousness of burning. Then suddenly the cool dark was before him, and he stumbled into it and blindly put Linette down.

He sank to the floor, shaking with sudden cold, his mind assailed with wings of darkness. His fingers went down to his scorched feet; the soles of his shoes were burnt almost through.

With a noise like the crashing together of mountains, the crack closed. He did not know whether they were out of the Otherworld or not, but they were out of Caer Sidi.

12. The End of the Quests

There was dark, and a cool wetness around his face; and his hand seemed to be closed on a palmful of fire.

What was it? A cavern; a gold ring still hot from the dragon's inward fires. No; his mind struggled dimly toward consciousness; he had dreamed or read that. Confused images came—Linette's face under the blazing jewels of a crown; dark clouds heaped over the bay; sunlight, a roadside, faces; a bronze-helmed head and the glimpsed downflash of a sword.

The wetness came again around his face; he moved, opened his eyes, and raised his head.

He was looking out to sea; the strong moonlight shone clear and desolate over the dark-grey water. Before him, at the edge of the sand, heaps of seaweed were piled, and a small wrack of driftwood, black against the pallor of the sand. The water washed forward around his hands and drew softly back. The cold light glinted, a little way off, on a peaked goldish shape already islanded by the tide.

It was Morandir's helmet. All the threads of memory came together in a pattern—Linette, the quest, the hedged place, the battle. He stared at the helmet for a long moment. It was all real: the helmet, the pain in his hand, the quest that had to be finished.

He tried to get up, but he was still too dazed and fell back onto his hands and knees. Something hard shifted under his hand; he saw it was the knife, which lay where it had fallen. He let it lie for a minute and held up his left hand in the moonlight.

It was dark with blood. He washed it in the next wave, with a renewal of the sharp, stinging pain. A long gash scored across the palm and between thumb and forefinger; fresh blood came in it while he looked, so he could not have been unconscious long.

He bandaged it awkwardly with his handkerchief, then cleaned his knife in the wet sand, dried it on his shirt, and put it away. For a little while longer he sat still, gathering strength. The moon shone down, cold and bright; he thought vaguely of Malory, of the moon shinning clear over Carbonek Castle when Lancelot came there, Carbonek by the sea, where Lancelot saw the Grail in a little room. But when he would have approached it, there came a breath intermeddled with a hurtless fire, which struck him so that he fell down like a dead man: and it was left to others fully to achieve the quest.

The quest, Anthony thought with renewed urgency. The night air had cleared his head now; he listened to see if his watch was running, looked at it, saw that it was a little past eight. Slowly he rose, still feeling unsteady and a little sick, and walked to the river's edge, glad that the tide had covered whatever was left of Morandir. He stood at the river mouth, on the pale moonlit strand between the dark marsh and the lead-silver sea. The moon shone strongly, paying no more heed to him than to all the other solitary men who had ever lifted their eyes to its brightness. The measureless immensities seemed to lay hold of him as he gazed; he thought of the unimaginable cold vastnesses beyond the sun, the galaxies spinning outward beyond gaze of eye or lens, every infinitesimal spark of them a sun from which Sol was a bright pinpoint and the circling orb of Tellus an invisible grain of dust beside it, and himself an unthinkably small particle on that grain, swallowed up in the huge, thoughtless glory of the heavens.

He turned his gaze from the stars to the dark river before him. There was nothing else to do; he fastened his shoes to his belt, waded in, lost the bottom, and struck out across the black width. The water was deadly cold, taking his breath away. He was in midstream now, in the salt upriver current of the tide. But the cold and the weight of his clothes seemed to clog his movements, and he felt himself tiring. His hand hurt, as if cold sharp metal had again been dragged through it. And the bank seemed to get no nearer. I should have rested longer, he thought. His strokes were getting shorter; he could feel his legs sinking into the deeper, colder levels, pulling him down. A desperate fear of drowning seized him. Wildly he thrashed forward and with his last strength seized the roots of the marsh grass on the far bank, and clung there, panting.

When he had got his breath, he crawled out onto the beach and sat there, shivering in the cold moonlight, like a mariner wrecked on a desolate and unfriendly shore. July though it was, a chill wind blew off the marsh and through his dank clothes. His hand seemed to grow hot and cold with pain; and that and the loss of blood and utter exhaustion weighed down on him, so that to move was an immense effort. An overpowering desire for sleep came on him; he could have lain down on the sand, despite the cold and the pain, and not stirred any more than one of the dead, drifted trees that lay white above the tideline.

But after a minute, he pulled himself heavily up, tried to brush off some of the coarse, clinging sand, and trudged northward. The wind off the marsh bent down the reeds and made him shiver; but it cleared his head, so that after a few minutes he began to walk faster. Now his earlier headache, from hunger and the daytime glare, returned in force; it ached behind his eyes like a heavy weight on the eyeballs, so that he felt sick and isolated from the cold dark-and-light shore on which he walked. As time wore on it grew worse, tightened like a burning cord around his brain, till even his shadow trailing black across the sand seemed distorted, grotesque, and strange.

Lights showed faint and far at Deer River Point, a bleak glimmer like lost fireflies. Other lights, colder and more alien, glowed up from the floor of the marsh; at the sight of them a chill, irrational dread rose in him, primitive and compelling as that of benighted hunters in forests aeons gone. His head and hand seemed to burn with an unconsuming fire; but a fixed, emotionless perseverance kept his feet moving on.

After a while the marsh ended and tall woods loomed again on his left, black and somber under the moon. An elder tree leaned out across the shore, its ghostly blossoms mixed with a few tufts of unripe berries. Anthony's hunger stirred at the sight of them, and he wondered whether eating would stop the pain in his head. A half-remembered literary allusion stirred in his mind—wasn't the elder one of the sacred trees of ancient Britain, a witch-tree and a tree of death, the garland of Blodeuwedd and the wand of Cerridwen? That memory of ill luck might underlie his grandmother's saying that eaters of elderberries would always be poor. But surely the British elder was a different variety; there was no need for this haunting sense of unease.

The berries proved sour, setting his teeth on edge; but he was too hungry to stop till he had eaten a large handful. Well, he thought, compared with green elderberries even bread was a luxury.

He went on past Deer River Point, staying far from the lights to avoid meeting anyone. A new stretch of coast spread before him, less desolate, the last long sweep between himself and Dog River. A few lights glimmered among the trees, but they only increased his sense of solitude. The headache had lessened a little, and with it the feeling of nausea; but his arm as high as the elbow seemed a bar of fire. He held his hand against his damp shirt, but felt no change except the burning heat of it against his body; he began to wonder a little if Morandir's blade had been poisoned.

The scattered points of light shone half-obscured, remote, indifferent as the fiery constellations that wheeled above him. It was nearly ten now; the people in those houses would be asleep or getting ready for sleep, or maybe sitting up late to play cards or read paperbound detective novels. They knew nothing about him and would have looked at him fearfully and with rejection if he had appeared in the light, with his torn clothes and cut forehead and handkerchief-bandaged hand. There must be plenty of dirt to complete the picture, he thought; and by now the bruises on his face must have turned blue. He knew how those people would look quickly away, pretend not to see him. And yet, he thought soberly, if I fail, they might all be dead before morning.

It was a solemn and terrible thought. He straightened, as if to adjust a weight on his shoulders, and looked up gravely and evenly at the sky. The moon made a great pool of radiance; around it the summer constellations burned in their never-ending processions.

I never expected this, he said. Here am I, a scholar, a medievalist, in a situation that men of action might hesitate at. I wanted to undertake the Grail quest, but I never thought I would get this far or that it would be like this. What is the quest of the Grail?

He stood shivering, suddenly cold, his mind trembling on the edge of an answer. Bodb, Morandir—part of a pattern—what pattern? He almost knew, almost could guess at the missing pieces. But the stretch of the mind was too far; the perception broke and fell away and left him standing empty-minded in the moonlight.

As he collected his thoughts, he was startled by a movement on the shore. It was close though not quite, just this side of a clump of trees some way ahead. A large black mass hesitated in the uncertain moonlight, then moved slowly and unwaveringly toward him. He stood still; perhaps it would pass him by. He saw now that it was some kind of beast, dark as its long shadow that stretched across the sand. Fear curled and twisted inside him; it was some unearthly thing, some creature of the Otherworld which had been sent for him. But then there was no use waiting for it; in a blind boldness of nightmare he strode forward.

The creature hesitated as if startled by his approach; and as he came nearer, he could have laughed. After all it was only a horse—a black horse, quite earthly, and one which seemed to him slightly familiar. He reached it; and it stood still, looking at him steadily.

"Solario?" he said experimentally, putting up his good hand to touch its mane. The horse gazed at him with dark, frightened eyes; he saw now that its ears were laid slightly back and that it trembled a little. But he was sure it was Julian's horse, though he could not imagine what had frightened it or what it was doing loose on this side of the river.

"Good fellow," he said, stroking its neck, "good fellow," and wondered disquietingly what had happened at Silverthorne.

As he talked to the horse and quietly stroked it, its ears straightened and the wild look went out of its eyes. It seemed glad to see him after its wanderings through unknown country in the desolate moonlight; and after a few minutes it let him gently turn it around the way it had come. He coaxed it close to some driftwood to give himself a mounting block, grasped its mane—with some difficulty because of his bad hand—and climbed on. In the absence of a bridle, he did not know how to guide it; so he nudged it gently with his heels and let it make its own way northward.

Solario, sensing home in that direction and no longer troubled by Morgan's bewitchment, set off at a good walk along the hard sand by the water's edge. Anthony, once he got used to staying on without a saddle, relaxed a little as he rode. His hand still hurt, and his headache was not entirely gone; but not to be walking was a relief, and he looked quietly at the dark trees and the rare glimmer of houses and the untroubled stars. Again an overwhelming sleepiness came on him. He sat motionless, still aware of the horse's head and the lapping of the waves, of the chiaroscuro of moonlight and shadow, of the steady motion beneath him and the pain of his hand. But all these things seemed remote, as in a waking dream; and strange images seemed to move between him and them—wastelands full of ruins, a barbaric stone Ozymandias that looked up through the choking vines with live eyes, Linette crowned and dead in a roofless ruin of columns. And steadily the moon-washed scene and the movement receded from him and were present only in dim glimpses, seen like a clouded moon breaking out barely from the sinister interweavings of dark dream.

Then suddenly he was wide awake and cold, in a place that should have been the forested river point but had gone terrible as a wood in hell. The moonlight was shut out by the close branches of old trees, their leaves black like decayed leaf mold in damp woods. There was a faint pallor ahead where the trees ended by the river mouth, but around him the shadowy trunks closed in like subterranean pillars. A formless horror brooded under their dark arches, oppressive, choking like a wet miasma. Solario stood still, his ears laid flat back, his hide twitching and shivering. The chill of winter hung in the air, moving with a slow, frosty stir; Anthony felt it pierce him to the bone. A sense of extreme evil oppressed him, as if some power to which his previous enemies were as children waited, watching, in that freezing silence. Thoughts of cold and deadly things crept through his mind, as if from a source outside him—quicksands and tangled swamps where feverish phosphorescence rose from decay; human faces blasted with madness and hideous disease, and with corruption within new graves; vast wastes of broken stone that were once a city, now utterly poisoned and dead, the very river a channel of grey dust; venomous great serpents like fireless dragons, crawling over the ice of dead worlds; the last utter desolation and horror of the frozen abyss.

An extreme horror of that wood filled him; the air seemed ready to choke him, the trees to close in on him so that he could never escape. He kicked the horse's sides, but it would not move; it trembled and shivered as if with fever, and turned its head to look at him with mad, staring eyes. He bent low over its neck, stroked it, spoke to it; but his own hands were shaking, his palms wet with a cold sweat. At last, shuddering and straining back, the horse began to move. Anthony could see the river now glinting dark beyond the trees; the terror enfolded it too, turning it to the glacier-cold river that at nightfall cut suddenly across men's path. All other rivers, broad, cold, or deep, were small matters beside it; this was the true Acheron, that river of woe, that sunless tide icy with the bitterness of death. The dread of that water pierced him like cold swords; there was no fierce joy of battle to warm the iciness of that crossing.

He could see the bridge now, white as ice in the cold moonlight; it too was terrible to him, an austere span that seemed to glimmer with a beautiful and fearful light. The cold had become more piercing, and the sense of evil was so strong that he could hardly breathe.

Suddenly Solario gave a high scream and shied violently. Anthony, clutching at the mane to stay on, saw over the horse's head a shape towering, lit up with a grey, unnatural light. He was aware in an instant's glance of a cloak like darkness and the cold sheen of steel mail. But his eyes were drawn to the face and could not leave it. A helm glittered icelike in the bitter, clinging light; under it the features were stern, perfect, and still, and the freezing eyes pierced him with a terrible brightness. A power went out from them and fixed upon Anthony, holding him like the steel so that he could not move; their gaze impaled him like thin daggers, pinning him to the rock of the grey desolate edge of the universe, while the unruled winds of chaos blew freezing around him.

He said in a dry, unreal voice, "Who are you?" But no words came in answer; only then he understood, transfixed by that bitter gaze, that he was before inexorable Angoré, Lord of Ruin, in whose breath all things withered, who had struck cities and empires into dust.

"What do you want?" he cried in an almost soundless voice, and then, remembering in a flash the old counterspell, rapidly traced the sign of the cross.

The Ruiner did not shudder at the holy sign; only the wood seemed to darken, and the grey eyes pierced Anthony like a sharp stab of pain. The knowledge came upon him under that gaze, that this was the greatest of the Otherworld lords who turned to darkness, as Lucifer was greatest among the angels.

And slowly, as though a grey mist came rolling around him, he felt himself cut off from the living world, adrift in a chill void where there was neither sky nor ground. Angoré seemed to be left behind; he was alone in a sea of cloud, that was cold and vague and faintly sad. Or not faintly; he felt an undertone to it, like the sound of the ocean, a desolation so ancient and profound that it could find no voice but a silent movement of air; and yet the whole gently swirling ocean of mist was full of that lament.

Then the cloud withdrew into a windy grey sky above him. He stood now on a vast grassy plain that stretched unbroken behind him and on either side, but before him a low ridge rose sharply against the sky. Upon him rushed a longing he had known many times before, a painful desire that did not know what it wanted but was keener than all other things of the earth. It seemed to drive him toward the ridge; if he climbed that abrupt height, where the wind bent the grass low along its top, he might know at last what it was that he wanted. He climbed, strangely without effort, getting handholds on the tough dark stems of grass. And when he stood on the top, he saw the plain also on the other side of the ridge, on all sides great spaces of windswept grass that stretched away beyond sight into the grey edges of the clouds. There was nothing else, neither tree nor living thing; he stood alone in the wind, between earth and sky.

Something compelled him to look down into the grass at his feet. A small red fruit like a crabapple lay there. He knelt and picked it up to examine it; and as it lay in his hand, a knowledge came to him that he should make a hollow under the grass and bury it. He obeyed without knowing why, and remained motionless, looking at the place. A green shoot appeared above the grass roots and grew before his eyes into a small dark tree. Leaves unfolded on it, then white flowers like those of dogwood. Anthony rose and watched it; the petals fell, and in every flower-place swelled out small red fruit like the one he had planted. No more surprised than in a dream, he plucked one and smelled it; it had a sharp, sweet scent that seemed one with the grey sky and the windswept expanses of grass that reached to the clouds. It woke in him the same piercing desire; but now with the scent everything grew keen and clear around him, and he seemed to see every blade of grass solid and sharp-edged like a sword. He looked down; and the grass and earth and rock under his feet seemed to become transparent like water, and he saw as down a shaft into a place under the ridge where a king of forgotten ages lay in white bones amid his gold, with his bronze sword beside him and a circlet of wrought gold around his skull. And Anthony understood as he looked that if he ate this fruit he would know all the things he had ever desired to know, the histories of forgotten peoples and the causes of the rise and decline of kingdoms and nations, the thoughts and motives of men, all possible patterns of the universe and how the actual might have been different by the changing of some minute thing, the pattern too of all that would happen till the end of time. Nothing would be hidden from him; he could read men's deepest secrets, he could look into the uttermost mysteries of the hierarchies of being, intelligences more than human clothed in terrible power; and by his knowledge he would be master of all. This knowledge seemed to blaze whitely before his mind, the discovered object of that sharp desire; he thirsted for it as for clear water in a desert. He looked at the apple, and with closed eyes nipped it slightly, piercing the peel. The taste came into his mouth, sharp and sweet like the smell; and with it came a cold, bright comprehension like a draught of icy springs. He remembered the quest. And at the same moment he understood with a shadowless clarity that if he ate the fruit, he would know how to command wind and water and fire, to cure all diseases, to make the earth fruitful and impose justice on all mankind; but that he would never see the Grail.

His mind hung poised, drawn in one direction and in the other. Surely he ought to choose this knowledge and be the benefactor of mankind. Surely there was another way of stopping Morgause, even if he himself never finished the quest. He would have no chance of coming back here after the quest was over; surely an opportunity in the hand was worth more than a vision he might never see. It seemed hard to be tempted with good instead of evil; but, in fact, which was the temptation?

He looked at the apple; its sweet scent rose to his nostrils, and the desire became almost more than he could bear. Suppose, then, that nobody stopped Morgause. Think like a philosopher: surely the sacrifice of one city was not too high a price for such far-reaching benefits to mankind. He put his mouth to the fruit, tasting it through the place he had bitten before. And with the taste came the certainty that outside the quest there was no way to stop Morgause. His mind hardened against the thought; what was one city, balanced against all mankind? Three hundred thousand people at most, counting the outlying areas; suppose they did all die. What was that compared with all the billions in the world, with all the billions yet to be born?

Then another thought cut like sustained lightning through his mind, scattering the chaos of numbers. He had been contemplating the death of three hundred thousand people. Suppose tomorrow it were three million, six million, a hundred million. He was not strong enough for limitless knowledge; it would wither him, it was withering him already. If three hundred thousand people were nothing to him, three hundred billion would be nothing. He would not use such knowledge to benefit the world; the best he could hope was to be utterly possessed by it, lost in it so that he would have no strength to act, burnt up by the sight of too much strangeness and power. But it was also likely that he would not be, that the hunger for ever more knowledge would consume him, driving him to who knew what evil, even to the destruction of the earth.

But now the desire had seized on him, ravenous as eagles. How could he live, knowing he had refused this knowledge? Bodb and Morandir had been strengthless compared to this; his mind swayed in indecision like an agonized flame. Slowly, very slowly, he willed his hand to move away from his mouth; he could see the apple, and stared hard at it as if he could not look away. In another moment, if he lingered, he would not be able to stop himself from biting it. With a wrench as if he were pulling the life out of his body, he hurled it away out of sight, out of reach, off the ridge into the plains of windswept grass.

And then suddenly he was again in the dark wood, mounted on Solario, and transfixed with a cold gaze of hate and rage. Angoré had gambled, that Anthony might see his deed clearly and be utterly lost. His throw had failed, but he was not conquered.

Anthony felt his eyes caught and held. He was looking into silver depths of ice, bitter-cold, almost translucent, like chasms of glaciers irradiated by a dim, colorless light. They seemed to receive him into the company of the lost. He had tasted the fatal fruit; he had thrown away for it his hope of saving his people, his hope of Linette, his hope of seeing the Grail. And as he thought this, the joy of that nameless desire brushed past him once more very faintly as if leaving him forever; and he knew that it was not for the apple's secrets but for the vision of the Grail. It floated upward from him with the terrible poignancy of a yellow-winged butterfly rising in the sunlight; but it was not rising, he was sinking, falling, through a dark void, watching the light of heaven and earth diminish to a point like the point of a pin. A furious regret and storm of memory tore him. Linette walking in the sunlight, his parents, Julian—all lost to him, all poised like figures in a photograph, motionless, about to be swallowed up in one wave of fire—grass, trees,

Silverthorne, home, pashed and burning, nothing left after, miles of scarred desolation and poisoned stone. And he had not even gotten the knowledge for which he had destroyed them. Why was he still alive; why live so long?

He did not know how the hunting knife had gotten into his hand. He could see it in that void by some preternatural light that seemed to come from the blade. He could hardly look at it; the brightness hurt his eyes. But it was the same color as that point of light infinite distances away. If it was kin to that light, why not die by it as some of that light had died by him? The throat was easier than the heart. His fingers found the vein; and now the point pricked against it, cold and sharp and hard.

He looked down at the knife to be sure of a good hold and aim. The light smote his eyes, bright and cold-seeming like lightning. It seemed to pierce into his mind; and something in the shape of the knife reminded him vaguely of something. What was that shape? At Silverthorne; the moonlight was shining on it; it was like bright silver, but the angle was different, upright. He seemed to be looking at it through someone else's eyes; and now he knew it was the delicate metal cross on Julian's altar.

With that, he pulled his mind together and it became abruptly clear. The spell shattered. He was in the wood, looking not into Angoré's eyes but at the real knife bare and moonlit in his hand. His heart seemed to rise in a sudden, irrational joy.

"Liar!" he shouted at Angoré. "I didn't eat your apple; and if I had, I could still have come back!"

He kicked his heels against the horse's sides. Solario, long past caring what he did, broke blindly forward as if he would ram Angoré down. Anthony ducked forward instinctively, expecting an impact like falling mountains. But at the last second the Ruiner was gone, like a flick of lightning; horse and rider shot through a sudden bitter cold as at the heart of an iceberg, trees fell suddenly away around them, hoofs clattered on the paved road. Under the glitter of its lights, the span of the bridge arched white before them.

Without slackening speed, they sped onto the bridge. The joy sang wild and unearthly in Anthony's veins; the wind rushing past his face, the white pour of moonlight, made it seem as if horse and man were swimming in air and moonlight as in a calm sea. There seemed to be music somewhere, behind, around, above him, just behind the edge of hearing—a faint rumor of music, too delicate to be heard with the ears, bell-like and crystalline as if the stars sang. This, he thought with a surprised, awed sense of revelation, is what the old poets meant by the music of the spheres.

They reached the crown of the bridge; and suddenly, as at the riverside with Morandir, Anthony saw incredible distances open out before him, visible miles in which everything stood out distinct as an architectural rendering. But it was not starry Eldis that glittered there, enforested, like crystal and pearl and moonlight. Spires, roofs, trees, squares—surely he knew some of them? And some he seemed to know but they no longer existed—that fantastic turret like a rose topaz had surely toppled last year for a parking lot? And those double towers away to the west, delicate-colored on the heights, between which a vast window blazed with the image of a woman golden-haired, red-gowned, cloaked in blue? There was no such building, never had been. And why was everything transfigured like this, all jewels and light and trees which by their color seemed to be undying? Other lights moved in it like planets against the fixed background of the heavens, converging on the basilica—if it was the basilica, for it seemed clung about with a light bright as flame, white and thin as moonlight, dazzling but not hurting the eyes. Around it, centered on it, that city existed splendor within splendor, drawn around it as if in the patterns of a dance; and that crystalline unheard music shaped the dance into secret harmonies that seemed to reflect the pattern of the stars. For one moment Anthony knew that he looked at Belmary the eternal, such of it as his human thought could grasp, complete and perfect as in the mind of God.

And then all was gone, as the horse plunged down the curve of the bridge. For a split instant Anthony had looked straight across the barriers of time at an image of completion. But now, cast back into the urgent present, he knew with a vivid, unexplainable certainty where he had to go. The basilica, tonight, would be the Chapel of the Grail.

Solario's hoofs clattered onto the black, white-lit road that plunged north into the city. But the moment of vision had left Anthony's gaze changed, sharpened; he could see through the common aspect of street, lights, and trees as through a thin haze, into the secret vitality of their existence in Belmary. The oaks and pines of Silverthorne loomed on his right, dark against the stars, intensely alive as if the power of the earth heaved them up like mountains and sang in them like the green sap of spring. Their reality dazzled him like a dark fire. The gate of Silverthorne stood out among them, glinting in the light like dull silver; the strength of the metal, the firm grace of the curves like frozen waves, astonished him and filled him with satisfaction like a great work of art. And then another blindness seemed to lift from his eyes. Out of the woods' edge came four lions and a white stag; a light, faint gold and intense white, clung around them and seemed brightest around the horns of the stag. With a slow and royal pace they came by him and passed through the gate into Silverthorne; and all the while, the gate was fast closed.

Solario tossed his head and broke into a gallop, racing through light and dark, between trees and open land and shadowed houses. It was late; the road, deserted, ran black and strange and exhilarating under the white light. As he passed Brookley, where the air base had been, Anthony looked toward it. And he saw for an instant, before the vision was lost behind the trees, the towering shape of Alandriel, the angel of the city, his ring-mail gleaming bright and cold like starlight, his spear in his hand, looming above the deserted airfield like an image of silver.

The night wind rushed past Anthony's face. A few cars passed now, their headlights piercing the dark; faces turned toward Anthony but were instantly whirled away. He noticed them with keen delight, as if he had never seen anything like them before. Then he was alone again in the wind, under the brilliant white stars, conscious of Solario's strong speed and of his own life like fire in his veins. He no longer felt hunger, pain, or exhaustion; there was only a blazing joy in existence itself, in conscious strength and the headlong following of the quest.

Lights glittered suddenly around him like festival fireworks; the road concluded in a sweep of town brilliant and deserted. Without thought he pressed his hand on Solario's neck and turned him unpausing into Government Street, which shot straight to the center of the city. The realization broke on him like the blaze of Roman candles: the horse had obeyed him. It was a startling glory, beautiful and awesome. The memory came, like the unshuttering of a window, that he had seen Julian use the same gesture; but this dominion, whoever exercised it, seemed preternatural and dazzling like a miracle.

The white columns of the memorial park gleamed suddenly on his left, pillars and lintel rising out of dark gardens over a dim, smooth pool. As he looked toward them, he saw on the lintel a nest of gold-silver straw, and in it a large white bird like the pelicans on the fountains of Spring Hill. Small birds of the same kind clustered around it, so thin that the silver light that clung about the nest seemed to shine through them; their beaks moved, as if they cheeped faintly with hunger, but he could hear no sound. And the large bird struck its chest with its beak, which was long and sharp, as if it would feed its starving young with its blood. The next instant the sight was lost behind oak branches, as Solario sped onward between the vast trees; but it seemed still to glimmer before Anthony's mind, with an aura of solemn significance he could not read. Of course it was a common symbol; the fountains of Spring Hill commemorated it. Like the white stag, it was in medieval literature; it was in Malory. But it conveyed to him a sense of imminence, of urgency; not timelessly but now, something was happening which he did not understand.

The dim houses and moonlit trees flowed past like water. Anthony, gazing down the wide night-emptied street, began presently to think something white was moving among the trees, at the same speed as Solario, keeping always some distance ahead. It gleamed in the moonlight, now hidden by the massive dark trunks, now running clear in a shaft of radiance. He saw now that it was like a horse, slender-legged and swift, its mane and tail streaming out brighter than silver. Then he saw with a shock of wonder something else: between its ears grew a thin, long dark-blue horn that gleamed like lapis lazuli in the moonlight. Wind-swift, solitary, and untameable, a unicorn was running there under the dark trees; and even in the shadows it sped with a faint moonlit shining.

The trees became scattered now along the silent emptiness of the street. The unicorn ran ahead in the moonlight, wild and beautiful as a star, its hoofs making no noise on the pavement. Suddenly it shot away into a side street; and Anthony, turning Solario after it, saw the basilica towers rising tall and noble against the dark-blue sky. The unicorn sprang in through the ironwork gates of the basilica close, and seemed lost to sight behind the shadowed mass of the building.

Anthony slowed Solario outside the gates and looked up at the basilica, its vast eastern portico washed silver with the clear moonlight. The worn steps, the massive towers, the gleaming stone filled him with an awed stillness. This was the place, the end of his quest. Slowly he dismounted and led Solario between the heavy gates of the close.

Julian leaned sideways in her chair, her hands clenched tight on the arm, her eyes closed. Her mind seemed to be falling headlong into an interior darkness. How could Morgan do what, before Julian's appalled and unbelieving gaze, she had just done?

But she did do it, thought Julian firmly; I am not mad. She opened her eyes. The candles burning on the table dazzled before her; but they shone on the scattered translation of the *Llyfr*, on the familiar Chaucer open at the Knight's Tale, on the abandoned and half-buried papers of the *Edda*. She glanced toward the door; it was still shut.

Impossible, she thought; but quite real. Through the window she could see a glimmer of green light in the Atlantis Tower; Morgan had gone back there. And she would certainly have locked herself in; she could not be stopped from whatever she was doing now.

Once again Julian's mind accepted the realities of the situation.

Morgan at this moment was calling dark forces to her aid. The moon stared through the eastern windows, white and unmasked; but the air of Silverthorne was charged as before a thunderstorm. Julian felt that she could hardly breathe. I am imagining it, she thought; it is not the presence of evil which is stifling me.

An inertness seemed to lie on her; she did not want to move. It would be good to sleep. The carved chair did not seem hard; the candlelight weighed on her eyelids. What could she do after all, now that Morgan was locked in, and in this heavy air full of undischarged lightning. . . .

She straightened with a start. For a second she had been asleep; the dropping forward of her head had wakened her. No, she must not sleep; and she must not stay in this library with its crowded, unbreatheable air. She must at least get up and move around.

She went down to the kitchen; Aramelissa was not there, though the lamp on the table was burning and Aramelissa's Bible lay open in its amber radiance. A sense of urgency filled Julian. She made some coffee rapidly and swallowed it black; it was hot and she felt it burn in her throat. Her mind came fully awake, and she knew more clearly what she meant to do. In a moment she went purposefully up to the round room in the top of the tower.

Emerging into it, she stood motionless in a pallor of light. The moon coming through the saffron-colored glass laid a goldish cast on the white stone of floor and wall and altar, and on Julian's hands and face; her purple dress looked black in it. There was no other color but the red spark of the sanctuary lamp, no sound but her breathing and the distant movement of the tide.

For a second she thought of other times here, Masses before the churches were built, the smell of baked grass in the summer, the chill of the winter stones. The people that used to come then, faces of twenty and thirty years ago—the old were dead now, the younger changed or gone.

Only you are unchanged, she said, looking at the tabernacle. Only you, in all this tide of years.

A deep peace reached out to her; she drew a long breath and opened the windows. The amber stone was washed white. Across the court, in the Atlantis Tower, there was a greenish glow.

Julian sat down on the low step that made a platform for the altar. Turned toward it, she could see over the altar to the glinting dull-gold of the tabernacle in the wall behind. The delicate metal cross on the altar cut across her gaze; its back was to her, so that she saw only the smooth surface washed pale-gold by the moonlight and shadowily intersected by the lines of the figure's arms.

It is twenty-six years now, she said. Suppose it all fails and we die tonight: yet I have been happy. I thank you, Lord, for my life.

Images of it passed through her mind like a scattering of pictures: a child Julian sitting in sunlit grass with others whose faces she had forgotten; herself older, on the steps of the school at recess, reading astronomy and mythology and the *Golden Legend*; the face of Christopher Marion, seen first backstage at the convent high school after she had played St. Catherine of Alexandria; that same face in a bleak dawn still terrible to the memory, herself trying crazily to wipe the water from it long after the artificial respiration had been stopped.

That was the worst grief I have ever had, she said. I thought he had drowned himself because we quarreled. And yet, if I had married him, I would not have been satisfied.

And so I returned to you, she said—to my old love again, as Malory would put it. But no, I had not loved you before as I did then. And I can hardly believe how little and how shallow my love was even then. And now after twenty-six years it is still not enough.

But her mind had gone to Anthony, whose mother was Christopher's sister. I have no children, she said suddenly. And yet—are you not more to me than many sons?

Anthony, she thought, leaning her head against the cool, carved marble of the altar front. She saw him before her mind, small-seeming on the vast dark land, his shoulders bent under an invisible weight—an Atlas-like figure, carrying the earth or the heavens.

The dark land around him became real to her—the city falling asleep in its security in the July night, trees hanging their boughs like shadows around the houses, lights turned off, heads alone or in couples above white sheets. Children, eyes shut, curled themselves around loved toys; long-married couples slept peacefully side by side, vulnerable and trusting; lovers in their ecstasy clung to one another, their faces full of effort and passion; near the waterfront, sailors and their women tried to stifle loneliness in a different kind of loneliness. And over them hung this: to die, not sometime but between now and morning, scorched out of life by a blast of withering fire. And with them would go the familiar streets, balconies, church bells, pots of fern, a certain cast of light around old walls and trees, a certain look of the sky. It had happened before, sudden destruction falling on Knossos, Pompeii, Lisbon, Saint-Pierre.

Julian raised her head and looked out at the moonwashed shape of the Atlantis Tower. It was hard to imagine that Morgan realized all this; but she had lived so long, had seen so much death and so much devastation of nations and kingdoms. That might have broken something in her: what could a few lives mean to her now?

She fixed her eyes once more on the slender bronze doors of the tabernacle, with the metal cross intersecting her gaze. I saw her, she said; I was looking directly at her and she was gone. Something is loose here which shouldn't be, and I have no choice but to believe in the danger. What are you going to do about it?

No words answered her, but calm once again invaded her soul and she drew a long breath. While I have you, she said, nothing can harm me, not even death. My Lord are you; apart from you I have no good.

But, she said, there are those others. What should be done for them? What would you have me do?

There was a charged silence. Julian saw nothing but the wash of moonlight on the bronze doors, but there was a sense of the meeting of eyes; her own were caught and held more intently than ever by Morgan's. Her being seemed suspended in that gaze, drawn out of her towards the doors. For a moment her mind hung utterly still, forming no words, seeming to rest instead on the mind of that other.

Very well, she said in a while; I will take this burden on myself as far as I may. I have belonged to you for a long time; surely you can use me for this.

She rose to her knees, leaning her forehead on the top edge of the altar and holding to the same edge with both hands. And slowly something began to happen in her mind. Her thoughts sank deep, into an image of the world that was submerged far within—a true image, reflecting events that were happening at that moment in the real world. But here there was another dimension; she could see not only visible actions, but other forces which stirred around them like shadows or qualities of light. In a golden firelike radiance Aramelissa sat two floors below, with her Bible open on the table; and Julian could feel the tension in her, the fear, the fatalistic loyalty of love. She could hear in Aramelissa's thoughts the words that she was reading on the page: *But a certain one of then, Caiaphas, being high priest that year, said unto them, Ye know nothing at all, nor do ye take account that it is expedient for you that one man should die for the people.*

What does this mean? said Julian, looking up. Surely not Anthony.

She knelt motionless, the cross and the bronze doors before her eyes; but sight did not disturb the inwardness of her gaze. With the words she became aware of Anthony as he rode half-asleep into the dark wood. She felt his waking and his fear, as if they were her own but removed to a great distance. The dread of the wood crept upon her, oppressive, brooding; she knew, though she could not feel, the unnatural cold. And suddenly Angoré was there, his colorless eyes freezing into Anthony's. She was aware of Anthony's horror, though in her passionless remoteness she felt none. She watched the tree grow and flower on the windy hilltop, saw the fruit and knew the convolutions of the hard choice. The black void opened around him; she saw the knife drawn, and her mind seemed to leap from its detachment and clash suddenly against his. There was a second when she seemed to look with a double vision through his eyes, seeing simultaneously the gleaming knife and the moonlit metal cross before her. Her mind recoiled into solitude; she saw him break forward and the Ruiner vanish and Solario streak toward the bridge.

Then her gaze went beyond Anthony's. She saw towering at the other side of the bridge the armored angels, Alandriel in star-white steel, Mor in bronze that gleamed as with the reflection of firelight; and they strove with one another in mind, Alandriel to show Anthony the way to the Grail, Mor to hurl new barriers in his path. Neither looked at the other; their eyes were fixed on Anthony; but Julian could feel the striving of their power like the tension of heat lightning.

Another dimension seemed to open in Julian's mind; she saw, in remote simultaneous dramas along the shore, Anthony's encounters with Bodb and Morandir. She understood that he was hurt and worn down with battles, and that he had been overwhelmed by Morandir's end. A sense of urgency filled her; he must not be slowed or hindered by any more such; he must ride fast now, fast, for the checkmating of Morgause. The combat of the angels' wills seemed even, suspended; there was no time for it to work itself out, no room to risk Mor's victory.

From a source she well knew, the knowledge came to Julian that she could challenge Mor. She could absorb his force and leave Anthony free for the straight ride to the Grail.

There was no need for decision; it was already made. She abandoned herself to the power that was gathering in her, and with all the strength of it concentrated her mind on Mor. He felt the touch of her thought; she was aware of his attention piercing after her, groping for an instant, then transfixing her as with a sharp, thin spear. It was as if she were pinned to a wall with it, under the glare of a blinding searchlight. His eyes seemed to sear into her, burning coldly and explosively into her mind. Was she going to stand in his way? Very well, let her take the horrors till she broke and let him pass.

His gaze and hers dropped together; she saw Anthony for a split second, horse and man poised in mid-rush at the top of the bridge. Then suddenly she seemed to see through Anthony's eyes. The land spread out before her like a table model of a countryside, every detail small and clear. And it was a ruined land, a terrain out of nightmare—grey, flat earth, covered with a fine dust, grassless, treeless, revealed in long, wavering distances by a reddish light. In the midst of it, lighting the plain with its faintly changing glow, rose a vast irregular wall that seemed made of red-hot iron, crowned with fantastic deformed pinnacles and spires, broken only by a towering gate like the gate of a prison. She could see over it as into a bowl. Smoke hung over it, grey billows from vast fires, sick-green poisonous fumes that trailed serpentlike out of black mill-chimneys. But she could see through the haze the immense ant-heap of the city. Buildings leaned this way and that, jagged, precarious, like the designs of a maddened architect. Against those which seemed to be factories, grey heaps of waste lay like sand; other heaps rose around them like extinct volcanoes. As she looked, she saw that the building was still going on. Tree stumps stood ragged in burned-over earth; vast trunks blazed in the bonfires. Creatures numerous as ants, dark with smoke, grubbed up the stumps and hurled them on the fires. Other shapes hurried to hide the scarred earth under black pavings and structures of iron. And Julian's eyes began now to trace a pattern in those areas of ruin. There, that space to westward where felled trees and wrecked boards were burning—the old Marion place? She looked for Silverthorne; she could find by the shape of the land where it should be, where polluted, nauseous water slid close to the wall; but there was no trace of it, only a vast black grotesquerie of iron. Away off there, one slender column still stood amid the ruins of a smashed house; it rose like a flower stem out of the wreckage and darkness. But the creatures had ropes around it; as she watched, a swarm of them heaved and it fell, and they hacked it into pieces and threw it on the towering flames. With the upflare her gaze seemed to sharpen; she saw that the creatures were not demons as she had first thought, but human or once human. Their faces were wild now, brutalized; they danced grotesquely around the fires, like crabs, yelling in horrible exultation. Then out of some of the mills, into great vats before them, rushed floods of a liquid like yellow-green fire. The hordes hurled themselves to it, drank barbarously and fought in the streets or lay down and coupled by the fires. Others ran off and circled in a ragged, shouting dance around a black tower that stood where the basilica should have been, skystriking, jagged and windowless and strong as adamant; on its topmost pinnacle stood an iron emblem, but she could not tell what its convolutions were.

These are my people, she thought in dull horror. My people. She felt a cry rising within her, but she had no voice to utter it. It isn't real, it isn't real, she said over and over like a spell.

Then it was gone, as Anthony plunged down the slope of the bridge.

No, it was not real; and she remembered for a second Mor's transfixing gaze.

The memory vanished, for she seemed still to look through Anthony's eyes. And nothing she saw gave her any joy. The landscape lay withered around her, its beauty quenched. The familiar bay shone faintly in the moonlight, its waves breaking softly against the shore; but the moonlight seemed stale, a souvenir of shallow loves that had turned to boredom; and the water was dirty and full of dead things, fish heads, rotting seaweed, drowned men. Weariness gripped her, as if she had walked miles and fought battles; her head ached and was light from hunger. As high as the elbow her left arm burned, and yet she felt shivers of cold. Poison, she thought sharply, seeing again for a split second the downstroke of Morandir's sword.

She knew obscurely that this transference was not sent by Mor; then her perception was drawn away to the next seeing.

Anthony rode past Silverthorne. Julian saw her woods towering in the moonlight, dead black against the cold glare. The gate reared sinister, ominous, portal to some decaying palace haunted with shadows. And something stirred, moving among the trees.

Her sight seemed frozen to a kind of slow motion. The thing crawled out into the moonlight, clangorous of wing, its scales glinting blue-black under the cold radiance. More fantastic in shape than any prehistoric saurian, it flowed over the rotting leaves; horny pinnacles rose along its back, and a barbed tail writhed heavily like a dead snake that would not be still. Foul it appeared; a black trail gleamed wetly in its track, and it moved slowly as with an endless unconsuming decay. Its neck was bent, the head hidden in inky shadow, as if it smelled along the ground. Then it reared straight; six cold eyes glinted ice-color, fixed on Julian. Her mind for a second could not take in the confusion: three necks branching out of the trunk, lithe as thick snakes; three heads with different metallic glints, fishbelly-white, grey-red, yellow like sick brass. And each, more dreadful than any fantastic contortion of bone, had an almost human shape. Its eyes, not animal eyes, stared at her; a piercing cold went through her, a sense of nausea. Then with a clash of wings it sprang over Silverthorne gate, and was gone like a smoke. Once more, for a flash, Julian was conscious of the bronze doors, of moonwashed stone, of Aramelissa sitting two floors below. Then before her again spread the lifeless road, asphalt darkly gleaming under the moon.

Anthony raced exultantly past Brookley. Julian saw in the dead moonlight a figure whose helmeted head seemed to strike the sky; its armor burned dull-gold like bronze, a tunic of joined plates like an armadillo's. It held a spear tipped with bronze, dull-gold also; and with the head of this spear it stirred the waters as if writing on the waves. Then Julian's eyes were drawn to the face, which shone with a pale phosphorescence like the whole form of the darkened angel, the cold perfection of the features still marked with the lost grace of heaven. Then, for the second time that night, the freezing eyes turned on her and pierced her as if she were made of glass. For a second she knew how the dark angel scorned her for all failures of heart and nerve, yet took delight in them because they gave him matter for scorn. Then she was gathered in by the power of that gaze. She felt the grief of Mor, the endless hate and despair: nothing was worth prizing in all creation, and nothing worth doing but spoiling the work of the Lord of Time who was blamed for that grief, no pleasure but a bitter joy in making others too taste of the same cup—the Lord of Time too through them, that he too might know it. And she saw now what was traced on the waves with the sharp spear, spells of hate to cause strife in men's minds and the undoing of the city. Gunshot in the streets, the crash of fire, shouting faces—the images rose to her mind like nightmare, the work of Mor, the unmaking of unity. She tasted the bitter exaltation of destruction, like a blind self-wounding pain, the mind's rending of itself; it pierced her heart like numberless knives, an anguish beyond weeping, a madness that sought to destroy itself by destroying all. Then, with a shock of recoil and separateness, she felt a horrified pity for Mor—why did he exist, in that anguish? The vision dissolved; once more she saw the road before her, and the city dead-seeming under the moon, desolate as the ruins of Charn.

Solario, his mane streaming back against Anthony's hands, rushed past the memorial pillars. On the lintel of the columns was a nest of small birds; a vast black sea bird stood over them with lifted wings dark as all darkness. Before Julian's eyes it bent down on the birds and bit their heads off, devouring them bone and feather. An incomprehensible horror struck through her, as if she were one of the birds with that black shadow towering over her. And yet it was worse, for she knew—it was not a natural hunger that drove the bird, it was an intense malignity deep upon deep beyond Mor's, and beside such knowledge the terror of bodily harm was a straw. The force of it beat against her like waves of dense darkness, of which that bird was the source like a sun of darkness, fountain of night instead of light, unnatural night stronger than a vast weight of waters. She felt she would drown in it; then the bird was whirled away in the wake of Anthony's speed.

The trees of Government Street flew past like ruined pillars on the banks of a torrent. Julian began to glimpse two shapes passing among the trees, weaving in and out, shapes clothed in a fierce reddish light

like that of smoky torches. Soon she could discern what the shapes were.
A spotted leopard, gaudy-pelted in black and gold, flowed along through
the trees; it was held on a golden chain by a crowned woman in a
shining garment of black, who flowed as lithely as that glowing beast.
Her hair streamed black and luxuriant; her face and arms and shoulders
were white as paper. The face was beautiful and hard, barbaric and a
little cruel; Julian sensed that no man could look on it and remain wholly
sane. The dark eyes of beast and woman noticed her and looked dis-
dainfully away, as if she were not worth their gaze. They twined away
gorgeously among the trees; but a suffocating darkness of the air flowed
out from them, nothing visible, but something that made it hard to
breathe. There was no scent, but a thickness in the air as in some hollow
underground place where a forsworn vestal had been walled up to die;
it was as if something good had been tormented and made foul. Julian
felt she could not draw breath; a weakness came over her, and a cold
dampness came out on her brow. Waves of darkness washed against her
mind; she felt that they would drag her down and drown her. She clung
to consciousness; and the face of Mor swam mocking against the darkness, the bitter eyes taunting her and telling her she could be free the
moment she willed. Beast and woman grew indistinct before her eyes;
but she fought off the darkness, and struggled for breath in that close
air. She was aware of Solario racing down a side street, with the leopard
and the crowned woman gliding ahead. She saw the basilica looming
in the moonlight like a cold ruin. And then suddenly it seemed as if the
woman and the leopard had struck against a wall of glass; for they
stopped, though no visible thing barred their way. Then they were gone
as if they had dissolved into nothing; and the waves of darkness drew
back from Julian's mind, and at the same moment the demonic veil was
lifted from her eyes. She could breathe, and the hold of Mor on her was
broken; and she saw the basilica standing solemn and beautiful in the
cold, pure moonlight.

Morgan stood trembling in the tapestried chamber, leaning for sup-
port against the wall. Her whole body quivered with the anguish of the
enchantment that had just passed. She heard Aramelissa's steps going
away down the hall, but she was too drained of strength to care.

In a moment the pain passed, and she stood upright in the moonlit
chamber. No candles were lit; but the draperies of the windows were
drawn back, and the room was filled with the white radiance as with
water. The tapestry of Atlantis stirred faintly on the wall; the wood of
the round table gleamed dark, except where the piled cards made a little
pool of shadow.

She went to the table and divided the cards once again—coins, staffs, swords, cups, Fool; earth, air, fire, water, the Sun Lord. With ritual care she laid out the Wheel of Power—the Fool at the center, and four spokes radiating to the four points of the compass, of the court cards outward from page to king. Then the numeral cards from two to ten she spread counterclockwise for the wheel's rim, each two next to its king, beginning at the north—fire, water, earth, and air. Outside each quadrant of the circle she placed one of the aces—earth outside the quadrant of fire, which had the spoke of water alongside it, because earth could be drowned or scorched dry; fire outside that of water, which had the earth-spoke beside it, because fire could be quenched with water or earth; air outside the quadrant of earth, which had the air-spoke, for air could be shut in the earth or vanquished with contrary air; water outside the quadrant of air, which had the fire-spoke, for fire and air could turn water into mist.

Nine times counterclockwise she circled the table, invoking the Goddess in chants of a language lost to time. Then she stood still at the north point of the circle and looked through the window at the clear moon.

"O Arianrhod, Blodeuwedd, Cerridwen," she prayed in the same tongue, "who are called all these and mightiest Druan Gwen, white oak-queen, maiden, mother, and wise princess of the final kingdom, grant that these mysteries I perform in your name may be made effective by your power. Your foes I place in the hollow of your hand. Power of earth and air I have against them, power of water and fire. Power of vision I have against them, to behold what will come to pass. Your justice is almost accomplished, and the recapture of the holy Sword that was lost to you long ago. Grant that it may come to my hand, and that your servant Morgause may obtain her desire concerning this Cup of which she speaks. What is it to me and to you, who are keeper of the mysteries of the holy Cauldron? But, mother, Druan Gwen, this one thing I ask for myself: let my task draw quickly to an end, that I may behold your true face and be received into the starry circles forever."

A mood of sadness was on her as she looked at the white radiance, seen how many times in its bright phases down the weary length of years. Fourteen centuries, was it, a long service of heartsickness and hope deferred. Now the tears of desolation and loneliness came to her eyes, as she thought of the words given in the oak grove and saw in spirit the deep eyes of Druan Gwen, mother of the living and the dead.

But she turned again to the cards and passed her hands to and fro over the quadrant of water, closing her eyes and fixing her mind on water—springs, rivers, seas. She thought of rain falling on the earth and feeding small cold springs, which flowed over white sand into streams, and swelled slowly into creeks and rivers, wide-watered under the stars, and poured at last into the ever-murmuring sea where the moon shone on the tide. And with dawn the waters would be drawn up again, to fall in rain and sunk into the earth, and flow down through springs and rivers to the sea. And slowly a little mist gathered on the surface of the table, and thickened and condensed; and when she opened her eyes, the quadrant of water was spread over with a thin pool, in which the moonlight was caught as in pools that lie smooth after rain.

Morgan gazed on the bright pool as she had gazed that day on the pool of ink in her hand. Shapes appeared against a background of night woods. Bronze-armored warriors strove to beat down the Pendragon with their spear-shafts, while he struck at their captain with a bronze sword and Morgause stood by in Linette's shape. The bronze sword snapped, but the Pendragon wounded the Captain slightly with the broken blade; and the Captain sprang at him and flung him down.

Morgan released the pool from her thought, and it became again a film of moonlit water. Her mind went questing after Morgause.

Sister, sister, sister. Come to me when you can.

A tongue of green flame flicked out from the card of the Queen of the Air. "Sister," came the melodious voice from the flame. "Why do you call me?"

"What fortune have you had with the girl?"

"She will fall at the next assault. Meanwhile she and the Pendragon are captive in Caer Sidi."

"Can they escape before you take possession of her?"

"The Gate of Fire is hard to open, and there are few that dare pass it. When I have possession of her, I will lead the Pendragon out by secret ways and return with him to where he entered the Otherworld. Then your spells must draw him back, and me in her shape."

"What of the one that seeks the Cup?"

"I have sent Angoré against him. And if Angoré fails also, I can command Mor. I must strike at the Cup before power flows out from it, in the narrow instant between its coming and the beginning of the mystery. It will not come till he reaches the very door of the place of the mystery, and he must be delayed until we command the Sword. Fire and air have power over water; shall not I, the Queen of the Air, with the fiery Sword have power over the Cup?"

"Sister, I grow uneasy about this cup. I would sooner let it alone."

"Do you want my help to recover the Sword?"

"What do you want from me?"

"Your skill is in the mysteries of Druan; and in the moon's full they are stronger than the mysteries of the Shadow. You must use the Wheel of Power against Cup and Sword when the time comes, and strengthen the power of the air."

"How shall I know when the time comes?"

"By your own skill. Pour all your strength into this magic. I go now for the last assault."

The green flame sank away, and Morgan looked once more into the water and saw by her magic what she sought to see. She drew out of the near past the entrance of Rhodri and Linette into Caer Sidi and the closing of the hill. The darkness and the dim halls of the lords of the dead were not forbidden to her gaze, though she feared to behold there the one who was called Anu and Bodb and Macha, on whom she might not look. The shadow-shape of the Goddess by the holy Cauldron was not strange to her. But as she watched the phantom, she felt a slow cold come over her. How dared Morgause wear that shape? How dared dark Morgause's face pretend to be the radiant countenance of Arianrhod? How dared she show that look of unholy desire, as if Blodeuwedd had acted from that and not in fulfillment of a fate foreknown? And what was that witch-shape that hung at last over the Cauldron? Cerridwen did not look thus; even in crone-shape her eyes had not that look of malice but kept their immortal calm. Was it Druan's image at all? And at the thought the cold horror seemed to reach Morgan's heart. Surely this was the shape of Anu, who was called Lilith and Hecate, the triple shadow of Druan Gwen's triple light. Was this not a false and blasphemous seeming, as if that accursed image were Druan? No luck could come of this; Anu was a shadow without strength, and this mockery would provoke the anger of the Lady of Light.

Rhodri and Linette sank down into the rock chamber, and Morgause entered into Linette. Morgan placed the Ace of Staffs within the quadrant of the air, as a focus of concentration to lend strength to Morgause. She poured her own power into her sister, felt Morgause's triumph, heard the wild words that were cried out in the chamber. But she sensed that a part of the power was pouring away, like a lake's waters spilling over a waterfall. Cristant, Cristant—what was that name? Why was the Pendragon crying out to it, in shame, in sorrow, out of the dark of Caer Sidi where no such name was known? And suddenly Morgause was gone. Morgan stood nonplussed, shaken; the pictures in the water wavered like disturbed reflections. Gone, gone where? She put forth the powers of her mind, questing, not finding; a cold fear filled her, as if a great cliff had suddenly appeared at her feet. But she snatched at her failing courage; she must keep her head, she must not lose sight of Rhodri and Linette. She pushed aside part of the water with her hand and laid the Ace of Swords in the emptied space, and placed the Ace of Cups in the quadrant of the air. On them she concentrated the force of her power, to dominate them to her will; only a little was left free, what was needed to keep her watch on the pool of water.

She saw Rhodri, head bent, holding Linette's hand. The flame guttered in the lantern; they watched it and spoke, sadly, wearily, then dropped into silence. And Morgan, watching them sit silent before the dying flame, felt her heart strangely moved toward them. She wondered at that; she had not thought, any more, that she could feel pity towards anything. So many lives, so many deaths; one lost the power to feel, one was deadened at last. But now, painfully, she felt the stirrings of a forgotten poignancy. Something about Rhodri, his youth perhaps or the way he sat looking at the flame, reminded her of Owain, her son, dead fourteen centuries ago in star-crossed battle. Owain, Owain—he had sat like that, yes, gazing into the fire at Gor, the night he stopped her from killer Uriens. From Avalloc he had had his dark hair, and from Uriens, maybe, his strength and bigness of bone; but his eyes were her own eyes, violet and deep. The low fire had cast a reddish glow on him, except where his hair caught pale gleams; his head was bent, and his eyes were pools of shadow. Looking at him across the firelight, she had repented her act, if only for her son's sake. Owain belonged to the newer world, Arthur's world; the old ways, which he could not understand, could only cause him bewilderment and pain.

And now this young man—the girl too in a way, who with her dark hair looked somehow like the young Morgause. Morgan saw Morgause suddenly, standing in the sunlight on the cliff of Tintagel the day Ygerna and Avalloc rode away. She had climbed to the highest place, to see them as long as possible—the more so because Cynddeleu rode with them, Cynddeleu whom she was to have married, who died defending Avalloc when the sortie was surrounded. Ah, Morgause as she had been then, wild in her fashion but straight-souled and fair—one could say she had been killed with Cynddeleu and Avalloc, and that what spoke out of the green flame now was the very ghost of a ghost, for she had been a ghost while she lived.

And now Linette would die, and that ghost of a ghost would live in her body—was it not the destroying of Morgause all over again? And Owain, no, his name was Rhodri—he would grieve for her even if he was not destroyed. Morgan remembered that he was her own kin, son of Arthur through many fathers, Arthur who was her own mother's son. And a doubt struck her: did the Goddess indeed want the Sword back? It might be fated otherwise; *Three Pendragons of Arthur's line. . . .*

Her reverie was shattered. The lantern light had died in the pool some time ago, but she had been conscious of Linette and Rhodri sitting in darkness. Now suddenly a light welled forth, pure and beautiful as clear water; she could see their faces and the rock walls. She recognized it as one of Druan Gwen's rarer magics, the Fountain of Arianrhod who was moon-queen and star-queen; and what was it doing now driving back the darkness of Caer Sidi? Where had it come from, indeed; and how could it fight the might of Cerridwen, who was Druan Gwen also? Cerridwen—or Anu? What did Morgause's apparition mean? And now the Gate of Fire opened, its red light streaming around the Fountain of Arianrhod like oil around water, unmingling. The Gate of Fire—that was some of Blodeuwedd's magic, it was the path of fire which the king's spirit travelled to the House of the Stars. And now the Pendragon stepped onto it, with Linette in his arms. Morgan could read the pain in his face, could see the beads of sweat standing out on it; with all the strength of her heart she was willing him to get safely across. And now he set foot on the other side.

Then with a rush the realization came to her: she had been wanting what would mean the destruction of her hopes, the overthrowing of her labors like uprooted trees. She realized that for this quarter-hour and more she had forgotten the domination of Cup and Sword, forgotten her task, forgotten all but the past and the pool. The Goddess's work, the Goddess's justice—forgotten, forsaken, undone. She drew herself together with an effort; let the fated outcome be what it might, she must do what was set before her. She bent her strength once more to the Wheel of Power.

"Rhodri," whispered Linette, "are you all right?"

She leaned toward him, shivering as with extreme cold after that fiery crossing. They were beyond the red light of the molten rock, but the crystal in her hand still gave off a faint radiance. By it she could see Rhodri leaning against the rock wall, slumped backward, with his eyes closed.

He shuddered and opened his eyes. "Yes, I'm all right—only dead tired."

Linette did not believe him. But she did not venture to ask any more; her concern was touched by a strange shyness, because she herself was unscathed.

"We should be going away from here," said Rhodri suddenly, gathering himself up. "They might follow us. And maybe we haven't much time." With the help of the uneven wall he rose, catching his breath sharply as the weight went on his burned feet. "Come on. We have to get on."

Linette was already standing, with the red-jewelled crown on her head. "Yes. I have a sense of being hurried on, towards something that's going to happen. Where are we?"

"Still in the Otherworld, I think. Otherwise I don't know. We walked a long way going down into Caer Sidi, but I don't know in what direction. But the tunnel only goes one way, so there's no choice."

They began to walk side by side through the subterranean dark, in the frail circle of light from the crystal. But this was no passage of built stone like the outer reaches of Annedd Cledd, nor corridor of hewn sandstone; it was rough and twisted, with a rounded shape that did not seem like the work of water in the rock. It looked as if some monstrous worm or snake or burrowing thing had gnawed or forced a way through the hills; and the imagination of this began to grow in Linette's mind, and she began to be afraid of the place. Now and then the mouths of other tunnels gaped suddenly on either side; she would hurry past them, glancing nervously into the blackness.

For a long time they went on, seeing nothing but the pale light and the writhed reddish rock, hearing nothing but their own breathing and the echoes of their steps. Neither spoke. Linette moved like one in a dream who climbs twisted stairways through endless dim halls; but the black tunnel mouths gave the dream a touch of nightmare, as she wondered what made them and what came there. Once she thought she glimpsed a faint light crossing the darkness far ahead, like a weak lantern carried from one tunnel mouth to another; but it was gone so quickly she thought it was an illusion from looking too long at the darkness.

A strange smell began to touch the air, cold and earthen and faintly foul, like the damp holes of snakes. And then, on the edge of hearing, came the sound of rushing water. Linette hesitated, wondering what they were coming to; she looked at Rhodri and saw that he had gone alert and tense, his eyes glinting darkly in the pale light.

All at once the tunnel opened out into a vast dark place where the sound of running water was loud. Their footsteps, as they moved cautiously into the vastness, set up reverberating echoes from distant roof and walls. The floor seemed smoother underfoot, worn perhaps by the passage of water long ago; it was not flat, but sloped downward from the walls like the bottom of a hole. The cold smell was very strong here, and the sound of water grew louder as they went forward; but the echoes of their steps seemed to fill the gloom like a clamor of drums.

"I hope there's nobody to hear us," whispered Rhodri. "We might as well have shouted, 'Here we are.' " And the darkness caught that too and whispered it back, magnified, from sightless distances, "Here we are . . . here we are." After that they did not say any more.

The dark seemed to press close around, too close. Strange drafts came from somewhere, stirring the hairs on Linette's neck, as if there might be more tunnel mouths in the invisible walls. She began to walk faster; this open space frightened her, the moving air made her feel exposed, the sense of urgency pressed upon her as if time were narrowing fast toward a crisis. How big was this place? Would they never get across? She was holding the light still straight in front of her, but straining to see beyond it into the distant blackness.

"Stop!" It was Rhodri's cry, and his hand grabbed her arm. She looked down; and while the walls yelled back "Stop!" like the clamor of a battle, she stared dazedly at a vast chasm that yawned a yard from her feet.

The light did not change in quality, but its reach seemed far as they bent over the chasm. Dark water showed at the bottom, running fast; the noise of it seemed almost to drown the echoes. The sides were sheer and deep, and far apart as the shores of a small river. From the long gleam on the water they could see that the gorge ran the length of the entire cavern; and it could not be jumped.

"Now what?" said Rhodri in a low voice. "Forget the echoes; anything that could hear us already has. We can't stay here. Give me the light."

He took it and lay down on the edge, holding the crystal as far down as he could reach. Linette, peering over his shoulder, heard him catch his breath sharply. "Look. Look down there."

Between the cliff wall and the water ran a narrow shelf on each side. A little upstream from where the two gazed, a strong, pale rope was stretched across from wall to wall, about a yard above the water, fixed into the stone with great rings of bronze. A small boat, moored with other ropes and rings on either side, was beached on the shelf nearest them; it had no sail or oars. Toward the boat, down each cliff, descended a ladder of bronze staples driven into the stone.

"Belongs to the Haldir, by the metal," whispered Rhodri. "They come here, then. Which means we'd better leave."

"We're lucky the boat's on our side."

"No, we could get it. Rope's fastened at each end. I'll go first in case something's down there. You hold the light."

He got up; and at the same second both of them realized that something in the darkness had changed. Instinctively they looked back. There, high in the wall behind them, a tunnel mouth opened; and in it, small and far away, gleamed warriors of the Haldir. A lantern cast bright reflections on their bronze armor and spears.

"Get on the ladder!" whispered Rhodri, thrusting his hands over the light.

But it was too late. A cry broke from the tunnel mouth, *"Edain! Sí edain!"* The tiny figures began climbing fast down a ladder of staples that descended from the tunnel mouth.

The cry broke Linette's frozen trance. She shoved the crystal down the neck of her dress and scrambled for the ladder, barely seeing the staples by the light that came through the fabric. Rhodri came after her, in the dark completely, groping for the holds.

"Linette!" came his voice, stifled in the hallow darkness. "Something's the matter up there. They've stopped; they're looking all around. They're going back—fast—up the ladder."

Linette stood still, straining to hear what might be stirring in the darkness. The rush of the water was in her ears; she could hear nothing else. "Get on *down!*" Rhodri's voice came with frantic urgency. "For God's sake, whatever it is—" She could see his scorched shoe-soles on the rung above her hands. Galvanized into movement, she scrambled down; her feet found the shelf, and in a second Rhodri was beside her. She had the crystal out; without a word he shoved her into the boat and pushed it loose from the shelf, then stepped in beside her and began hauling at the taut rope hand-over-hand. The boat edged out; they felt the pull as the swift-running current caught it, nearly wrenching the rope out of Rhodri's hands.

Linette clutched the crystal and stared up into the dark. She thought she could hear something above the roar of the water, a dry, heavy rustling as if something were dragged over the stone. It came. She could not scream; a small choked noise came in her throat. Rhodri heard it and looked up.

Over the edge of the chasm something white was stretching, catching the light from the crystal, triangular at first but growing longer and longer, huge, wider than the boat, longer than anything could be. It arched down; great golden eyes flecked with black, big as shields, stared at them as the vast serpentine length poured down. Grey-blue scales shone coldly in the light, edging the white underparts. Thicker than oak-trunks the vast body flowed out of the dark. With a cry Rhodri let go the cross-rope; the boat shot away from the head. But the mooring ropes caught it with a sharp jerk that threw both of them flat in the bottom of the boat. Staring, they could see the boat straining at the bottom of a U of rope, tipped crazily against the current, while a mouth like a cavern opened slowly above them, fanged like an array of swords. Then the rings, not meant to stand that strain, shifted in the soft rock; one gave way, and the boat swung round point-first into the current. It dragged there for an instant at the end of the taut line, while the yellow eyes stared; then the other ring wrenched out of the rock, and the boat plunged away straight for a tunnel mouth that gaped to receive it.

"What was it?" breathed Rhodri when he could speak.

They still crouched in the bottom of the boat where they had been thrown. The light from the crystal showed the reddish rock of the tunnel roof not far above the sides; there was not room to sit up. The current was still hurrying them along fast, an island of light, out of darkness into darkness.

"Not hers, I think," said Linette slowly. "She wants us alive."

"It wasn't after us at all. It had every chance. It just stared."

"And she's so far away I hardly feel her unless I think about it. But if it's not hers, whose is it? What was it there for?"

Morgan, watching in the Atlantis Tower, did not know either. She had forgotten the great Earth-Snake; and though it had once been sacred to the Goddess, she did not know who had called it to the place where it drank once in a hundred years.

The boat still sped through the darkness. Linette and Rhodri sat silent in the bottom, side by side, leaning against the seat; Rhodri's hand was clasped around Linette's. The Water of Vision lay between them, shedding its fragile light on the grain of the wood and on the rough rock of the roof.

"I'm so tired," said Linette in a low voice. "I don't think this will end; we'll go on in this boat forever. Forever and ever." She felt somehow that she wanted that to be so, so she would not have to part with Rhodri. A bad business enough; poor Cristant. But she had loved him. Did she any more? Too tired to know.

"How can she do it?" she went on, in a dreamlike tone. "Cristant. How can she take my struggle? Is she me?"

"No," said Rhodri, "not Linette Silverthorne. But maybe she is you in some other way. I don't know."

He thought about Cristant, that first night, brushing her hair in the moonlight—white gown, fair flowing hair. And now—it was good he could not see her now, not see Morgause struggling in that face. Good? He ought to be made to see it, made to see the cost. Once again the shame stabbed at him, and he rammed his fist hard against the wood. But Linette, Linette—No, shut up. An end to that.

"Look at the walls," said Linette in a different voice, wide awake, urgent.

The walls and roof were no longer solid sandstone. They were a reddish mist that shifted like cloud and faded into grey white. The two twisted round and stared ahead into the darkness. But it was not darkness. Water and tunnel shifted and moved like fog, pale fog that deepened ahead of them into a solid whitish wall. To both of them it seemed an opaque barrier like a wall of stone, at which the boat was rushing like a log in the race of a waterfall.

Cristant stood in the tower of Caernarvon Castle, in the dusty emptiness containing only herself and a pool of moonlight from a narrow window. Eight stone walls; stone steps leading to a locked door; stone floor, the lines of its pavement picked out by a spill of light. But she had no time to think of it, for Morgause's strength was beating down hers as the sea beats a shell into sand. Her frail mastery crumbled and suddenly broke, and once more her body was not her own.

The wild queen paced up and down the room, seeking some means to make fire—matches, flint, anything. But there was none, and nothing to burn, only stone and cold moonlight. She paused in the moonlight, breathless, raging with frustration; only one element was left her, by the law of the dark magic, and it was not to be found.

Cristant, buried as beneath dark waters, knew what she wanted and was afraid. Morgause was desperate now, she knew, and would find fire if she had to strike it from the stones. Surely there was some way she could fling off this mad queen, rather than suffer death by burning. Cristant wondered whether she or Morgause would feel the fire; they said witches screamed at the stake.

Morgause was aware of the thought, and a cruel smile touched her face. With her full force she dashed Cristant's fist against the stone wall.

It was Cristant who felt the pain and thought that Morgause had broken the bones of her hand. But even in rage the dark queen had more forethought than that; she might need that hand. She thought it likely that Cristant could turn her loose if she chose, and she wanted to make clear to her who would feel the fire if she dared face it. It would take time to raise the fire and destroy her with it; and Morgause was conscious of the precious seconds slipping away. If she could not control Linette in time—

The conviction grew on Cristant that she could get rid of Morgause, and that the queen guessed it. That would be the reason for the blow; Morgause was in a hurry, in no mood to waste time on wanton cruelty. Cristant tried to thrust the knowledge away, but it could no more be pushed back than smoke.

Morgause threw back her head and laughed in furious exasperation. Wretched, stupid girl, reasoning so doggedly—did she think she could resist indefinitely? Did she doubt Morgause's ability, because earthly fire was not there, to draw fire from the very stones?

She spun round like a dancer, her arm stretched out in a gesture of command. Thin green flames sprang round her, head-high, in a circle that left no stain on the moonlit stones. They swayed, nearly a yard still from Cristant, trembling and giving off a thin greenish light; then, slowly and hesitantly so that she could see every fraction of their motion, they began to draw inward.

She stood white and still, her arms pressed close to her sides. She felt no heat as yet; but a wild panic tore at her mind, so that her will flung itself blindly against Morgause, striving for control. Coldly Morgause pressed the knowledge in on her, that even if she won control she could not stop the flames. Cristant's thought reeled with the shock of it, as she watched the green tongues creep closer, curling, hesitating, always nearer and yet nearer. Her mind went blank for a second, her will motionless; then both whirled in a violent desire to throw off Morgause. The queen felt it; in a moment the bond would go and she would be free. Then Cristant's mind hesitated, confused by a thought. Rhodri . . . if Morgause got loose, what would happen to Rhodri?

The thwarted queen shouted, It isn't Rhodri, it is Linette, don't you understand? Linette, your rival, the one that wants to take the Pendragon's love.

Pendragon. . . . The word penetrated to Cristant's shrieking mind: *Pendragon . . . Logres . . . not let her harm. . . .* And then her mind cleared terribly and she knew that she was not going to thrust Morgause away.

The flames touched the wool of her skirt, but the cloth did not catch fire. It hung in the flame as if in water, quivering slightly. Cristant could not move; she stood in a hollow pillar of green flame. Then the fire licked across her hands and arms, and her spirit shuddered violently with the agony of burning. She would have screamed, but she could make no sound. She saw how the flames consumed nothing, left no mark on her skin; but with the withering pain of them her soul soared toward madness. *Logres, Pendragon, Rhodri*, the words meant nothing now, upswept in a furnace-draft of white-hot burning. Threads of green flame twined like serpents up her hair; her body felt the fire as if her clothes were all burnt away. She was lapped in flame as if in seawater; she strained her face back from it, and one thought came clear: No one will know how I died. She shut her eyes as the fire touched her face. It was the pain she would die of; her heart would stop with it, not long now. Rhodri's face flickered before her mind, without a name now; let go, why not, not hurt him, surrender or die it was all the same. But she knew blindly that she must not, and fought back as against a clawing animal, as if the pain could not kill her unless her will let go. Her mind cleared a little; she knew that if she tried she might hold on for a long time.

Morgause battered against this new resistance like a crash of waves. She was too angry now to know clearly what she did, only that she must beat down this obstinacy that outrageously raised itself against her. But slowly at the back of her mind an urgency was growing, a sense of something happening behind her, like flood-water creeping under a door. She paused in her fight, straining to know what it was. Across four thousand miles she felt the presence of her enemy. She abandoned all effort to possess Linette; she wrenched herself away from Cristant and rushed back like a dark wind to the Atlantis Tower.

Anthony stood within the basilica gateway, before the great steps that rose to the porch. A little wind blew in the dark trees of the lawn, and the moon shone brilliant and cold. Far off somewhere a chime struck midnight with a strong, sweet sound; and he thought that in the following stillness he could hear the sea.

All his senses seemed sharpened to the fineness of glass. Before him the noble porch of stone rose to the stars; behind him Solario stood still as a carved image in the moonlight. Anthony felt the life within him tremble and soar up high like a white flame; his adventure had come to him. Slowly, in a kind of awe, he mounted the steps toward the solemn porch.

He saw that the great doors stood open in the shadows of the portico, between the two angels of bronze. And as he advanced among the pillars that rose like a mighty forest, he saw that two lions guarded the doors. They shone bright in the shadows, great tawny beasts lit up as with unseen firelight, and watched him with immense, unwavering eyes.

But he went forward without fear; and as he passed through the white radiance and the pools of shadow, it seemed to him that here the darkness was not at enmity with the light, that for this one hour peace was between them as it had been before the dance of creation was marred, before any broke out of the harmony and called themselves the rulers of darkness.

He passed between the two lions, and they bowed their heads like the lions of Eden. He stood in the small entry of the basilica, where the painted saints showed dim in the glass of the inner doors; and he put his hand to one of the doors and opened it. And suddenly there was a brilliant light, as if the basilica had become filled with lightning; but it stayed and did not waver, and all light he had ever seen beside it was like a candle beside the sun.

Anthony went forward into the basilica. The place of the Grail was entered.

Linette had closed her eyes for the crash against the wall of stone. But there was no crash. She felt herself hurled with great force against what seemed like a wall of water; lights burst in her mind like red and blue stars in a black sky. And she was through the wall.

Dazedly she became aware of something cool and hard beneath her, and of Rhodri lying half on top of her where he had thrown himself to shield her from the crash. But most immediately she became aware that the dark burden had been taken from her.

"Rhodri," she gasped, trying to sit up, "move; I can't breathe with you on me." He drew himself upright, and she looked around. The crystal had gathered its radiance back into itself and lay in her hand like a faint star. She could see Rhodri by it; his face, tight-drawn and full of shadow, had a fire of excitement in the eyes.

"Look," he said, staring beyond the circle of light from the crystal.

There was no sign of the boat or the Worm's twisting halls. The walls of white limestone were once more around them, and beside them the blocking wall with the hole broken through. A cold draft blew through from the dark cellar beyond. "Well," said Rhodri, "we've left the tools in the Otherworld."

"And the lantern. Rhodri, listen—she's gone. Morgause is gone."

"Lantern or no lantern," said Rhodri, rising. "Hold up the crystal."

"Don't be such an archaeologist. This is important."

"More important is to find Excalibur. Fast."

But even as Linette was getting up, something began to happen to the stones. They were no longer dark beyond the small radiance of the crystal. The barrier wall and all outside it remained dark; but around them, walls, roof, and floor kindled to a dim phosphorescence like a faint luminous object in a dark room. The light grew even as they watched, flowing out till each stone was as bright as the crystal in

Linette's hand; they could see one another plainly, their tired faces washed over and smoothed by the radiance. Yet it remained subdued, subtle and beautiful like moonlight, as if each stone were alabaster and translucent with some light that burnt softly within.

"The beauty of one of the Ancient Things rises to greet another," said Rhodri softly. "The Grail must have come for Anthony. I am glad we have lived to see this."

"Yes," said Linette, remembering Celebrin under the moonlight of the Otherworld speaking of the price of return. But the bitterness that rose in her was washed away by the clear light as by lucent springs.

"Come, though," he said; "this is our moment too. We must go find Excalibur."

They went forward along the passage, slowly like walkers in a vision. The clear light shone all around them, shadowless and gravely beautiful, till they lost consciousness of walls and floor and felt as if they were walking in the very heart of light.

The passage opened out into a room, and they entered. The chamber of stone was filled too with radiance as with clear water; but here the light was more intense and full of a severe purity, more beautiful but austere like the beginning of dawn. In the midst of the room rose a low shape of stone, like couch or tomb; and on it lay a woman, still as a dead queen carved in stone on a sepulchre. She wore a long gown of a turquoise color like a bright sea, and from beneath a circlet of silver and pearl her red hair flowed down over the edges of the stone and touched the shining floor. Her face was white almost as the stones, terrible with an austere beauty and a remoteness infinitely beyond sleep, and with a look as if she had died fighting nobly.

Rhodri said softly, "She is Goeral, the maiden sister of Madoc, who lies in the deep trance before the door of Annedd Cledd. They say she will wake at the drawing of the Sword."

At his words they both looked beyond Goeral to the other side of the chamber. From another doorway light flowed, faintly enriched with the color of fire. Linette saw in her mind the fiery vision in the dark passage.

For an instant they gazed again at the awesome calm of Goeral's face; then without speaking they approached the doorway from which the gold-tinged light came.

Morgan, gazing into the film of water, saw Linette and Rhodri break through from the Otherworld. This should not be happening, not yet, with Linette still free. For a moment panic shook her: where was Mor-

gause? Words spun through her mind, out of some book read years
ago—

> Her strong enchantments failing,
> Her towers of fear in wreck,
> Her limbecks dried of poisons
> And the knife at her neck,
>
> The Queen of air and darkness
> Begins to wail and cry—

The green flame leaped up from the card of the Queen of the Air.
Morgause's voice rose low and wild, vibrant with controlled violence.
"The Cup is coming, and the girl is cut of our power! Why didn't you
keep her in the Otherworld?"

"I had nothing to do with that."

"Do you know this is the hour? You must seize the Sword—now—
and use it against the Cup."

Morgan did not waste time on an answer. She passed her hands
over the cards to see what presences would be shown. The Ace of Cups
began to shine like fire, and the Ace of Swords glowed faint gold in
answer. Morgan concentrated her mind on them, no longer aware even
of Morgause. With a fervent silent cry to Druan Gwen she picked the
Queens of Air and Fire out of the wheel and laid them on the Ace of
Swords.

The power of the spell came around her. She could still see the
cards, and beyond them the windows and the moonlight; but they were
like faint reflections in a pane of glass, indistinct and thin. Through
them, more real than they, shone a glowing chapel of white stone. She
stood both in it and in the tower room; it was smaller than the tower
room, vaulted with a low, round vault supported by short pillars; a small
plain altar stood at the end. But all the stones, pillars, altar welled out
a clear white light, as if a flame burned within each one and shone
through a translucent shell like alabaster. But the white light was pressed
back and almost drowned in a more brilliant light, gold and fierce, which
radiated from the center of the room. A block of stone rose there like
a short, square pillar; it was white like the rest and gave out white light;
but from it rose upright a sword in a jewelled scabbard. The light
seemed to burn through the scabbard, so that all the jewels were like
flames; but the hilt rose clear, so dazzling that she could hardly see it,
a blazing gold that seemed like the sun, cross-shaped and crowned with
a glint of purple fire. For a moment she forgot all about the magic and

the urgency; she stood without speech or thought, staring as if her entire life were in her gaze.

"Sister!" came Morgause's voice, furious and wild. Morgan saw her now standing beyond the Sword, no flame now but a phantom-shape, tall, beautiful, and crowned, with streaming black hair and eyes like blue flames.

"Seize it, sister! Seize it and turn it against the Cup!" Her eyes and hair and face were all like fire, unearthly and full of power; Morgan sensed in her a fury like a breaking storm.

But she did not want to hurry. Something in her resisted Morgause, resented the intrusion of her fury on this moment, when the only right act was to stand in awe before the beauty of this holy thing. She took one step toward the Sword and then stopped. There it burned; she was almost afraid to take it in her hands, because of the glory and the shining. She sensed an immense power in it and felt suddenly a nameless fear.

"What are you waiting for?" cried Morgause, almost screaming. "The Cup is here!"

On the edge of her gaze Morgan was aware of the doorway, of Rhodri and Linette appearing under its arch. But she did not pay them any attention; she stared back straight at Morgause across the blazing Sword.

Rhodri and Linette saw the chapel, saw the altar and the white stones; but their eyes were fixed on the fierce blaze of Excalibur, and on the two women facing one another across it with eyes like swords. Their shapes were clear, though a little unsteady like the shapes of waves; and their passion thickened the air like thunder.

"Why?" asked Morgan in a low, ominous voice. "Why all this noise? Have you no reverence for holy things?"

"Holy things!" Morgause began to laugh wildly. "Why, you did the magic yourself! You have no more reverence for the Cup than I do! Come on; one for you, one for me!"

"I felt there was something wrong here," said Morgan, standing rigid. "Now I know it."

Morgause's voice dropped its laughter and was again screaming. "Come on, you fool! It's here! Do you want it to escape?"

Morgan did not move. "Answer me. What is this Cup?"

"Nothing, nothing to you! It is not one of the four holy things! Do it, do it!"

"Did I say it was one of them? Not sword, dish, or spear—but the cauldron? What does it have to do with Druan Gwen's cauldron?" Ideas were coming together in Morgan's mind so fast she could not sort them out; she was dizzy with them, as if lightnings were flashing all around her.

"Cauldron, cauldron, nothing at all! Do what you have sworn to do! In the name of the Goddess you pretend to serve, draw the Sword!"

Anthony could see nothing for a moment because of the great light. It dazzled around him, seeming to run up and down like waterfalls of the sun, shimmering, singing, so that his mind too was dazzled.

Then he began to be able to see, and the basilica took form. The light came from no source, and did not light everything; twilight hung in the round vault and in the spaces between the rushing streams of light. Like veils of rain the light was now here, now there—now for a second sweeping across the painted vault, now flowing in swift undulations up the nave.

And he saw that the nave was full of people, a vast crowd, more than he had thought the basilica could hold. Out of the side of his eyes he seemed to see people in such multitides that they would have covered hills and fields; but when he looked straight at them, they were all inside the walls of the basilica. It was hard to see them clearly, because of the restless dance of the light; but now and then a gust of light would blow across a face or a group of faces long enough for him to see. A girl in turquoise, with long braids of red hair flowing from beneath a circlet of silver and pearl, stood gazing intently into the holy place. He glimpsed behind her a man, also red-haired and with features not unlike, clothed in scarlet and circleted with gold in the manner of eight hundred years ago. A black-haired girl, still younger but also crowned, turned to say something to a man in richly embroidered robes, who had slung from his shoulder what looked like the case of a harp. Suddenly the light ran across a face Anthony knew—Catherine Windeatt the poet, standing with her dark, proud head thrown back just as in the portrait at Silverthorne. Silverthorne—that couldn't be Julian there under the Immaculate Conception window, with Aramelissa and Linette on either side? And who was that slight fair woman in the scarlet robe, certainly not medieval, and the very young girl in the dark dress of no definable period, who was looking at him with a calm, interested gaze?

And then he knew who they were—everybody, all the people of the city, gone, living, and unborn, standing in some instant of life or death in the place of the Grail.

All this it seemed he saw and knew without any passage of time; it was still the same moment that he had begun to see. He looked at the high altar and saw the candles lit there for Mass. The shimmering, running lights did not go into the sanctuary; up there was only the brilliance of the tall candles, and a solemn darkness of shadows beyond and around them. Yet that simple brightness awed him more than the waterfalls of light; it was quiet, very distinct, with an air of intense waiting. He advanced slowly up the aisle, between the silent and expectant rows, and stood hesitant before the entrance of the sanctuary.

There was a single sweet sound, not very loud, as if the bells of the basilica swayed and struck in the wind. A priest stepped out of the shadows into the light of the candles. He wore vestments of gold, and in his hands he carried a golden cup that shone like fire. Anthony saw his face clearly in the light of the candles; he did not know him but thought he might be one of the young priests of the basilica. And yet it seemed to him that he knew the face from somewhere, that strong delicate structure of features, the dark hair and high forehead, the searching eyes.

The priest had reached the altar and set the cup down; it stood on the white altar-cloth, outshining the candles. He said, "I will go in to the altar of God."

And there was complete silence. Anthony did not look round; but he could feel the attention of the people in the nave, breathless with intensity; he could feel their eyes on him. And he realized that it was his place to speak for them. He opened the gate of the sanctuary, went and knelt in the server's place, and answered, "To God, who gives joy to my youth."

"Our help is in the name of the Lord."

"Who made heaven and earth."

Again came the silence, intense and devouring. Anthony, in a kind of desperation, began the Confiteor: "I confess to almighty God, to blessed Mary ever virgin . . . and to you, father, that I have sinned exceedingly in thought, word, and deed. . . ." And again came the overpowering sense that he was speaking for all of them, in behalf of all they had ever done or ever would do; that it was for that, all that, that the priest was now pronouncing absolution.

"O God, you will give us life again."

Anthony answered, "And your people will rejoice in you."

The priest's strong clear voice began the entrance chant: "Hail, holy mother, who gave birth to the king who rules heaven and earth forever." And there was something in his voice so direct, so personal, that Anthony looked up in surprise as if he expected to see Mary instead of the white statue overlooking the altar. But there was no one but the priest with his intense, luminous gaze.

The Mass went on. Anthony was tautened to the height of concentration; he could feel the wills of all those people flowing through him, the weight of their silent words on his tongue. Now and then would come the demanding silences, louder-seeming than thunder; in the middle of the Kyrie he had to say the "Christ, have mercy" three times instead of two. He got through the "Glory to God in the highest" without a flaw.

The words of the reading and then of the chant passed over his head: "Alleluia, alleluia. The rod of Jesse has blossomed: a virgin has brought forth God and man. God has given peace, reconciling in himself the lowest with the highest." And the meaning of the words broke in Anthony's mind like a crash of golden waves. The possible and the impossible, the real and the aspiration, the depth and the height—that was what it was, the reconciliation of these, not in an instant of time but in all time, everywhere and always the action of this reconciliation: that was the true work of God and man. He saw in his mind Mary standing on a meadow of the earth, stretching out her arms toward the sun, her long, unveiled hair tangled in its shining.

The time for the offering came. Anthony went to a small table at the edge of the sanctuary and brought back the bread and wine—fruits of the earth, the offering of the earth, on which the eternal miracle would descend. He placed them in the priest's hands; the shimmer of the candlelight got in his eyes and he could not see clearly. He knelt again in his place; the intensity of the others' silent wills shook his mind like a leaf in the wind: offer and be offered, offer the earth, offer the self, forever and ever for the reconciliation and the miracle. The words moved like thunder above his head, so that he hardly realized he was speaking them: "O God . . . grant that through the mystery of this water and wine we may be made partakers of his divinity, who deigned to become partaker of our humanity. . . ." And then, louder, came the voice: "Pray, brothers, that my sacrifice and yours may be acceptable to God the Father almighty."

And Anthony answered the words of ratification: "May the Lord receive the sacrifice from your hands, to the praise and glory of his name, for our welfare and that of all his holy church." And as he spoke, he remembered that *church* meant assembly—all of them, not only in that basilica but all and everywhere, the assembly of the earth.

Now began the words of the prayer of the miracle. Anthony felt an extreme tension building inside him, rising as the words rose, bearing him on towards something that was going to happen, something which he sensed but could not yet grasp. Above him the voice went on clear and unhesitating, "Everywhere we proclaim your mighty works, for you have called us out of darkness into your wonderful light. . . . From age to age you gather a people to yourself, so that from east to west a perfect offering may be made. . . ."

And now the momentous words of the consecration began, the final calling into being of the miracle. "On the night he was betrayed . . ." Anthony felt he could not breathe; the tension filled him so that he could hardly endure it; the words came in his ears like the sound of the blood pounding in his veins.

". . . he broke the bread, gave it to his disciples, and said, 'This is my body which will be given up for you.' "

The priest's voice seemed to change on the words. Anthony looked up. The priest's hands were stretched up, holding the wafer high above him; his head was bent back, his face etched out with a white-hot glare as if he were staring into a furnace; Anthony could see the muscles tautened and ridged, the eyes concentrating all intensity as if they would outburn the white furnace he held aloft—for it was not bread, it was something that scorched and dazzled as if transfixed with lightnings; it was transfixed with lightnings, Anthony thought; it seemed to whirl before his gaze like a consuming sun. Yet his eyes were not stricken by it; he seemed to gaze into an abyss of light in which three colors moved like fire, shaping—he could not see what, for his sight could go no further and sank back suddenly in a dazzle of darkness. And out of the darkness that covered his mind, Anthony felt a rumor like storm and seemed to see for a second a dark vision of piled rocks and thunderous sky. But it was not thunder that spoke; it was the priest's voice, like shouting from an extreme distance, ". . . this is the cup of my blood, the blood of the new and everlasting covenant. It will be shed for you and for all men so that sins may be forgiven."

A new glare struck away the darkness from Anthony's sight. The priest stood rigid, his body and head bent back; the red glow beat down on his face with a violence like the consuming of a world by fire. High in his hands burned the Grail, the Cup, not gold but a devouring red like scorching iron; the fierce light poured out of it and through it, turning the priest's vestments blood-red. The color dazzled before Anthony's eyes; he looked up from it to the face, which was like that of a martyr amid the flames, ridged with anguish but consumed from within by a power that outdared the fires. The Cup, caught in the intense concentration of that gaze, shuddered like a fire in the wind; shadows of darkness licked across the priest's face and hands. And in that rush of shadows Anthony for the first time saw the priest's hands clearly. They were scored with deep marks like wells of fire, from which poured a glorious and terrible brilliance of light.

Darkness again dazzled over Anthony's mind. As he rose out of it, he heard as from a distance his own voice crying out, "Christ has died; Christ is risen; Christ will come again."

He saw that the scorching brilliance was gone. In its place a cool light like dawn filled the sanctuary. The Grail stood like cold silver on the altar; and the same silver, like the whitening spaces of morning, tinged the metallic robes of the priest. Anthony sensed a freshness in the air, like the weight of dew on grass still grey with shadow. The priest's face was filled with an immense stillness as of rest. His voice was calm and not loud: "Lord, may this sacrifice, which has made our peace with you, advance the peace and salvation of all the world."

The words moved over Anthony's head like the delicate, light-stirring winds of spring. It seemed to him that the light grew slowly and was enriched, like the imperceptible steps of sunrise. The priest's voice rose suddenly loud and full of gladness, "In the unity of the Holy Spirit, all glory and honor is yours, almighty Father, forever and ever!"

And with that, as Anthony answered "Amen," a sudden golden light broke from the Grail, like the rising of the sun. Its brilliance colored the whole sanctuary, drowning the light of the candles in an intense golden wave. The priest's robes also blazed with it; his face seemed to answer, reflect, enkindle the very sunrise. A rush of life and strength swept through Anthony to the roots of his being; he found himself on his feet crying out the Lord's Prayer as if he had never dared the words before, as if he were shouting them to a morning sky.

And then the priest turned to him, with the wafer and the cup in his hands. Anthony could not look at his face now; the joy of it overwhelmed him like the blazing sun, and he had to close his eyes. He felt the wafer laid in his mouth; as he swallowed it he felt a sense of unbearable sweetness like the delirium of spring. The Cup touched his lips; the wine was like fire in his mouth and throat, and his mind seemed to burst suddenly upward through darkness toward a whirling brightness that seemed to change and rush toward him, and as it broke over him his exultation exploded in his mind with a golden violence and at the sudden end of his strength he sank, in the deep trance of a complete exhaustion, to the unfelt floor.

Julian saw, for a second more after Anu's vanishing, the solemn moonlit shape of the basilica with its towers rising dark against the sky. Then its silvered masses wavered like reflections in a swaying mirror; and the thread of vision broke, and she was leaning cramped and cold against the stone altar of Silverthorne. But she was too tired to move; she was drained of strength in both body and mind, as if after some fierce physical ordeal. With an effort she shifted her position and leaned half-collapsed against the stone, her eyes closed; her mind floated without thought, like a leaf on a dark heavy-flowing river.

A thin haze of dream drifted over her mind. She was a young girl at High Meadow, lying on her back under a flowering crabapple tree, watching the pink blooms move against the pale-blue sky. A light wind was blowing; a few petals drifted down onto her face. She thought Christopher Marion was there, though she couldn't see him; he would be beside her watching the same gently stirring boughs. She turned her head slightly and saw the indistinct outline of his dark hair against the moving branches. "Christopher," she said drowsily, putting out her hand a little towards him; she thought he was sitting up, with his back against the tree and his face turned slightly away. He turned and looked down at her; and it was not Christopher's brown eyes that she was looking into, but very deep eyes whose color she could not afterwards remember; and the face was not Christopher's, yet one that she seemed to know.

With that she awoke and saw the moonlight and cool stones around her. But she was no longer tired; she felt as young and vigorous as the Julian in the dream. Without knowing why, she rose swiftly and stepped to the north window and looked out.

Below her lay the lawns and woods of Silverthorne, the trees tossing darkly in the land breeze. But she could see beyond them, as if from a great height, yet clearly, as if the miles lay spread before her on a table. She remembered for a second her vision of the ruined city, seen through Anthony's eyes from the height of the bridge. But this was normal and quiet in the midnight silence, the shadowed tree-masses and the pinpoints of light, a watertower here and a spire there, the moon-grey grass of the park and its still lakes, the minute sharp outlines of downtown. She could see the fountain in Bienville Square and the twin towers of the basilica. A freshness of beauty and repose hung over it all, like the remote white brilliance of the stars.

And then she raised her eyes, or some further veil dropped from her mind; and she saw the woman who towered above the city. Her head was raised high against the stars, and the trees and buildings were like flowers and grass before her feet. A light, not moonlight but a gold brightness like firelight, clung about her without illuminating the ground. Her red gown and blue cloak glowed with the brilliancy of jewels; her hair, vibrant gold like grain or small flames, streamed down and curled like the crests of waves. On her head a garland of white azaleas shimmered like stars. Her hands were stretched out over the sleeping city and seemed to scatter grains of light that became invisible before they touched the ground.

Julian recognized the familiar ikon of Our Lady of Mobile. But this was real, a powerful spiritual presence scattering its grace; and Julian held her breath in wonder. Then it seemed to her that the lady stooped and picked up the city in her hands; it glimmered small there like an art object of crystal and jade, sprinkled through with wandering stars. And as she looked at the city in those strong, slender hands, it was not an art object any more but a child, about whom a delicate light clung, and who returned her gaze with calm and all-comprehending eyes. Julian ceased to think; she was lost, body and soul, in the contemplation of the glory.

At the same moment Cristant, lying half-conscious on the stones of the castle tower, felt the exhaustion and darkness leave her. Vitality and joy rushed up in her like springs; she sat up and saw an intense light around her like aerial gold. For a moment she did not even realize it was a vision. Then she looked down the golden tunnel of it, as it pierced across seas and lands like a stride of the sun; and as it neared the other place it grew brighter, so that she could hardly look at it. And she saw in the heart of the light, distant and powerful like a star, a golden cup that blazed like the sun. Then near it, awakened by its brightness, a sword-shape flamed and shone beside it down the corridor of light. She understood that they were Excalibur and the Grail. And then the second sight sharpened and, for a single moment startling as lightning, she saw them as the two principles of immortal justice and untransmutable love, and knew that they were one. And suddenly every particle of her being wanted to sing.

Aramelissa had fallen asleep over her book; she woke suddenly to a clear light she thought was morning, and to a confused sense of the coming of spring. Forgetful of her years, she flew to a window and threw it exultantly open. The summer night startled her; she looked up, and the whole sky seemed full of a rain of stars. They fell like drops of hurtless fire over the city to the north; some shimmered to the courtyard grass and vanished with a sweet scent like unknown bloom. Aramelissa felt a great happiness swell in her heart; words came to her and she was hardly aware that she spoke them out loud, "Wild beyond art or rule, enormous bliss."

*   *   *

Morgan faced her sister, with a cold fierce obstinacy in her eyes. The blaze in her mind had hardened instantly into that, and she wanted answers. Excalibur burned between her and Morgause, in its glory of jewels and fire. She did not touch it.

"No, answer me," she said in the same low, almost breathless voice. She felt a sense of crisis mounting in the chamber, like the prelude to an earthquake; but she would not pay attention. She was not going to yield, not to Morgause. "I want to know," she said, crushing down the rising urgency that almost stifled her. "What connection does this cup have with Druan Gwen's cauldron?"

"It's a hard question, and there is no time! Loose the fire!"

"Loose it yourself or answer me. I know you have no reverence for the Goddess; I saw the shadow-shape you made of her, in the likeness of darkness. You make me think the cup and the cauldron are one."

Morgause had bitten her lips, and flecks of foam stood on them. "You know I am barred from touching the holy things! Take my curse if you will not obey me, my curse unto the everlasting darkness!"

Morgan drew herself straight and rigid, meeting the frenzied gaze of Morgause. "You forget yourself, sister. I am the Goddess's servant, not yours. And if that cup belongs to the Goddess, I will not destroy it."

"You fool, it is the Goddess who commands you to destroy it! It is here, here; in a moment its power will break forth! Do you know why you are forbidden to look on the Shadow?"

"She is Anu, Bodb, and Macha, the threefold mockery of the Lady of Light; she is the mother and mistress of darkness, and sovereign of Annwm." Morgan was trembling with the sense of terrible forces building toward the breaking point; the wild voice of Morgause was intolerable in her ears; but she would not show fear.

Morgause was almost mad with the same knowledge; her eyes scorched like blue coals in her haggard face. She no longer cared what she said; she would make Morgan obey her if she had to blast her to ashes. Her voice screamed like the crash of swords. "Have you been blind all these centuries? Do you forget I can command the Shadow?"

Morgan had not thought about it; she stood rigid, with a sense that her mind was about to be overwhelmed by some terrible revelation. She half guessed what it would be but would not think that thought.

"Where was I, sister, in the hour of Anu? Do you think I am called queen for nothing? You were content to serve, sister, to be a handmaiden and deputy; did you think that was my character too? That I cared either for the House of Cornwall? A life for a life, Uther for Avalloc! Vengeance, yes, a devouring vengeance; but more, sister, more! I learned the dark mysteries; I learned what I could be. And century by century, power by power, act by act, and price by price, I gathered, I learned, I became. You gave yourself as the vessel of the Lady of Light; but I gathered into myself the being and the power of my Goddess, paying for it the price that had to be. This is the end, sister, you have broken your law. It is I you dare not behold, I, not Morgause but Anu, Badb, and Macha, the triple Sovereign of Darkness!"

Morgan reeled to the thought that Morgause was mad, then reeled away: it was too plain that she was telling the truth, it explained too much to be lie or raving. She stiffened against the shock, not fully grasping the implications, but understanding enough and accepting it without wavering. She drew herself straight and lifted a commanding hand. "Begone, spirit of darkness! I renounce my claim in you; you are not my sister, and I do not know you. Begone, shadow of light, before the face of the Sovereign Queen!" She pronounced the exorcism with ritual solemnity; the words seemed ponderous as marble, taking eternities. Her body and mind were in the grasp of the enormous force that was about to break; every movement seemed weighted with stone.

Morgause did not fade; she laughed, and her height and presence seemed to tower, and her lashing hair to fill the room with darkness. "Shadow of light! Fool, it is your Goddess who commands you to draw the Sword! Do you not know the Dark One is the other face of your Goddess? Did you think Druan Gwen was innocent?"

"You lie," said Morgan, white to the lips.

"I have become Druan Gwen! Worship me, sister; worship me!"

"No. I am the servant of the Lady of Light!"

"Light is only a mask of darkness! Do you think the Sun Lord is different from the Dark Lord? Do you think Arianrhod is different from Macha?"

"Yes!" Morgan felt her universe being whirled away by a dark flood; but she stood up against it, clung tight to this one thing and would not let go.

"It is I you have served all these centuries! From me you have had your powers! If there were light, you are too long steeped in darkness to touch it! It would burn you to ashes!"

"Druan, Druan, Druan, defend me from the powers of darkness!"

The pent-up force was released like a tidal wave. Linette and Rhodri saw what seemed like a flash of lightning above the Sword, and at the heart of it was the shape of the Cup. The Sword sprang a foot out of the scabbard and flared in answer. Morgause spun back against the wall as with the force of a blast. But Morgan saw above the Sword not the

Cup but a cauldron of red copper that shone like fire, and over it stood the form she had seen in the sacred wood, cloaked in nightblue, with shining white hair and unlined face and deep ageless eyes. The eyes, in a second of eternity, looked into hers: not Macha but Cerridwen the All-Wise, therefore not Anu but Arianrhod, not Bodb but Flowerface— In that instant all the lies and half-truths of Morgause lay bare before Morgan, and how far she herself had gone into the tides of darkness. But that was nothing to the sight of how right she had been, how the light was truly light and not darkness. A tremendous joy sprang in her like a fierce golden tide. And as she looked, the eyes of Cerridwen told her that this vision itself was a shadow and a disguise, that she must come nearer and deeper into the light if she would truly see.

She moved forward toward the light. But as she did so, she caught a movement through the edge of the vision—Morgause coming towards the Sword, glowering blue eyes and thunderous hair, a white arm raised to seize the Sword or bar Morgan's way—

"Leave me, Mistress of Darkness!" Morgan cried. "All my powers, all I have had from you, I cast in your teeth! You have no more claim in me! I am the servant of the Lady of Light!"

She seized with both hands on the fiery blade before Morgause could touch it. The iron burnt her hands; but from it a power flooded into her, and she cried out again to Morgause: "Go, Sovereign of Darkness! Go to your own place and do no more harm here!" And she saw Morgause, without a sound, fade to a phantom of burning eyes and dark mist, and mist and eyes dim out and go, withdrawn into the silent unsurrendering void. But the unearthly fires of the Sword had already seized on Morgan and wrapped themselves around her like a garment, consuming nothing but enfolding her in an agony of flame, an intensity like a holocaust that roared through her so that she was conscious of nothing but the pain; she knew she was still holding the Sword, but instead of letting go she clung tighter, tighter, while the violence of flame surged over her; her mind sank backward suddenly towards darkness, and as it sank she seemed to see herself running down a twilit road toward an indistinct distant light which grew larger like an aurora borealis. . . .

When Morgan cried out that she renounced her powers, Rhodri and Linette saw Morgause fade as if into nothingness. For an instant longer they saw Morgan clinging to the Sword, a wraith-shape wrapped in flame. Then she and the flames were gone in a bright flare like a match blown out, and at the same instant the form of the Grail vanished like the cease of lightning. The House of the Sword stood quiet in the golden light that still flowed from the central stone.

Rhodri and Linette stood motionless in the doorway, in awe of the Sword. It still stood half a foot out of the scabbard, but its flames had died; the bare six inches of blade kept only a gold incandescence like burning coals. Otherwise it was cool, cool and beautiful in the rich light. They could see it clearly now, long and wide-bladed like a cavalry sword at the end of Rome, with a fineness about it like some perfection of balance; something in its texture suggested that when it was not shining, the light would ripple on its blade like water. It was not heavily jewelled, but cleanly made as for use; the hilt was of some bright metal, gold perhaps or bronze, inlaid along the shoulders of the crosspiece with what might have been silver. A single jewel, a great square amethyst, burned in the pommel with a cool violet flame.

Rhodri's hand touched Linette's; she looked at him and saw the light in his eyes, the archaeologist's passion mixed with awe. "With this," he said hardly above a breath, "Arthur defended Logres long enough for something to be saved. With this he will be summoned at the end. Not with something like this. With this."

Slowly, hesitant with reverence, he moved away from her towards the Sword. She saw the chastened pride and exultation in his face; he moved, she thought, like a king going to be crowned, like the Pendragon of Logres going to the summit of his life's glory. And in that instant of admiration she felt a sharp pain, because he was going away from her. She broke her trance and followed him; but the irrevocable moment of severance would not be undone, and she did not touch him.

Under the golden light letters of gold shimmered on the stone around the Sword. She guessed that the words were Welsh, but Rhodri read them aloud in English in a voice breathless and full of passion.

"The sword of Arthur. Let no man draw it till the intensity of the hour of darkness, when Arthur shall return for the renewal of justice on the earth.' "

Linette, listening, felt a strange joy blaze through her. She had an instantaneous vision of green hills near the sea under an immense red-tinged sunrise; and on one of the hills, a remote dark outline against that beautiful and terrible sky, stood a man leaning on a sword. The lonely and piercing glory of it rushed on her with a poignant splendor; and she remembered suddenly her own words the night Rhodri came. No, one was not born to sit and look at the rain.

They stood silent before Excalibur, still marvelling at its beauty. Rhodri's hand went slowly, hesitantly to the hilt, as if he longed to draw the Sword out and try its balance; Linette saw that he had the feeling for fine weapons that some women have for jewels, and again she felt the sharp stab of loss. But at that instant, as he touched the hilt, the blade blazed out a sudden lightning like thirty torches. The room was lit to every corner with the golden fury of it. Rhodri did not take his hand off it; he gave a tremendous exultant laugh and seized the hilt with both hands, his face in the golden glare full of triumph and joy. "Let all hear that can hear me," he cried, "living or dead, from highest heaven to the deeps of the pit. I, the Pendragon of Logres, have found this sword. I set it in its sheath; let no man draw it before the appointed hour!"

And he thrust it down into the scabbard with a great ringing sound; and the glory of it blazed through the scabbard like the fires of the setting sun.

At Silverthorne, Julian stood without moving at the north window. The vision had gone; but she stared out unseeing into the darkness, trying to fix the memory of it in her mind and heart.

Suddenly her reverie was rent by an outbreak of blinding brilliance. She looked across the court. A fierce light poured out of the Atlantis Tower, coloring the white walls of Silverthorne a terrible red-gold. Great curtains of flame broke out of the tower windows; the whole top of the tower blazed like a fountain of fire towards the sky.

With horror Julian remembered that Morgan was in there. She raced down the winding stairs into the kitchen, where Aramelissa was rising wild-eyed out of her chair. "She's done it!" cried Aramelissa. "She's let loose the fire to destroy us forever!"

"Call the firemen, then!" demanded Julian without heeding. "I've got to get her out. Where's the key?"

A numb look came over Aramelissa's face. "I threw it in the court-yard. To lock her out—couldn't. Oh, God—"

"Call the firemen!" repeated Julian, and seized a hatchet from the tool cupboard and ran out through the arched walk. The roar of the fire rushed toward heaven; all the upper part of the tower seemed like a pillar of flame. Julian ran up the north stairs and reached the tower door in the up-stairs hall. She felt the door, but the wood was so heavy she could not tell whether the flames were near. Fiercely she slammed at the door with the hatchet; she could not break it down as Rhodri had done, but she would break the lock. As she struck she shouted Morgan's name; there was no answer but the roaring of the fire.

Aramelissa thought numbly of the phone and remembered that there was no telephone at Silverthorne. She ran out to the cars and found them all crouched crazily over flattened tires. Julian's radio, she thought, and flew back into the kitchen, trying to remember how it worked. Her hands were shaking, and her memory seemed paralyzed; a concert burst out, then something in Spanish. Then she hit the police band, and cried out desperately that there was a fire at Silverthorne, and heard the promise to send help. She ran out to Silverthorne gate to be sure the firemen found the entrance; looking back, she saw the towering glow against the sky.

Julian struck and struck at the heavy oakwood around the lock. Chips of wood lay on the floor, but the door refused to give. The savage brightness of the flames poured through the windows and lit all Silverthorne with a grim red light. The rush of the fire was like a high wind; and the wild intensity in Julian's mind rose to the same turbulence like a hurricane blowing without hindrance. She had little hope now of finding Morgan alive, but she hacked on without thought of stopping.

Suddenly she became aware that the noise of the fire was much less than it had been. The change itself had not been sudden; it had been so gradual that she had not noticed it till now. At the same time she saw that the violence of the light had also grown less; the far side of the courtyard was once more drowned in moonlight and shadow. And through the night came to her ears the long wail of the fire engines.

She did not cease her blows on the door, not even when the fire trucks arrived shrieking before Silverthorne; but all the while she was aware of the fast sinking of the noise and flame. She heard the firemen coming in up the stairs; and then they were all around her, a haste of fire helmets and firemen's coats, one with an ax in his hand, others getting a hose through a window in one of the rooms. But by now the sound of the fire was lost in the noise of their feet and voices, and only a flicker of red light came fitfully through the windows of the Atlantis Tower.

Julian stood out of the way while the fireman with the ax aimed a blow or two at the hopelessly jammed lock and then with the tool's powerful weight split the door away from the lock. The wood splintered; the door swung crashing against the inside wall. All of them had stood back clear of the doorway, but there was no need. A breath of heat drifted into the hall and died. But in the Atlantis Tower there was no flicker or flame, only the grave moonlight. Julian, gazing in, saw the tapestry of Atlantis stirring a little in the night air as if there had been no fire in miles.

The firemen had gone in, but almost at once one of them returned to her side. "It looks as if we're no use here, ma'am. Your fire's burned out by itself. I never saw anything like it. The police said that whoever called sounded as if the whole house was on fire."

"That would be Aramelissa," said Julian, with an instinct to conceal the incredible under an appearance of calm. Perhaps all was well; if the tapestry had escaped, Morgan might have. But another sense would not listen to this reasoning and waited with foreboding.

"I never saw anything like it," said the fireman again. But she guessed that he was groping for words, feeling for a way to break some news to her.

"I think someone was in there," she said. "Did you find—?"

"Yes," said the fireman; and a look came into his face, a numbed and puzzled look that broke through the accumulated horrors of years. "I never saw anything like it. What a terrible, strange thing it was to happen." He hesitated. "Maybe you would want to identify him or her. It's all right; there's nothing very bad to see."

Julian went with him into the room. The stones of walls and floor, that should have been stained and blackened with fire, shone in the moonlight as white and cold as bone. Only the table stood charred and blackened across its top, under a dark blur of soot on the ceiling; and on it, among the frail grey-white ash that had been cards, a blackened candlestick lay overturned on its side. And on the floor lay something as light and pale as the scraps of burnt-up paper; its size and outline were faintly human, but there was nothing to be seen but a layer of dust or very fine ash. By it, as if fallen there, lay a silver dagger slightly marked with fire; and in the dust, at the place of the neck, Morgan's necklace of twisted gold. Close by one of the hands, as if it had been held to the last, was a half-burnt fragment of a card. It was the Ace of Swords.

Julian stood stunned by the completeness of the catastrophe. All she could think of was Morgan as she had seen her last, in the instant of fading, the pallor of her anguished face and the closed eyes. Then she thought for an instant of waning Roman Britain, and of sunlight on the pebbled shores of Tintagel.

The fireman shook his head with a dazed sadness. "Fire doesn't do that, not like that. It's as if there was something other than the effects of fire."

Julian, kneeling by the ashes of the dead queen, did not answer. But the words stirred in her mind the image of a half-forgotten tale, of the marsh-king's daughter who had looked for three minutes on heaven, while many centuries passed on earth. She had come back for one moment to mortal lands; then her earthly body had fallen away in dust, and her spirit had gone back to gaze forever on the immortal glory. The tears fell down Julian's face; but when she spoke her voice was quiet, unable to express the sorrow and regret which had no words.

"Yes, this was my guest, Morgan Cornwall, a British subject. I will notify the proper authorities."

She thought of all the things that had to be done; but she remained kneeling a moment, looking at the shadow-shape of dust, thinking, I hope that at the end she found her Goddess.

Epilogue

"Well," said Rhodri somberly, "a truce to Schliemann's ghost."

It was Sunday evening, a warm July night full of poignant softness; a wind off the river stirred the heavy-branched oaks in the square and let through glimpses of the slowly waning moon. Bienville Square was deserted except for the two of them. Across the street the silent shop-fronts spilled a lonely light; and up Dauphin Street the towers of the basilica lifted their crosses against the sky. Rhodri and Linette strolled slowly up the solitary walk, under the dark, murmurous oaks, and leaned on the rail that encircled the tall fountain. From basin to basin the water fell, splashing softly, gleaming a little in the radiance of the old gaslights; now and then some sleepy pigeon or sparrow in the trees made a low twittering sound, fragile and soon gone.

Rhodri stared into the dark, gleaming water of the lowest basin, saying nothing, seeming to watch the occasional loom of a heavy goldfish in the smooth depths. Linette watched him from the side of her gaze, thinking of the time, so little time, that she had known him. Only a week, but her life would never be the same after. She thought now of what had happened after he had thrust the Sword down in its sheath, in that blaze of sunset glory. He had stepped back from the Sword and looked at it for a moment, and she had seen tears standing in his eyes. Then he had grabbed her hand wordlessly and pulled her out of the golden chamber, and led her rapidly after him through the passage where around them the light was dying. Without word or pause he brought her straight out of the house to the car, and did not speak till they reached Silverthorne.

They had arrived in the middle of the furor and the fire engines, but it was over by then. They were too tired to grasp yet even the news

of Morgan's death. Linette had found her way dazedly to bed, overwhelmed with the sudden burden of exhaustion, and slept beyond the
depth of dreams.

When she and Rhodri rose late next morning, Anthony was at Silverthorne. After the firemen left, Julian had taken Rhodri's car and gone
to look for him. She had found him in the dark basilica, lying unconscious before the high altar, and brought him back to Silverthorne. He
had not been awake since; the doctor had examined him without waking
him, but had found nothing wrong and had told them to let him sleep.
Linette had slipped in once to see him; he lay quiet in the Eagle Tower,
without mark or bruise except thin scars on forehead and hand. Julian
had spoken of the healing power of the Grail. The mark on his forehead
would fade soon, like the already fading signs of Morgause's scratches;
but the mark scored across his palm he would carry to his grave.

"Rhodri," said Linette, almost hesitating to disturb his reverie, "do
you think Anthony will wake up?"

Rhodri looked at her as if she had startled him out of some dark
vision. "Yes, I think so."

"But will he be all right, or will he be—changed?"

"I don't know. Changed, I think—nobody could see what he saw
and not be—but not for the worse. Not in any way you would have to
fear."

Again silence fell; they were both tired from the exertions of the
day. There had been Morgan's funeral; Rhodri had dug the grave in the
woods of Silverthorne, overlooking the sea. They had buried her ashes
in an alabaster box Julian had, with the dagger and the necklace and
the half-burned Ace of Swords. Julian had spoken the burial service
over her grave, simply but with the poignancy they all felt. Linette could
forgive Morgan now, and be sorry for her passing; it was enough to
remember that she had been unique and beautiful and was gone.

Then there had been the council of decision. Julian had thought it
best to close the passage, taking nothing out, so that there would be no
need for any kind of inquiries. She had gone with them, standing silently
for a moment before the tombs, helping them put the jewels back in the
chest; they kept nothing but a couple of silver coins for Rhodri to take
back with him. And Rhodri and Linette had spent the afternoon filling
the passage back in, bricking up the opening in the cellar, plastering
over the bricks as if the place had never been disturbed. Linette had felt
sad all through the task, as if she were sealing up the grave of part of
her life; and Rhodri had hardly spoken the whole time.

She looked at him now; he was still staring somberly into the dark
water. "Rhodri," she said, "what are you thinking?"

He did not look at her. "I will never see anything like Excalibur. There is an emptiness in my hands, because I have touched it and will never touch it again."

Linette thought of saying that there was an emptiness in her heart because she had loved him and he was going. But that would not be good to say; it would be a last futile reaching-out to what was over, and it would make the parting harder for both of them. She guessed that his longing for Excalibur only made more poignant his own longing for that brief bittersweet time. A chill suddenly went through her; she saw herself for an instant standing on the high crags of a mountain, in a tumbling mist where a pale ray of sunlight shot briefly through and faded; and the cold of the high lonely places pressed around her, and a harsh, freezing wind beat against her face and hair.

"And what will you do now?" she said.

"Well, you know that—I'm getting the early plane to New York. I'll be in Caernarvon day after tomorrow. And then—I'll have to explain to the Society what I did with their money. One twelfth-century wall and a few coins; everything else destroyed when the house was built. I'll show them the coins and the photographs of the wall. Well, it constitutes proof, anyway; and it's all they were after."

His hands tightened on the iron railing, and he stared blankly into the water. "It wasn't what I was after. If I could tell, I'd be in the ranks of fame like Schliemann. If I hadn't found Excalibur, if I hadn't been obliged to leave it in its place, I could have told about the passages at least—a great discovery, a unique thing; it would have made my career—" He shook his head. "And yet—it is worth it. Infinitely worth it to have found something like that, even though I can't tell. Only—after this, what can I do that would equal it?"

"Who knows," said Linette with forced lightness, "you might dig up Camelot."

His face livened, and she saw that he took her words seriously. "Yes, that's true. They're doing a dig at South Cadbury; they think they might find it. I could get in on that."

Linette noticed that the archaeologist's light had come back into his eyes. She smiled a dark, stiff smile; he seemed to have forgotten she was there.

"And Cristant," he went on; "she can stop working in that shop. Ah—Cristant—" He was silent; and his expression had turned inward, so that Linette could not read his thoughts.

"Rhodri—I'm sorry, if that's worth anything."

"Sorry?" He seemed to take a second to grasp her meaning, as if his thoughts had sunk to a great depth. "No; I don't blame you. You wanted something, just as I did; it was natural to try to get it. It was my fault for not mentioning Cristant at the start."

He paused a moment, reaching into his pocket. "There is one more thing. I kept something besides the coins; Julian knows and said it was my right. This."

And he drew out the box that contained the Water of Vision, and began to undo the wrappings of gold and silk. Linette, watching, realized that he was sharing this one last thing with her, as a parting gift.

The crystal, freed from its wrappings, now lay in his hand, delicate, gleaming only with the lights of the square. Very carefully he drew out the stopper and held out the flask over the smooth, dark water of the fountain pool.

"Brigid, or whatever greater power rules this water," he said, "let us see whatever it is good for us to see."

And he let a single drop of water fall into the pool. The ripples spread out in rings, disturbing the reflections in the water; and as stillness returned, the wavering lights and images did not form into the lights and shapes of the square. Instead, indistinct moving images appeared there, very bright against a great depth of dark; and as the two watchers gazed at them, they began to understand the images, and were drawn into the vision so that they seemed to see not pictures but reality. Men in strange armor fought on a dark plain; Excalibur blazed in the hand of one, like a long flame. Then that was gone; Roman columns showed for a second wrapped in fire. A dark river flowed through a wood; in its shallows a man in ring-mail lay dead, his dark hair in the water, a dragon-banner trailing beside him in the stream. Morgan stood in a stone room, white-gowned, her fiery hair streaming back, her face uplifted as if she prayed. Small ships sailed out across a vast ocean; on one stood a red-haired man with a circlet of gold. For a moment the face of Goeral looked out of the dark, then the Princess Christant's as Linette had seen it once before. Then for a moment there was darkness; and then a face shone out fair and solitary, a delicate face amid long pale-gold hair. There was something grave and a little strange in the expression, something lonely and too wise; Linette sensed in it a wildness as of desolate windswept places, as if the owner owed no allegiance to human conventions and might do anything. It was a frightening quality, unveiled there without the softenings of social intercourse; but there was a terrible splendor in it, like a lonely fire burning on a hill. This was Cristant, she guessed, Cristant in the silence of her secret thoughts, beyond the reach of life's hardness or love's treachery, wrapped in a stoical not-caring as in ice. No, not Cristant now, she thought; Cristant as she would be without happiness, yet not passion's slave. In her mind, suddenly, she had the image of that hilltop fire suddenly blazing up to a sky-lighting radiance, the gold of a festival, showering sparks of light over flowering meadows; when she looked again, the face was gone, and only the dark water gleamed glasslike in the lights of the square.

"It was—," began Rhodri.

"Yes," said Linette. "I know."

Once more the quiet fell. Linette stood motionless, trying to hold this moment, feeling it slip away from her, the last up-flash of the glory, being caught now with the quests into the immutable crystal of the past. Let me remember, she prayed suddenly, closing her hands on the iron rail; let me remember.

I am twenty-five, she thought. What I am going to have in this world, I had better have quickly.

"And what will you do?" Rhodri asked, breaking the silence.

"I don't know." She looked up suddenly, as if surprised by her own conclusions. "I keep thinking of Anthony. I wonder whether I loved him all the time."

"And so it ends," said Rhodri. "You go to Anthony and I to Cristant. We didn't think that once. Still, we had something, the four of us together."

The moon by now had risen clear of the trees and stood straight above them in a sea of calm blue, considerably waning. Linette looked at it and knew she would never see it again without thinking of Morgan and the luminous skies over Eldis.

"We should go back now," she said. "Aunt Julian'll be waiting for us; and Anthony may be awake."

And they turned away under the shadows of oak branches to return to Silverthorne.